TWO FOR ONE . . .

"AN ALMOST PERFECT HEIST"
by Carolyn G. Hart
Retired reporter turned journalism professor Henrietta O'Dwyer Collins follows her instincts and calls on Homicide Lieutenant Don Brown when a student doesn't show up for class because she's hit a deadly delay. . . .

"SEASONS OF THE HEART"
by Ed Gorman
A gunshot shatters the peace of a country farm when an enemy from the past starts stalking retiree Robert Wilson, and his granddaughter Lisa becomes his ally in his plan to hunt down the hunter.

"OIL AND WATER"
by J. A. Jance
Kings County Detective Phyllis Lanier grits her teeth when she pulls duty with womanizing, smart-mouthed cop James Joseph Barry, whose own past may get in the way of investigating the death of a battered wife.

"SEE WHAT THE BOYS IN THE LOCKED ROOM WILL HAVE"
by Bill Crider
Mystery authors Janice Langtry and Bo Wagner collaborate on bestselling mystery novels, but when a real locked room mystery has the police stumped—can the authors put their heads together and come up with a killer?

PARTNERS IN CRIME

A MYSTERY ANTHOLOGY

EDITED BY

Elaine Raco Chase

A SIGNET BOOK

SIGNET
Published by the Penguin Group
Penguin Books USA Inc., 375 Hudson Street,
New York, New York 10014, U.S.A.
Penguin Books Ltd, 27 Wrights Lane,
London W8 5TZ, England
Penguin Books Australia Ltd, Ringwood,
Victoria, Australia
Penguin Books Canada Ltd, 10 Alcorn Avenue,
Toronto, Ontario, Canada M4V 3B2
Penguin Books (N.Z.) Ltd, 182–190 Wairau Road,
Auckland 10, New Zealand

Penguin Books Ltd, Registered Offices:
Harmondsworth, Middlesex, England

First published by Signet,
an imprint of Dutton Signet,
a division of Penguin Books USA Inc.

First Printing, October, 1994
10 9 8 7 6 5 4 3 2 1

 REGISTERED TRADEMARK—MARCA REGISTRADA

Printed in the United States of America

PUBLISHER'S NOTE
These are works of fiction. Names, characters, places, and incidents either are the product of the authors' imaginations or are used fictitiously, and any resemblance to actual persons, living or dead, events, or locales is entirely coincidental.

BOOKS ARE AVAILABLE AT QUANTITY DISCOUNTS WHEN USED TO PROMOTE PRODUCTS OR SERVICES. FOR INFORMATION PLEASE WRITE TO PREMIUM MARKETING DIVISION, PENGUIN BOOKS USA INC., 375 HUDSON STREET, NEW YORK, NEW YORK 10014.

Contents

Introduction

There is a definite ring of truth to that old proverb: "Two heads are better than one." Especially when it comes to solving crimes or committing them.

In this collection of short stories, you will sample the unique styles and voices of some of today's award-winning mystery writers.

Dark and intense; gritty and taut; sharp and humorous; or just plain heart stopping—these stories all share the same theme: Partners.

Now some partnerships are definitely for the better; others just bring on a more fatal companionship. But all will leave you wanting to read more by these talented storytellers.

I know you'll enjoy becoming involved with all of these *Partners in Crime* . . .

—*Elaine Raco Chase*

Death Sentence
Jay Brandon

Jay Brandon started two careers at once when he financed his stint in law school by publishing his first novel, *Deadbolt,* which won the Editor's Choice Award from *Booklist Magazine.* He then went on to serve as an attorney with the District Attorney's office and the Court of Appeals, both in his hometown of San Antonio, and with the Court of Criminal Appeals, the highest criminal court in Texas.

Although he still practices law occasionally, Jay now concentrates on the written word. He is the author of five mystery novels, including: *Rules of Evidence*; the Edgar nominated, *Fade the Heat,* whose protagonist, Mark Blackwell, appears in *Loose Among the Lambs.*

In this short story, you meet two minor characters from *Fade the Heat,* Marilyn Ebbetts and Frank Mendiola. They were partners then, now they're adversaries.

Frank was defending a man everyone knew was guilty and Marilyn was having a tough time proving her case. She needed some help. So she turned to her old partner, Frank. Was he still one of the good guys? You decide; become the thirtoonth juror and see if you hand out the "Death Sentence" . . .

"In your hearts, you know he's guilty. You only have to find the courage to say so."

Those had been her last words to the jury. Marilyn had stood before them sympathetic to their dilemma but stern as well. Her eyes bored into theirs as if daring them to acquit, or, she hoped, as if she were trying to lend the hesitating jurors some of her own strength.

But that had been yesterday, and the jury was still out.

The thing was, they probably did know that Joey Lezar was guilty of capital murder, just as everyone in San Antonio knew it, but Marilyn hadn't been able to prove it, precisely because Lezar was a cold-blooded murderer.

He sat almost alone at the front of the courtroom, arms stretched out extravagantly across the chairs on either side of him, his ankle chains clanking when he crossed his legs. And wearing that grin that would make any self-respecting person want to slap the shit out of him, just for the sake of the grin itself, not knowing any of Joey's history or the mind that lay behind the grin. But Marilyn knew both, and the grin not only drove her fingernails into her palms, it made her deathly afraid.

The defendant's lawyer rose from the chair beside him, clapped Joey on the shoulder, and strolled through the gate toward Marilyn, wearing a grin almost as evil as his client's. Frank Mendiola could have played the role of the devil on a soul-buying spree. He wore a double-breasted black pinstriped suit, its creases sharp as razors, the sheen of his shoes matching his hair. Since becoming a defense lawyer Frank had started slicking his hair back, as if he *wanted* to look like a mob lawyer.

"How can you touch him?" Marilyn asked when Frank stopped in front of her.

"Ease up, Marilyn." With the same hand with which he'd patted Joey Lezar's shoulder, Frank stroked Marilyn's upper arm. She shrugged him off with a grimace—not for the first time. That only made the defense lawyer's smile grow brighter and more intimate. "He's not a bad kid, once you get to know him. He's just a product of his environment. Just because he's the best at what he—"

"Save it for punishment, Frank."

"Punishment?" He laughed. "We'll never get there. Seriously, though, Marilyn, maybe you should get to know Joey better. He's going to bring me a lot of business after this case is over. I could use a partner.

You were a good one." This time he touched her arm with only a finger, stroking slowly. Marilyn stepped away. "Of course, you wouldn't want to leave the D.A.'s office to join me immediately after the trial, that might look"—he waved a hand in the air, dismissive of the ethical rigidity of public opinion—"but after a month or two—"

"I'd rather push a wheelbarrow at the stockyards."

Frank laughed again. "Maybe that *will* be your next job, after this trial."

He walked on past her and out, with what could only be called a swagger. *I should have slapped him,* Marilyn thought—again, not for the first time.

I should have been nicer, Frank thought. Ol' Marilyn might actually come around if he just smooth talked her a little, instead of coming off like such a jerk. Frank knew the impression he left. He was far from an idiot; hadn't he just proven, over the course of the last two weeks, what a sharp lawyer he was? But there was something about Marilyn Ebbetts's sternness that brought out the worst in him, and the truth was, Frank liked himself best when he was at his worst.

Why was he worrying about her, anyway? There were other women, and there'd be plenty of others after he won this trial. He'd wasted too many hours wooing Marilyn. Besides, soon he'd have his satisfaction of her in another way. He was about to do to her publicly, in open court, what he'd tried so often to do in the privacy of their shared office.

"Any messages, sweetie?" Frank leaned casually against the phone, watching the hall.

Really he should be back in the office, working on other cases, but no case he had was remotely as important to him as this one. He was content to be idling at the courthouse, basking in the admiration of his peers. There'd been other lawyers in the audience of the trial; he'd won their respect, he knew. Frank waved lazily to a judge passing in the hallway, flashing his smile. The judge nodded judiciously back to him.

"Okay, well, I'm still in the courtroom. Call me if there's anything important."

Besides—Frank could admit it to himself, even while bestowing another confident smile on a lawyer conferring with a miserable client in the hallway—it was best that he be here with Joey, to keep him in line.

Frank had prepared his client, hammering it home over and over, for a guilty verdict. "It won't matter a bit, Joey, understand? It'll just mean a delay while I appeal the case. Even if the stupid jury comes back with a guilty verdict, the evidence wasn't there to support it. I guarantee it. I've tried a lot of cases, right? I know when the state hasn't proven its case. The appeals court isn't like a jury, they look at the case real coldly. They'll see in the record there just wasn't enough evidence to convict. It's an absolute cinch they'll reverse it, which is just like a not guilty. Understand? They couldn't try you for it again. You'll be free as the breeze."

And Joey had agreed, after Frank's repeated explanations of the appellate process, that he understood. "But, Frank," he'd said in that soft voice that chilled even his lawyer, "it'd be a lot nicer to walk out of the *courtroom* free as the breeze."

"I know, Joey, I know. Maybe we'll get that instead. It's looking good."

But still, it was better to stay right by Joey's side during the waiting period, where he could see Joey's thoughts in his face and soothe his concerns, keep his mind from wandering. Joey was paying a lot for Frank's representation, and he expected a lot in return.

And when Joey was displeased, he didn't keep it to himself. His relationship with his last lawyer had ended rather badly, when Joey had gotten probation and been damned lucky to get that. But Joey hadn't been happy with the fact of conviction. Ed Perry, his lawyer, had actually gone into hiding for a while after the case, until Lezar was known to have calmed down.

That had been a crummy car theft, not the capital murder and possible death sentence that faced Joey Lezar now. Frank would never admit it, but anyone who knew the players would understand that the defense lawyer's main worry was not losing the case, or the decline in business that might entail. It was the more immediate consequences of such a loss that concerned Frank. Joey was an impulsive guy.

Look at him, Marilyn thought. *Little punk.*

The phrase wasn't nearly harsh enough an indictment of someone who was responsible for so much terror and human agony, but it was what inevitably leaped to the mind of anyone gazing at Joey Lezar. At twenty-two Joey was getting a little long in the tooth for the youth gang of which he was master, but he still looked like the sixteen-year-old punk who'd leer through the window when pulling up beside you at a stoplight. He turned lazily and gave Marilyn such a leer at that moment.

She didn't react at all, didn't glare, didn't turn away, just studied him as if she were a scientist and Joey a newly discovered fungus that might prove poisonous. Did she really see the capacity there for the horror of which she suspected him?

As if he'd heard her thought, Joey's grin changed from sexual to plain arrogant. *Oh, yes,* his face said. *I did it. I did it all.*

Marilyn believed his face. She wouldn't have believed a word that came out of his mouth. But his whole expression was too self-satisfied to lie. She found herself walking toward him, as if drawn by his magnetism.

Joey's grin reverted. His eyes traveled down and up her body, and down again. Marilyn knew how asexual she looked in her gray suit—it was an effect she strived for—but then, Joey had been in jail a long time.

"Hey, baby," he drawled. "I'll probably be outta here by tonight. You got any plans?"

"I'll be drinking champagne to celebrate your death sentence."

Joey's grin just widened. He liked girls with spunk. It was so much fun watching them lose it.

His long arm came off the back of the chair.

"You want to lose that hand, go ahead."

Joey reached for her anyway. Marilyn slapped his hand away. She glanced up at one of the three bailiffs, sitting at his desk only a few feet away.

"Hey!" Richard, the bailiff, said, struggling to rise to his feet. "Keep your hands to yourself," he ordered the prisoner.

Joey turned toward him. "Watch *yourself,* man," he said softly. Richard stayed on his feet for a minute, glaring, but didn't approach.

Joey Lezar shouldn't even have been in the courtroom. He should have been in a holding cell, or a few blocks away in the jail, while waiting for the jury to come back. But Joey had expressed his desire to spend his idle time out in the world, in the relative expanse and brightness of the courtroom rather than a cramped cell, and the bailiffs had let him have his way. They knew—everybody knew—what Joey was capable of accomplishing, even from his jail cell.

"Why don't you just step away from him, Ms. Ebbetts?" the bailiff suggested gruffly.

Good advice. Frank was still outside the courtroom. Marilyn had no business talking to his client while Joey's lawyer was absent. But court rules didn't mean much to her at that moment.

"You think you're going to get away with this, don't you?" She leaned over close to Joey's face. He smiled up at her. "You know if that jury comes back with a not guilty, I can't touch you for this murder. Nobody could, even if you gave a press conference and confessed it. But this isn't the only trial you're going to have. I'm going to put together a good case against you, one of these days."

"If you still have your job after this one," Joey drawled. "You just can't stand the thought of not being close to me anymore, can you, lady? Go ahead, ask me. You don't have to do it the mean way. You'll like me."

She wanted to spit. Marilyn felt her face twisting in revulsion.

Joey loved it. "Maybe I'll look you up one of these days after this is over," he said. "At home. I can find out where you live. Frank probably knows, doesn't he?"

Marilyn knew, in that moment, that she was going to buy a gun. An idea she had resisted for years—its time had come.

Her face must have changed again, revealing the sudden fear she felt. Joey liked this expression even better. He smiled at it lovingly.

"I'd appreciate you not talking to my client behind my back, Marilyn. I thought you knew the rules better than that."

Frank was back, standing stiffly beside her. Next to his client, Frank looked sober and respectable. Marilyn slowly straightened up. *Rules,* Frank had said. But there were no rules, she suddenly realized. Certainly not for Joey Lezar. Why should there be for her?

"I have a note from the jury."

Behind their backs, Judge Marroquin had taken the bench. He was one of the rare judges who didn't care for ceremony; he never bothered to alert his bailiff when he was about to reappear, so Richard never got the chance to order everyone in the courtroom to their feet.

Judge Marroquin looked at Marilyn sympathetically, and her heart froze. A note from the jury might mean they had reached a verdict, and from his sympathetic expression the judge knew the verdict was not a good one.

But the news wasn't *that* bad. Not yet.

Judge Marroquin donned his black-rimmed reading

glasses. " 'Your Honor,' " he read aloud, " 'we cannot agree on a verdict. What should we do now?' "

No one moved. Frank looked pleased. Marilyn was momentarily relieved just at the bad news being delayed.

"Well?" the judge asked pleasantly. "Reactions? You have a motion to make, Mr. Mendiola?"

"No, Your Honor." Frank had already thought out this possibility. He could move for a mistrial, based on a hopelessly deadlocked jury, but if the judge granted the motion all that would get Frank was a new trial: starting all over. It was better to let this trial proceed to conclusion, one way or another. If it ended in a not-guilty verdict, Frank and his client would be golden. If guilty, better to let the appeals process that would eventually free Joey anyway begin now.

Besides, if the jurors couldn't agree, that meant at least some of them were voting for acquittal.

"The defense is content for the jury to continue deliberating," Frank concluded.

"Ms. Ebbetts?" On the record, Judge Marroquin was always formal with her.

"The state agrees, Your Honor."

"Very well. I will instruct the jury to continue to try to reach agreement."

The judge gave Marilyn a slight shrug of comradeship as he left the bench again. He would do what he could to help her, as always. The judge had already done her a great favor by denying the defense's motion for a directed verdict at the close of the trial, when Judge Marroquin knew as well as the two lawyers that the prosecution's evidence had been insufficient for conviction.

"This Joey Lezar is as bad as they come," the judge had told Marilyn in the privacy of his chambers. "If the worst we can do to him is let him sit in prison for a year before the appeals court gets around to reversing his case, we'll still be saving lives. This boy—

he's evil. I've seen it in his face. Nothing means anything to him."

"You don't know the half of it, Judge."

"Yes, I do." The judge had nodded. "You don't think there are any secrets in this courthouse, do you?"

So the judge knew about her lost witness. Marilyn hadn't told him, but she was glad he knew—knew that she hadn't deliberately presented him with an insufficient case.

Marilyn had been in Judge Marroquin's court for almost two years. From the beginning he had taken her under his wing, as if he were her training officer rather than the impartial arbiter of her work. Judge Marroquin made no secret of which way his sympathies lay in most cases. He was as tough a judge as the building held. The judge had been a gang member himself forty years earlier during his teens. "But gangs were different then," he always pointed out. "We'd help old ladies in the neighborhood with their groceries. And the worst thing we ever did to each other was maybe a fistfight. Or something really terrible, pull a knife. None of this drive-by shooting where you don't even have to look your rival in the face."

Rising from his background had given the judge a great respect for responsibility, and contempt for defendants appearing before him who claimed they were victims of society. Defense lawyers knew not to go to Judge Marroquin for punishment.

By the same token, Marilyn knew she could expect from the judge whatever help he could give her. He was her partner in this prosecution. But no one could help now.

Except, she suddenly thought, and the idea almost made her laugh aloud, the only person who could help her was her old partner . . . Frank Mendiola.

"I don't want to increase the pressure on you, Marilyn, but you know, we need this conviction."

"Gee, Mark, I hadn't realized that." Her sarcasm

was a sign of how far Marilyn's spirits had fallen. Usually she felt intimidated by her boss.

Mark Blackwell let the remark slide by without visible reaction. The District Attorney leaned against
Marilyn's filing cabinet. To make his intervention appear less formal, he'd done her the courtesy of coming
to his assistant's office, instead of ordering her to appear in his. Marilyn had been sitting there dejectedly,
sorting idly through her thick file on Joey Lezar as if
something would occur to her. Nothing had.

"What can I do to help?"

"Can you bring my witness back to life? I'm sorry,
Mark, I'm snapping. I've reached my limit. Nobody
can do anything. The evidence is over, the jury hasn't
bought it, and even if they do—"

The District Attorney nodded. His voice was quiet,
but steely. "Everybody knows Joey murdered that
store clerk. Everybody knows he had the only witness
to it murdered. And everyone knows what he'll do if
he goes free. If we can't stop him, what use are we to
anybody?" Blackwell saw that he hadn't told his assistant anything she didn't know. His voice became more
brisk. "Sorry. Let's talk about your options. How
about if *you* ask for a mistrial? Judge Marroquin
would grant it, wouldn't he?"

"Oh, yes."

"And that would give us time to come up with more
evidence before the new trial."

"I don't think there *is* any more evidence out there,
Mark. Even if there's another witness, who would
come forward now after what happened to Mona?"

"Then let's look at Mona's murder." Mark Blackwell was tall and fit, but he looked his age, fifty. His
face bore its experience. But when he talked it was
with the eagerness of a young prosecutor. "That was
capital murder too, and we have a good idea who
carried it out. If we could turn one of them— Ordering a hit is also capital murder. Maybe we could get
Joey on that one."

"Get one of his own gang to testify against him?

They already know very well what happens to people who plan to do that!" Marilyn said, her skepticism edging into scorn.

"But we'd have a possible death penalty case to hang over their heads."

"One kind of death sentence is a lot like another, Mark. I think they'd be more worried about the one they know would happen sooner."

"Yeah." Blackwell's enthusiasm hadn't died, it had compressed into deep thoughtfulness. "You let me worry about that case, then," he said distractedly. "I'm *not* going to let this punk kill one of our witnesses and get away with it."

"Mark." Marilyn stopped his departure. "You're dead serious about this?" The D.A. didn't have to answer, he just looked at her. "Will you give me a free hand?" Marilyn continued.

"Yes." His brow arched. "To do what?"

She chewed her lip. "I'm not sure, but ... First I have to talk to Frank."

"Frank? What on earth would you say to him?"

Marilyn laughed humorlessly. "Nothing I wouldn't want his client to know. But you know, those gang members aren't the only possible witnesses against Joey."

"Frank's not your partner anymore," Mark Blackwell stated soberly. "He never was much of one to begin with."

"No, but I owe him something."

The D.A. frowned. "What?"

"A chance."

As she made her way back down to the courtroom, Marilyn thought about the jury. The sixty-seven-year-old Mexican-American grandmother Frank had probably left on the jury in hopes she'd be sympathetic toward Joey. Marilyn had left her on because the woman had children in Joey's kingdom; she should know what a threat he was. Then there was the thirty-eight-year-old married man, father of two, who'd admitted he had a brother in prison serving time for robbery, and cousins and nephews who'd also been in and out of the joint. It was obvious why Frank had left him on—hoping the man thought the system ground down innocents. But the juror had never been in trouble with the law himself. Marilyn hoped he believed that a man could and should resist his criminal impulses.

But choosing a jury was all shooting in the dark. Who knew what potential jurors were really thinking during jury selection, or what they'd do in the privacy of the jury room? She wondered which of the ones she'd let on the jury were betraying her now.

She also thought about something her boss had said. "Everybody knew" that Joey had committed murder. *Everybody knew.*

And Joey didn't mind that a bit. Look at the manner in which he'd had Mona Calloway killed. Joey didn't want to be convicted for his crimes—he damned sure didn't want to land on death row for them—but he was happy with the idea of everyone knowing what he was capable of, what he could get away with.

"Talk to you, Frank?"

Frank grinned broadly for the benefit of his client sitting beside him. "Going to offer us a deal, Marilyn? Or is it"—he deepened his voice—"something personal?"

"Maybe we could work something out."

She walked out and she could feel Frank following her, feel his eyes. She pictured the bad-little-boy swagger that only made him look pathetic. Turning quickly in the hallway, she caught his exaggerated ogle. Her stern look only made his smile broaden.

"Frank, this is serious."

"For you it's serious, Marilyn. For me it's pure pleasure."

"It's serious for you too, Frank. It's *about* you. You want to talk here, or go upstairs?"

He lost his stupid look. "Let's find a quiet spot."

At the far end of the hallway they found an isolated

bench. Marilyn sat on it, Frank put his foot up on it and leaned close to her.

"Frank, we know Joey had Mona Calloway killed."

Frank's features gave nothing away. But Marilyn knew her former partner well. She'd seen that same blankness on his face when a defense lawyer had stumbled across the weakest part of their case. Frank looked most guileless when he was most vulnerable. "That's another case," he said. "That's got nothing to do with anything."

"It has to do with you, Frank. Mona Calloway's name was on our witness list. You told Joey she was going to testify against him."

"Of course I talked to my client about the witnesses, asked if he knew what they might say. It would have been incompetent of me *not* to. You don't know anything about defense work, Marilyn."

"Yes, I do, Frank. I know what goes beyond the bounds of representing your client, too. Joey was in jail when Mona was killed. He had to get word outside. And you were his only visitor, Frank. His little thug henchmen don't like going into the jail, and he doesn't have any other friends. Even his mother won't have anything to do with him anymore. You were his only link to the outside world, Frank."

Frank didn't answer hastily. She could see him thinking. Nothing could have better confirmed Marilyn's suspicion.

"He was allowed phone calls," Frank said.

"He wouldn't have trusted jail phones for a message like that."

"Well, he didn't trust me with it, either. Jesus, Marilyn, what do you think I am?"

"I think maybe you're his dupe," Marilyn said carefully, watching him. "That's what I'm hoping, Frank. Now that you know what happened to the witness, maybe you can realize that Joey gave you some kind of message that you passed on without knowing what it meant. Did he, Frank? Did you pass word to somebody on the outside for him?"

Frank's face was thoughtful, but he spoke by rote. "I'd better not say any more. I wouldn't want to violate the attorney-client privilege."

"That privilege doesn't extend to the planning of crimes, Frank. Now that you know that's what Joey was doing, you don't have to keep quiet about it. *You* can testify. *You* can be my witness."

"What?" He hadn't even known what she was driving at.

"I'm dead serious, Frank. You're the only one who knows Joey ordered a murder from his jail cell. We can prove the murder. All we need you to do is link Joey to it. Who did you pass his message to?"

"You're crazy!"

Marilyn studied him. "Have you really changed so much, Frank? Remember how we used to work together to go after guys like Joey? How you'd work late and call cops and do all those extra things to get a conviction? And now you're going to help Joey Lezar get away with this cold-blooded murder of an innocent girl?"

Frank looked appalled. But there was still that slowness to his speech. "I didn't help him do anything."

"Do you know how he did it, Frank? How he killed that poor girl who didn't do anything to anybody, who just had the bad luck of having Joey brag to her about killing a store clerk during a robbery, because he thought it would impress her?"

"I don't—"

"Not just a clean shot through the head. That's all he needed to do to silence her. But that wasn't good enough for Joey. He ordered his thugs to make it look good. So they terrorized Mona Calloway. They kidnapped her, and held her, and took turns raping her, until finally they strangled her and dumped her body in her own yard for her mother to find. That's how your little friend did it, Frank. To *my* witness Just because I talked her into testifying!"

Marilyn knew she sounded hysterical. Frank's tone of voice said that he knew it too. "I'm sorry, Marilyn.

But I didn't have anything to do with that. I don't think Joey did, either."

Marilyn's voice was low again. "So, it was just one of life's weird coincidences then, Frank? Because the timing was pretty delicate. This case has been pending for months, but they didn't take out my witness until the trial had begun—as if Joey had obtained legal advice. As if a lawyer told him that if my witness disappeared once the case had already started, and that caused a not-guilty verdict, Joey couldn't be tried again, ever."

This time Frank didn't answer at all. Marilyn stood up. Her old partner hadn't moved, so she was looking down on him. "There's nothing wrong with being his lawyer," she said coldly. "But you're something more than that, Frank. You're now his partner."

"No, I'm not, Marilyn," he said to her back as she walked away. "I would never do something like that."

At least I'd never get caught at it, Frank thought. They couldn't prove anything. Not against him. He'd made damned sure of that. He'd told Joey not to spell things out for him. He didn't mind doing little extra favors for the gang leader, as long as they could both pretend Frank didn't know exactly what he was doing.

He stayed at the end of the hall for a minute, thinking frantically. *Raped and strangled.* The murder of the witness hadn't been real to him until Marilyn had described it. It made something else make sense, too: the way Joey had blown up at him when giving him the message to deliver.

"Tell the boys to have fun," Joey had said in the privacy of their jail conference room, grinning.

"Yeah, yeah," Frank had said, anxious to leave, already turning toward the door that led to the outside world.

"Frank!" Joey's cold voice had stopped him. "Tell 'em. Exactly that, just like I told you. Tell 'em to have fun."

"All right, Joey, I'll tell them." As if Joey's gang

members on the outside wouldn't feel authorized to enjoy themselves without explicit instructions from the boss.

Now, in memory, the words, the ones Frank had faithfully passed on as ordered, took on a whole new meaning.

He exhaled noisily. But it was nothing to do with him. His job was just here inside the courthouse, and he'd done his job damned well. That was Marilyn's problem. She couldn't stand losing to him. By the time he caught up to her, he was almost jolly again.

"The trouble with you prosecutors," he told her, putting his hand on her arm, "is that you're used to having all the cards, and when you don't all you can do is whine."

" 'You prosecutors—' " she echoed him contemptuously. "You've really gone over, haven't you, Frank?"

Frank lost his smile and leaned close to sneer. "Maybe I *should* still be in the office with you, Marilyn. Maybe I would have liked to stay."

"I'm not the one who reported you, Frank. Which means I'm not the only one you harassed. If you—"

"Ah, who cares?" he said loudly. "I'm better off now anyway. After this case—"

"This isn't about just a case, Frank."

"Sure it is, darling. You've just got to learn to take it like a man."

"All right, Frank. I felt like I had to give you a chance."

"What do you mean by that?"

But she turned aside and walked off without another word.

There is no feeling in the world like having a jury out. Waiting for a baby to come doesn't equate, because there's joyful anticipation in that. Waiting for a jury is just misery. The longer they stay out, the worse it gets, until the lawyers on both sides are convinced they've lost. They go over all their mistakes while waiting. There's nothing to do but wait. You can't go to the bathroom; they might come back while you're gone. You can't use your phone; the court coordinator might be calling to say they're back. You can't think about anything else; forgetting that jury might put a hex on your case.

Feeling that way, there was no reason for Marilyn to stay away from the courtroom. Frank was there too, as if it were his home. So was Joey.

This time when Marilyn entered, Judge Marroquin was also in the room, casual in shirtsleeves. His bailiff crossed from the back door and whispered. "We have a verdict?" the judge asked. Richard nodded. "Guess I'd better get myself dressed, then." The judge left the room.

The pain suddenly intensified. Marilyn felt immobilized by the dread churning her stomach. It was a long moment before she could force herself to hurry forward.

Frank was conferring with his client, talking quickly. Joey was nodding, but barely seemed to be listening. "I get it!" he finally snapped. "I walk now or I walk later. I get it!"

"All right, Joey, all right. Just don't worry about what happens here. I'll be—"

Marilyn walked right up and leaned over him again. "That's right, Joey, it doesn't matter. You're still worthless scum no matter what."

"Get out of here, Marilyn," Frank ordered.

"Is he telling you that if they say 'Not guilty' in a few minutes you'll be free of this crime forever, no matter what kind of perfect evidence I could uncover after the trial? Is he?"

Joey's grin answered.

Marilyn's voice rose even higher. "That's right, Joey, you little punk. But you won't have anything to brag about. If they acquit you it'll just be because the evidence wasn't there—not because you got away with anything. You're not smart enough to get away with anything."

"Marilyn—" Frank was standing. Richard, the bailiff, had come over too. Not because they were afraid of what Marilyn might do. It was the look on Joey Lezar's face that had brought them to their feet. His grin was gone completely. He glared at Marilyn, and his hands were on the arms of his chair.

"You think like a rat, Joey, but you don't even have a rat's brains. You're too stupid to get away with anything important. If they say you didn't do it I guess you didn't, because you could never pull off anything that required thinking, or manhood. You're too much of a—"

"Come on, Marilyn," Richard said softly, pulling her away. "You're just making it worse."

"Hide and watch, lady!" Joey screamed after her. "You think I can't do whatever I want? Watch and see!"

Frank was trying to shush him. Joey pushed him away. Joey's eyes were blazing. His fingers were opening and closing. When the jury box began to fill, he didn't even look at them. He was still glaring at Marilyn.

Frank didn't look at the jurors either. In fact, he hadn't paid much attention to them even during jury selection, Marilyn had noticed. She had wondered then how he could be so casual during the all-important business of picking the people who would judge his client. Frank had barely listened to their answers. Later Marilyn had understood. For Frank it didn't matter what these people did. He was certain of an acquittal now or an appellate acquittal later. Either way he'd win.

The people in the jury box looked a little confused. A couple even flashed nervous smiles. Their big moment always makes juries nervous, Marilyn thought. A few of them looked at her, which was supposed to be a good sign—but their looks were questioning.

Frank was watching the back door of the courtroom, the one through which Judge Marroquin had disappeared. "Come on, Judge, come on," he said under his breath. Let the ride begin.

Marilyn saw the clerk receive the verdict form from one of the jurors, open it, read expressionlessly, and lay the paper on her desk. "Now she knows," Marilyn stated softly.

Frank looked in the same direction. Together he and Marilyn studied the placid clerk. Another minute passed. Two. "Doddering old fool," Frank muttered, not so quietly.

"What's taking the judge so long?" Joey said loudly.

Marilyn was suddenly on her feet, walking briskly to the clerk's desk. "Just a peek, Belinda."

"Hey!" In the next moment Frank was beside his former partner.

"You'll have to wait for the judge like everybody else," the clerk was telling Marilyn.

"Please, Belinda. It means—"

"Don't be so stingy," Frank snapped, reaching past Marilyn. "What's it matter to you?"

He snatched up the paper. Marilyn and Belinda were equally motionless. Frank quickly scanned the printed page, to the line on which the jurors had been instructed to write their verdict. Frank's hands clutched the form. His eyes lifted skyward, and closed. "Yessss!"

Marilyn tore the paper out of Frank's grip. She stepped around him.

"This is your verdict?" she almost shouted at the perplexed-looking people in the jury box. "*Not* guilty?"

A few of them nodded. The man at the front corner said, "That's right, not guilty. The evidence just—"

"Is it, Frank?!" Now Joey was on his feet as well, causing the bailiffs to start nervously to theirs.

"It is, Joey," Frank said in a voice like prayer. "It's not guilty!" He took the verdict form from Marilyn and read it aloud:

"In the case of the state of Texas versus Joseph Anthony Lezar, we find the defendant not guilty of capital murder. Not guilty," he repeated.

Frank raised his arms as if leading a chorus. Life was beautiful.

Marilyn slumped onto the edge of the table. Her face was grim, as if it didn't matter, as if her work had just begun. But then, as if without her volition, her hand turned into a fist and slammed down on the table.

The courtroom had turned noisy. There were reporters present, other lawyers, spectators. The jurors sat patiently, beginning to turn to one another. Richard was talking to them. Frank was shaking hands with someone, some lawyer or other crony. The noise level was about to rise to a burst of celebration or commiseration.

Then the noise was pierced by a sound that froze everyone it touched. A quiet sound, building only slowly. A sound menacing and cold and completely out of character with what it was:

Laughter.

Joey Lezar was laughing, slumped as if boneless in his chair. He turned his face up and sent the evil laugh heavenward. Then he, too, slammed his fists down on the table, in joy.

"Not guilty!" he shouted. "Right?" He looked at the jurors. One or two of them nodded. "Did you write that down, lady?" Joey yelled at the court reporter, who was still transcribing every word spoken in the courtroom. "Did you hear, my man?" Joey shouted, rising to hug his lawyer. Frank cut off his own celebrating to try to calm his client.

But Joey was still building toward his greatest moment. He leaned around his lawyer, out into the narrow space between the defense table and the state's. His voice lowered. "Did *you* hear?" he asked Marilyn softly.

"I heard." Efficiently putting away her files, Marilyn didn't look at him. "Just remember what I said, you little shit. Don't think you—"

"Did you hear these *morons* say not guilty?!" Joey screamed.

"Joey, shut up." Frank began to worry about contempt of court. But Judge Marroquin still hadn't returned. The court wasn't formally in session. Joey began to rave without restraint.

"Now I'm golden, right? No matter what?"

"Right, right. But—"

"Because these *idiots* did just what I wanted them to do, just like I'd given them orders." Joey grinned at the jurors, who looked back at him placidly. Their calm expressions launched Joey even higher.

"You think I didn't do it?" he screamed at them. "Of course I did it, you morons. 'Course I shot that clerk. Because he was as stupid as you are. I could see what he was thinking. I saw him studyin' me, thinkin' he was gonna identify me later. So I blasted *that* stupid thought out of his head. 'Cause where was he when the case got here? Did you see him? No! 'Cause I blasted his stupid ass!"

"Joey, shut up!" Frank was finally looking where his client was, into the jury box. He looked into the peaceful, almost perplexed face of a middle-aged black woman, who nodded back to him as if being introduced. Frank's eyes widened, and moved. Within seconds they were scurrying frantically from face to face.

"Where's—?" he said softly. "Who are—?"

Frank gripped his client's arm. His voice when he spoke had changed so much that it halted Joey's ravings even though Frank's voice had fallen to almost inaudible. "Joey, shut up. These people, I've never seen them before."

"Thanks, folks," Richard said to the people in the jury box. "You can go on back now."

They began filing out of the jury box by ones and twos. Joey watched them, mouth open. He didn't recognize them either, but then, he hadn't given a damn who was on his jury. His lawyer had told him it wouldn't matter.

"What have you done, Marilyn?" Frank asked his former partner. He would have been dismayed if he had been aware of the pleading note in his voice.

"I just let some spectators into the room, Frank. Just some people who wanted good seats for a confession." People she'd chosen to resemble the real jury as much as possible, at least in gender and age and race, in the short time she'd had.

"But the judge—"

"What judge, Frank? Did you ever hear court called back into session? I just borrowed the courtroom while we were waiting for the jury. Of course"—she gestured toward the court reporter, who was packing up her narrow slips of paper, the ones recording Joey's outburst—"I asked Anne to make a record of anything anybody said. And I think we had a few witnesses to Joey's announcement of guilt. I certainly heard it."

"I heard it," Richard said, walking by.

Frank looked dazed. Even his client's suddenly punching him in the shoulder didn't seem to register with him.

"That wasn't the jury!" Joey screamed. "And you didn't notice, you stupid bastard!"

"You didn't notice either, Joey."

"But you're the lawyer, man. You picked those people! And you don't know *strangers* when they come in here?"

"You talked too fast, Joey." Frank was starting to talk faster himself. His color didn't improve, but Marilyn could tell from the flash of his eyes that he was starting to think. "I was telling you to keep quiet."

"After you'd already told me it would be okay! That I could say whatever I wanted after—"

"After the verdict," Marilyn said. "Which we don't have yet."

Judge Marroquin entered the room briskly. This time he was wearing his robe. "All rise!" the bailiff said triumphantly.

"This court is now in session," the judge said. "I have another note from the jury. They say they're still deadlocked."

"In that case, Your Honor," Marilyn said from her

seat, "the state requests a mistrial. I don't see any hope that this jury will ever reach a verdict."

"Neither do I," Judge Marroquin agreed. "Defense?"

"Objection," Frank said in a dead voice.

"Well, that will be overruled. I hereby declare this case a mistrial. You'll both let me know when you're ready to begin the retrial?"

"Very soon, Your Honor," Marilyn said.

"Your Honor!" Frank called out, to stop the judge's disappearance. "Your Honor, I want to register an objection to what just happened in this courtroom before the new note from the jury."

"Something happen in here while I was gone?" Judge Marroquin asked innocently. "Well, whatever it was, it was unofficial. I don't see how I can entertain an objection to something that wasn't part of the trial. So . . ." And he walked out again.

"Don't worry about it, Joey," Frank said quickly. "This'll never stand up on appeal. They can't—"

"Why not, Frank? What was improper? I think we're free to do as we please when court's not in session. Including confess. I've heard of defendants confessing during trials. Haven't you?"

"Shut up, Marilyn, I'm talking to my client. Forget her, Joey, she doesn't know what she's talking about. I'll keep that confession out, trust me."

"Judge Marroquin suppress a confession?" Marilyn merely chuckled.

Frank kept talking. Now it was his client who had gone mute. But Joey's eyes were very lively. He no longer paid any attention to his lawyer. He shook off Frank as he would have a gnat buzzing around his ear.

Marilyn started up the aisle. Frank gave up on Joey and hurried to catch her. He grabbed her arm and pulled her around to face him.

"You know what you've done to me?" he said softly. It was the first time during the whole trial that he'd spoken to her without sarcasm or bitterness or hostility. His voice sounded as if it would break.

Marilyn looked at him without hatred or pity. "Just what you did to Mona Calloway. Isn't that right, Frank?"

"Exactly the same," Frank said harshly. He didn't even realize he was confessing. He had more immediate worries.

This was where Marilyn had planned to deliver her prepared speech, the one where she told Frank that the only way to protect himself now was to come to her, to agree to testify against his former client.

But Frank's inadvertent confession shocked her. Until his few words of admission, she'd tried to hope that whatever he'd done had just been accidental, that her old partner hadn't really turned into something despicable. But there in the aisle of the courtroom she looked at him clearly and saw through his fear to his guilt. His client was only a few steps behind Frank, and in that moment Marilyn couldn't have picked out which of them was worse.

That was what caused her to say the most terrible words she'd ever spoken.

"Thanks for your help, Frank." She smiled and clapped him on the shoulder.

Frank just stared at her, openmouthed. Behind him, she saw Joey Lezar look surprised too. When his gaze left Marilyn and landed on his lawyer, it changed character.

Marilyn turned and walked away, shaking off Frank's reaching hand for the last time.

Soon to Be a
Minor Motion Picture
Barbara D'Amato

Multitalented Barbara D'Amato is a playwright, novelist, and crime researcher. She won the Anthony Award for Best True Crime for *The Doctor, The Murder, The Mystery,* the true story of John Branion, which later formed the basis for a segment on the TV series *Unsolved Mysteries.*

Barbara writes three mystery series: *The Hands of Healing Murder* featuring forensic pathologist Gerritt DeGraaf; *The Eyes on Utopia Murders* under her pseudonym, Malacai Black; and Chicago freelance investigative reporter Cat Marsala, who you can catch in *Hard Women.*

The Chicago Police Department's Marine Unit is the temporary beat of Susannah Figueroa and her partner Norman Bennis. It was a cushy assignment until they encountered a deadly problem that was "Soon to Be a Minor Motion Picture" . . .

It was the hand of Lady Luck, I suppose, that led me to watch the television news just before we found the actor and the one-man film crew. But I like to think Norm Bennis and I would have seen through their story anyway.

My name is Susannah Figueroa and I'm a Chicago Police officer.

My partner Norman Bennis said, "Is this living?"

"This is living!" I said.

"I mean, this *is* living!"

"You can say that again."

The sun struck glints from the waters of Lake Michigan. A warm hint of breeze caressed my face as I sat in the open cabin. Our small boat, its motor off, rose slowly and lowered almost imperceptibly on a glassy calm sea. "Like being rocked in the arms of Morpheus," said Bennis, who was in back at the helm, ostensibly observing. I could see that his eyelids hung lower than a furled mainsail.

"I didn't know you could wax poetic," I said.

"Hey! That's the way I wax when I wax."

I was eating my lunch at the table in the tiny cabin of the Chicago Police Department Marine Unit powerboat. We had decided that I would eat while Bennis stayed at the wheel, then vice versa. As I watched, a wave thrown up in the wake of a passing water-skier slapped the boat and tossed a few drops of spray onto my partner. He didn't move.

If we had been on patrol in the city, the only spray would have been from the spitting of air conditioners in high-rises. The breeze would be automobile exhaust funneled down urban canyons over superheated road tar. The only rocking would take place as our squad car bumped into potholes.

The CPD goes through off and on stages in its use of the Marine Patrol. More than once the unit had been cut out of the budget entirely, the City Council having decided it was too expensive. Then somebody would drown or a tour boat would capsize and the next day they'd have a Marine Unit patrol again.

Bennis and I were not regular Marine Unit officers. I had put in two months on it early in my training. And Bennis, who is ten years older than I am, had been in the Navy and had spent one year in the Marine Unit back in 1987. We'd been roped into duty this week in late August because of an unfortunate accident.

Some genius at the central cop shop had decided that the least expensive way to fuel the Marine Unit humans was to have sandwiches made downtown for their lunches and put aboard in a cooler. Somebody had neglected to keep them cool enough before they were put into the cooler. Salmonella can take twelve to twenty-four hours to develop, so before anybody realized what was happening, everybody had eaten the sandwiches. Seventy percent of the Marine Unit staff was now hors de combat. All experienced personnel and all half-experienced personnel were being called in to take up the slack. We'd got the call at the crack of dawn: report to the dock.

This was fine with me and Bennis. We like each other, we're longtime squad car partners, and we thought a few days on a boat would be a splendid vacation. Our first really plum assignment in ages, in fact.

Bennis leaned back and said dreamily, "Figueroa, my man, I had this case a few years ago."

I knew I was about to be instructed in some point of policing. "Yes, Norm?"

"This guy—you know how Stibich always says the average crook is terminally stupid—this guy decides to rob a bank. But he's too lazy to scope it out ahead, see?"

"I know the type," I said.

"He figures he can just go in and muscle it. Takes his .38 and his seriously dangerous-looking black pants and black shirt with the cutout sleeves that show his delts and biceps and figures that's good enough to scare the piss out of any teller."

"Which it probably is."

"Oh, no doubt. Scares *me*. The gun anyhow. But see, he forgot one thing. He's got the bank all picked out. He's been passing by the building for years. One of those big banks made out of red polished granite, with the name carved across the front and big granite pillars and carved acanthus leaves—"

"Acanthus leaves! I didn't know you were so erudite, Bennis."

"Yes, you did. Probably a Louis Sullivan—"

"Who is Louis Sullivan?"

"A major architect of the early twenties, Suze, my man. I'm astonished you didn't know. Designed banks all over the place. Also the Chicago Opera House.

And Carson Pirie Scott. And many more architectural triumphs."

"My, my!"

"In any case, a big bank. Impressive. Big steps leading up to the front doors. You know the kind of step that's so wide you have to take two steps on it?"

"Yeah. Not user-friendly."

"But stately. So he stashes his gun in his pocket and goes in. But unknown to him, the bank moved out years ago and the building has been taken over by a firm of lawyers. There's a big sign in one window, all gold letters, perfectly clear, but our guy doesn't bother to read it. In he goes. Doesn't even notice that the tellers' cages are gone. He marches up to a receptionist behind a mahogany desk at the back and says, 'Gimme all your money.'

"She says, 'I don't have any money. What do you think this is, a bank?'

"So he looks around now, and by that time one of the lawyers is coming over to the desk. He says, 'What's the trouble?'

"The secretary says, 'This man wants to rob us.'

"The lawyer says, 'This is a law office, young man.'

"By now our perp is mad, and he says, 'I don't care if this is a bank or an office, get all your money together and put it in a bag.'

"So they get some money out of wallets and purses and stick it in a paper bag, but the lawyer says to the guy, 'Okay. But you know I'm gonna have to charge you for this.'

"Perp says, 'What?'

"The lawyer says, 'I get $200 an hour and I'm gonna have to charge you for my time.'

"Perp looks at him, blinks, and says, 'Oh, hell! Forget it then!' and he throws the money bag at the lawyer and runs out the door."

I laughed so hard I spilled my Coke on the bench seat and had to wipe it up. It's very important to stay shipshape on a boat.

Bennis said, "And the moral of the story, Figueroa

my man, is that they always do *something* stupid. In some cases you gotta look for it, but they always do something stupid."

I watched the noon news on a television set about the size of a large grape. There was some doubt about whether Chicago schools would open next week as they were scheduled to do. Apparently the teachers and the board had not yet agreed to come to the bargaining table.

Newscaster Bob Cole reported that there had been a morning rush hour pileup on the Edens Expressway. Finally he turned to his coanchor.

"Now, Heidi Amurao has the entertainment news," he said. "Heidi?"

"Thanks, Bob. Tonight is your last chance to see Frank Sinatra in concert. He's giving his farewell performance, "My Kind of Town" at the old Chicago Theater. Tickets are said to be scarce. And Emeraude is in town. She's finishing filming of the major motion picture *Maid Marian* directed by Steven Lagerfeld in which she costars with Collum Greene. Emeraude, known for her austere profile and cool-cool-cool air on-screen, has finally agreed to film a torrid nude love scene for the picture. Rumors are that the segment is being filmed in deep secret somewhere on Lake Michigan. And in a surprise development, a reliable source states that despite earlier announcements, Emeraude is going to pull out of the forthcoming Lagerfeld remake of *Dark Passage* starring Collum Greene. Our source cites artistic differences that cropped up during the filming of *Marian*. On the music front, the search goes on for a new conductor for the Chicago Symphony Orchestra—"

Bennis said, "Emeraude? Nude? Where, where? WHERE?" and leaped up on the rail, balancing precariously and scanning the horizon with his hand shading his eyes.

"Please! Spare me. And besides, if you fall in, I won't fish you out." He stayed on the rail. "You know, that's odd about *Dark Passage*. The *Enquirer* said it was a done deal."

"She shouldn't have let that leak while she was still making this picture." He jumped back down.

"I don't think she let it, Bennis. I've heard Emeraude and her current guy Mitchen are fighting. She hit him with a pineapple from the centerpiece at a dinner last week. He probably ran to the gossipmongers with something she'd told him in confidence."

"Ah, pillow talk. Always very foolish."

I folded up my sandwich paper and lobbed it into a trash can. "Well, she changes men every three weeks whether they're used up or not. She used to be an item with Lagerfeld, and Collum before that."

"Fickle."

"Speaking of fickle, how's Annabella?"

"Annabella's history. I'm dating this Felicia now. She really is the one, Figueroa."

"We'll see about that."

Bennis went to the table to eat and I took his place at the helm. I noticed the start of a sunburn on my arm. Not bad, though. If we were out again tomorrow, I'd have to bring sunscreen. Still—thank goodness we got to wear short sleeves. A full uniform out here would be deadly.

When Bennis had finished lunch, we tooled around some more, first up toward Belmont Harbor, then down past the Planetarium. Since it was Thursday, not a weekend, and since Labor Day was still a week away, there were one or two boats visible, but not the armada that would be out on Saturday.

"My favorite," Bennis said, "is when we get boats as far as the eye can see and then some guy trails a water-skier down the middle, right in front of cigarette boats going at top speed."

"Top speed and drunk," I said.

Half a lazy hour later we issued a citation to one motorboat operator who was laying down a serpentine track on the calm water.

"Fueled by gasoline and vodka," Bennis said.

Then, with not much going on, we ran farther out into Lake Michigan and stood half a mile offshore with the engine off, surveying the city. That was when we heard screaming.

We looked around, not seeing where it was coming from, and I actually stared down into the water. Then Bennis's eye picked up a motorboat coming toward us. Somebody on deck was waving.

As it got closer, I said, "Speak of the devil!"

It was Steven Lagerfeld and Collum Greene. What they were screaming was, "Help us! Emeraude's drowning!"

I stood on the deck of their twenty-five-foot cabin cruiser. I almost said, "Gee, you look just like in the movies," but that would have been naive and also trite, and a Chicago cop can't act that way. Collum Greene did look just like in the movies. He was the "new" style of hunk, red-haired, white freckled skin, although his nose and forearms were looking sunburned now, probably having exhausted the protection of his sunscreen. Collum's appeal was said to be of the boy-next-door sort. There had been nobody next door to me like that, unfortunately.

Lagerfeld was bony, swarthy, and dark-haired. He was more like the mugger next door.

Both men were extremely upset as we stood there on the deck in the sun. It was a warm day, and Collum was wearing a short-sleeve terry-cloth shirt over a skimpy bathing suit. His hair was wet and he was shivering. Lagerfeld was beautifully dressed in white linen pants and a cotton shirt, but he was shaking too.

"She fell overboard," Collum repeated several times. He kept grabbing at my hand when he said it. Bennis, in our boat, was on the radio, giving our position to the dispatcher to relay to the Coast Guard. At Meigs Field, which jutted out into Lake Michigan only a mile or so away, there was a rescue helicopter already taking off.

After Lagerfeld and Greene flagged us down, we

had motored together to where they thought the movie star had gone into the water. But there was no sign of her. Behind us Chicago was almost out of sight in the haze. There was nothing ahead but open water, and the coast of Michigan eighty miles away.

I checked that we had lashed Lagerfeld's and Greene's cruiser tightly enough to ours and that the tires we used for bumpers were in place between us. The CPD doesn't like its boats banged up. I heard Bennis say into the radio, "We'll hold the boat," meaning the cruiser. Bennis would stay on our boat. I was guarding the scene of the crime—or what could potentially be a crime. We had agreed to this in a glance, without a word. Bennis and I have been together long enough to communicate without speaking.

I said to the two men, "Okay, now tell me again. What happened to her?"

"Oh, God!" Collum groaned. "She was so beautiful! And she must be *dead!*"

His voice was that of a soul in genuine torment, grief-filled and raw. I reminded myself that he was a very fine actor.

"Tell me what exactly happened."

"We had finished the scene," Lagerfeld said. "It was our third time through, and I thought it was fine. With this kind of a scene, really torrid, if you do it too much, it doesn't get better."

"I see."

"So I told them it was a wrap. It was the last bit to be filmed for the picture. Collum turned to go get dressed, and he said something about celebrating, and Emeraude was stretching and reaching for her robe. Glad to get it over with, I think. She must've just put her arms in the sleeves—"

"Must have? You didn't see?"

"Well, no. I was setting the camera down."

"Did you see, Mr. Greene?"

"Yes."

"You tell me what happened next."

"Um. She leaned back against the rail while she was

tying the belt of her robe. And—I don't know. A wave may have hit the side of the boat. It was calm, but maybe there was a wave from some ship. I didn't see one. It would have had to be pretty far away, but there are waves sometimes that come along and you don't see what caused them—"

Lagerfeld said, "Get to the point, Collum."

"Well, she pitched backward over the rail. Just like that! It was so fast I just stared for a second or two. I mean it was like in *The Deep* where the wife just vanishes from the lifeboat while the husband is looking ahead—or maybe it's *Beast*—?"

"Go on with it," Lagerfeld said.

"So I ran to the side and looked over and I couldn't see her. I grabbed the life preserver, the round one, off the wall bracket and threw it in. Then I grabbed one of the vest types and jumped in. I swam around looking for her for—for just about forever—and then finally we decided we'd better go for help."

I said, "And you never saw her surface?"

"I never saw her after she went over the rail. I heard a couple of splashes before I got to the rail and that was all. She must have sunk like a stone."

"She had put on a long terry-cloth bathrobe," Lagerfeld told me. "Maybe it dragged her down."

"And you, Mr. Lagerfeld—you didn't dive in?"

"I can't swim."

A helicopter whump-whumped over us. Collum, Lagerfeld, and I sat at the table in the cabin of their boat.

"There was a story on Channel Four news at noon that she was going to pull out of your next picture. Did you three have an argument?"

"No! We never heard it!" Collum said.

"We didn't watch the news," Lagerfeld stated more firmly and less agitatedly. "Over lunch we critiqued the last shot."

I noticed with mounting suspicion that he did not say "Omigod! You mean she planned to pull out of *Dark Passage?*"

Lagerfeld pointed at the small television set on the table. "That monitor's probably why you thought we watched the news. We use it to play our tapes through for checking."

"Does it pick up the local TV?"

I was convinced Collum started to say no, but he had hardly drawn a breath when Lagerfeld said, "It can. But we didn't watch. We were working! I told you, we spent the whole lunch critiquing the morning's filming."

"Anyhow," Collum continued, "after lunch we did the scene over again. Emeraude wouldn't have done that if we'd had a fight, would she?"

"I guess not. Can you show me the film?"

"Well, it's uh—"

"A nude love scene," Lagerfeld said.

I was about to tell them I knew about sex and stuff like that, but you're not supposed to get sarcastic with the public. Fortunately, Lagerfeld jumped at the chance, and I had the feeling that I was being manipulated. Did they actually *want* me to see the tape, to prove they'd made it?

They turned on the monitor. Yes, the scene was steamy. Emeraude was a glossy, tawny woman, with tan skin and very blond hair. Collum was pale-skinned with red hair. They were quite a sexy pair of lovers. Collum was naked, but no frontal views. Emeraude wore nothing and was seen from all angles. This apparently reflects current values in some way.

"It isn't film you know," Lagerfeld said apologetically. "It's tape."

"What's the difference?"

"Film gives better definition. But Emeraude wouldn't do the scene in front of anybody else. At all. No crew."

"So that's why just the two of you."

"Yes. Plus, we had to get way out in the lake, out of sight of buildings and other boats. I had to do the cinematography alone, so basically we were limited to tape. Film is so much more cumbersome to get right.

The lighting is much more tricky. I wouldn't have been able to do it by myself. I hope the tape's going to look compatible with the film in the final—" He stopped, realizing that he was worrying about the movie, when he should be worrying about Emeraude.

We saw all three scenes. We were inside the little cabin, and even so there was a hood over the screen to keep the bright spill of daylight off the image. Lagerfeld had filmed—taped—from many angles, apparently dashing from port to starboard while his two stars made love on the deck in the sun. In the second take the angles were different and included a lot of shots he must have made sitting on the roof over the cabin. Then the third and last time through he filmed from the deck.

While we watched, the helicopter passed over again, and I could hear Bennis on our boat sending his suggestions through the mobile relay.

The third love scene came to an end. "That's it," Lagerfeld said.

"How long does one scene take to film?"

"Oh, half an hour or so, but we talk it through first. An hour altogether."

"So you taped the first scene when?"

"About ten."

"And the second?"

"About eleven."

"And the third?"

"We broke for an hour's lunch."

"Where did you eat?"

"Out on the deck. Emeraude and Collum wanted to go right ahead while they were still made up and in costume, so to speak."

"And you filmed the third at what time?"

"About one."

"So you were finished about two?"

"Right."

And they'd approached our boat, screaming, at 2:13, or 1413 hours as the CPD and the military say. You couldn't fault the two men's testimony on the time element.

Collum said suddenly, "Why are we just sitting here? Why aren't we looking for her?" He went out on deck and Lagerfeld and I followed.

I said, "The helicopter can cover a lot more area a lot faster."

Bennis had been standing on the deck of the CPD boat listening to us in between transmissions. The deck of the cruiser was a little lower, and he leaned down to us over the rail. "A second helicopter just took off from Glenview Naval Air Station, Mr. Greene."

"Oh. Good."

Bennis glanced at me, knowing my suspicions. "Mr. Greene, we're out here right where you think it happened. You said there's a life preserver floating around someplace?"

"A—a ring life preserver and one of those orange vest things. Both. I threw one to her and then took one in when I jumped in."

"I don't see them. The helicopter doesn't see them, either."

"Maybe it was farther out," Lagerfeld said.

"Like how far?"

"I don't know. It's all just water out here."

I heard Bennis saying "Forty-five seventy-two."

"Go ahead seventy-two."

"Try farther east. My informant isn't sure how far."

I turned to Lagerfeld, "Couldn't you have called for help on the ship-to-shore?"

"We don't have one."

"All this filming equipment and you don't have a radio?"

"It's a rented boat," he said sharply, and then wiped the annoyance from his voice. "We didn't know we'd need one."

"Of course! How could we know there was going to be an accident?" Collum said.

Lagerfeld shot Collum a glance and he shut up.

None of us spoke. Collum shrugged and the two men went back into the cabin to sit down.

Collum Greene was nervous. In fact, Lagerfeld was nervous, too, though he showed it less, but to what extent did nervousness indicate guilt? A lot of perfectly innocent people can't even say hello to a police officer without stuttering and fidgeting, let alone somebody who has just been involved in a suspicious death. My instinct, however, was that they were guilty of more than watching Emeraude pitch backward overboard. How could I jog them a little?

Bennis was on the radio again with the Coast Guard, and we could see the helicopter making a slow run east from our position.

Bennis said into his radio, "It may have been even farther east than that—well, give it a try."

The rules are you can question witnesses without cautioning them. If you question suspects, you have to give them the Miranda warning. If I gave these two famous people the Miranda warning, it could make them very angry, and they would have no trouble kicking up a fit in the media. Stars understand media. CHICAGO COPS BULLY ACTOR AND DIRECTOR. Wonderful! I didn't have much time to make a decision about what to do. Whichever I did could be wrong and could botch up the case.

And then my name would be mud.

However, right now they were rattled. They may have made up this story, and if so, it was still new to them and they wouldn't know whether it would fly. By the time they got to shore, they would have perfected it by rehearsing it on me.

I wandered over to the rail of the cruiser. Bennis leaned down closer to me over the rail of the CPD boat. I asked softly, "What do you think?"

"I think they pitched her in the drink."

"It's just their word. I mean, there's no evidence."

Bennis said, "Even if her body's found, there won't be. Not if she just drowned. If we don't find a bullet

in her head. Which I doubt. These guys are not idiots.
Impulsive maybe, but not idiots. Who's to say from a
drowned body whether these characters were throwing
life preservers at her while she drowned or driving the
boat in the opposite direction?"

"Hell!"

"Well, I hate to have them get away, too, but what
are you going to do?"

"What about the tapes? Say they made the first tape
at ten, the second at eleven, the third at twelve. Then
say they heard the news, got pissed off, and pushed
her overboard. Then say they waited until about two,
just to be on the safe side, and then went roaring off
screaming for help. If we could prove the three film-
ings were done before lunch, we'd have them cold."

"I don't see how you'd do that."

"The angle of the light? At eleven the sun is a little
to the east and at one it's moved farther west."

"Yes, but the boat can motor around and face any
which way. You won't be able to tell that unless you
get some city background in the shot to tell you.
Was there?"

I shook my head. "No. Just deck and a little water
beyond the railing."

"If we had a consistent chop from one direction,
you might get an idea which way the boat was facing.
But as far as I can remember, it's been glassy calm
all day."

"Glassy calm in the tape, too. Damn!"

Bennis had a radio call and turned away.

I didn't believe their story. It was all just too convenient. The breaking news, Emeraude's threat. I looked
up at the bright yellow furnace of the sun for
inspiration.

And found it.

I went back into the cruiser cabin.

Lagerfeld and Collum were still nervous. They had
not been talking together while I had talked with
Bennis. They were beyond earshot in the cabin, but I
had watched them out of the corner of my eye. Proba-

bly they didn't want to look like they were colluding. I sauntered casually—as casually as possible on a boat deck—over to them. Then I just stood next to them, gazing out at the lake. The second helicopter was now quartering the area in tandem with the first. A Coast Guard cutter appeared from the south.

My presence made the two men more nervous.

"You say you took a break for lunch?"

Collum jumped and Lagerfeld blinked. "Yes, I had a sandwich," Collum said.

Lagerfeld said, "I think Emeraude didn't even eat. She was a little seasick."

I glanced pointedly at the extremely calm water.

"Or maybe dieting," he added.

Or maybe they were trying to cover for the fact that Emeraude's body would be found with no food in the stomach. Maybe she had drowned before they got around to lunch. The news item had been on at 12:07, 1207 hours.

I said, "So did you stay in your—ah—acting garb for lunch?" Birthday suit.

Collum tossed his handsome head. "Sure. It didn't seem worth it to dress. And like I said before, we were rehearsing."

"And the final tape was shot at one?"

"One, one-fifteen. Something like that."

I pounced.

"So, when we get your tapes enlarged, they'll show you a lot more sunburned in the third version than you were in the first two run-throughs?"

Collum's mouth dropped open. Lagerfeld's eyes narrowed.

Collum said, "I guess—"

"I wonder. It's odd that your arm is turning red up to the sleeve. White underneath."

I pointed, not touching him, at the sunburn that went up his arm and ended at the short sleeve of his shirt. "You'd think an easy-burning redhead like you had had that shirt on a couple of hours now. Since, oh, maybe noon?"

Collum stared.

But Lagerfeld, who was smarter than Collum, spoke up, "He did it! He pushed her in and ran into the cabin and grabbed the wheel and drove away from her. And by the time I got hold of the wheel and came back, I couldn't find her."

"That's a lie!" Collum shouted.

"And then I was scared that the police would blame us both, so I went along with his story. I mean, he was the one who wet his hair and said he'd been diving for her. I didn't tell on him, but I never hurt her."

"No, he did it!" Collum said. "He was screaming at her because she was pulling out of *Dark Passage* and he'd lose his backing and all the money he's put in it so far."

The helicopter sighted the life preserver and life vest quite a bit more to the east. A couple of days later, Emeraude's body was sighted, considerably farther north. Either she'd drifted, or they'd motored a mile or two before dumping the life preservers in the lake.

Bennis and I wrapped the case up. With both Collum Greene and Steven Lagerfeld accusing each other, it was never possible to decide who did which thing first. My guess was that Lagerfeld and Emeraude argued, struggled, and she fell overboard, whereupon he and Collum both just decided not to go in after her. It turned out that Collum had backed the *Dark Passage* project heavily with his own money and was every bit as angry at her as Lagerfeld. I could bring myself to believe that after she went down, they relented and tried to find her, then panicked, then made up a good story. They were charged with manslaughter, which seemed about right to me.

Our commander was amazed and delighted, which is one of the best things that police commanders can be. Then they make flattering notes that get filed in your personnel jacket.

The regular Marine Unit personnel recovered from

their attack of salmonella in two days, which was a pity. As I said, to Bennis, "I could cruise around out here another week, best buddy."

"Suze, my man. Likewise."

Old Rattler

Sharyn McCrumb

Sharyn McCrumb is an award-winning Southern novelist whose mysteries explore the politics of culture. Her skill as a lecturer, her wit, and her wicked satires of the pretensions of society have inspired critics to compare her to Mark Twain. She is a member of the Appalachian Studies faculty at Virginia Tech and has brought the area into literary prominence.

She won the Edgar for *Bimbos of the Death Sun*; an Agatha winner and nominee and an Anthony nominee too many times to count. *Lovely in Her Bones* won Best Appalachian Novel. The *New York Times* cited *The Hangman's Beautiful Daughter* and *If Ever I Return, Pretty Peggy-O* as Notable Books of the Year. And *Peggy-O* was nominated for the Pulitzer Prize.

Sharyn brings that prize-winning style to this heart-stopping partner's story featuring Sheriff Spencer Arrowood from her last two novels. Another young girl has disappeared in Wake County and the sheriff enlists the help of a man with the Sight known as "*Old Rattler*" . . .

She was a city woman, and she looked too old to want to get pregnant, so I reckoned she had hate in her heart.

That's mostly the only reasons I ever see city folks: babies and meanness. Country people come to me right along, though, for poultices and tonics for the rheumatism; to go dowsing for well water on their land; or to help them find what's lost, and such like; but them city folks from Knoxville, and Johnson City, and from Asheville, over in North Carolina—the skinny ones with their fancy colorless cars, talking all educated, slick as goose grease—they don't hold with home remedies or the Sight. Superstition, they call it. Unless you label your potions "macrobiotic," or "holistic," and package them up fancy for the customers in earth-tone clay jars, or call your visions "channeling."

Shoot, I know what city folks are like. I could'a been rich if I'd had the stomach for it. But I didn't care to cater to their notions, or to have to listen to their self-centered whining, when a city doctor could see to their needs by charging more and taking longer. I say, let him. They don't need me so bad nohow. They'd rather pay a hundred dollars to some fool boy doctor who's likely guessing about what ails them. Of course, they got insurance to cover it, which country people mostly don't—them as makes do with me, anyhow.

"That old Rattler," city people say. "Holed up in that filthy old shanty up a dirt road. Wearing those ragged overalls. Living on Pepsis and Twinkies. What does he know about doctoring?"

And I smile and let 'em think that, because when they are desperate enough, and they have nowhere else to turn, they'll be along to see me, same as the country people. Meanwhile, I go right on helping the halt and the blind who have no one else to turn to. *For I will restore health unto thee, and I will heal thee of thy wounds, saith the Lord.* Jeremiah 30. What do I know? A lot. I can tell more from looking at a person's fingernails, smelling their breath, and looking at the whites of their eyes than the doctoring tribe in Knoxville can tell with their high-priced X rays and such. And sometimes I can pray the sickness out of them and sometimes I can't. If I can't, I don't charge for it—you show me a city doctor that will make you that promise.

The first thing I do is, I look at the patient, before I even listen to a word. I look at the way they walk, the set of the jaw, whether they look straight ahead or down at the ground, like they was waiting to crawl into it. I could tell right much from looking at the city woman—what she had wrong with her wasn't no praying matter.

She parked her colorless cracker box of a car on the gravel patch by the spring, and she stood squinting up through the sunshine at my corrugated tin shanty (*I* know it's a shanty, but it's paid for. Think on that awhile.) She looked doubtful at first—that was her common sense trying to talk her out of taking her troubles to some backwoods witch doctor. But then her eyes narrowed, and her jaw set, and her lips tightened into a long, thin line, and I could tell that she was thinking on whatever it was that hurt her so bad that she was willing to resort to me. I got out a new milk-jug of my comfrey and chamomile tea and two Dixie cups, and went out on the porch to meet her.

"Come on up!" I called out to her, smiling and waving most friendly-like. A lot of people say that rural mountain folks don't take kindly to strangers, but that's mainly if they don't know what you've come about, and it makes them anxious, not knowing if you're a welfare snoop or a paint-your-house-with-whitewash conman, or the law. I knew what this stranger had come about, though, so I didn't mind her at all. She was as harmless as a buckshot doe, and hurting just as bad, I reckoned. Only she didn't know she was hurting. She thought she was just angry.

If she could have kept her eyes young and her neck smooth, she would have looked thirty-two, even close-up, but as it was, she looked like a prosperous, well-maintained forty-four-year-old, who could use less coffee and more sleep. She was slender, with a natural-like brownish hair—though I knew better—wearing a khaki skirt and a navy top and a silver necklace with a crystal pendant, which she might have believed was a talisman. There's no telling what city people will believe. But she smiled at me, a little nervous, and asked if I had time to talk to her. That pleased me. When people are taken up with their own troubles, they seldom worry about anybody else's convenience.

"Sit down," I said, smiling to put her at ease. 'Time runs slow on the mountain. Why don't you have a swig of my herb tea, and rest a spell. That's a rough road if you're not used to it."

She looked back at the dusty trail winding its way down the mountain. "It certainly is," she said. "Somebody told me how to get here, but I was positive I'd got lost."

I handed her the Dixie cup of herb tea, and made a point of sipping mine, so she'd know I wasn't attempting to drug her into white slavery. They get fanciful, these college types. Must be all that reading they do. "If you're looking for old Rattler, you found him," I told her.

"I thought you must be." She nodded. "Is your name really Rattler?"

"Not on my birth certificate, assuming I had one, but it's done me for a raft of years now. It's what I answer to. How about yourself?"

"My name is Evelyn Johnson." She stumbled a little bit before she said *Johnson*. Just once I wish somebody would come here claiming to be a *Robinson* or an *Evans*. Those names are every bit as common as Jones, Johnson, and Smith, but nobody ever resorts to them. I guess they think I don't know any better. But I didn't bring it up, because she looked troubled enough, without me trying to find out who she really was, and why she was lying about it. Mostly people lie because they feel foolish coming to me at all, and they don't want word to get back to town about it. I let it pass.

"This tea is good," she said, looking surprised. "You made this?"

I smiled. "Cherokee recipe. I'd give it to you, but you couldn't get the ingredients in town—not even at the health food store."

"Somebody told me that you were something of a miracle worker." Her hands fluttered in her lap, because she was sounding silly to herself, but I didn't look surprised, because I wasn't. People have said that for a long time, and it's nothing for me to get puffed up about, because it's not my doing. It's a gift.

"I can do things other folks can't explain," I told her. "That might be a few logs short of a miracle. But I can find water with a forked stick, and charm bees, and locate lost objects. There's some sicknesses I can minister to. Not yours, though."

Her eyes saucered, and she said, "I'm perfectly well, thank you."

I just sat there looking at her, deadpan. I waited. She waited. Silence.

Finally, she turned a little pinker, and ducked her head. "All right," she whispered, like it hurt. "I'm not perfectly well. I'm a nervous wreck. I guess I have to tell you about it."

"That would be best, Evelyn," I said.

"My daughter has been missing since July." She opened her purse and took out a picture of a pretty young girl, soft brown hair like her mother's, and young, happy eyes. "Her name is Amy. She was a freshman at East Tennessee State, and she went rafting with three of her friends on the Nolichucky. They all got separated by the current. When the other three met up farther downstream, they got out and went looking for Amy, but there was no trace of her. She hasn't been seen since."

"They dragged the river, I reckon." Rock-studded mountain rivers are bad for keeping bodies snagged down where you can't find them.

"They dragged that stretch of the Nolichucky for three days. They even sent down divers. They said even if she'd got wedged under a rock, we'd have something by now." It cost her something to say that.

"Well, she's a grown girl," I said, to turn the flow of words. "Sometimes they get an urge to kick over the traces."

"Not Amy. She wasn't the party type. And even supposing she felt like that—because I know people don't believe a mother's assessment of character— would she run away in her bathing suit? All her clothes were back in her dorm, and her boyfriend was walking up and down the riverbank with the other two students, calling out to her. I don't think she went anywhere on her own."

"Likely not," I said. "But it would have been a comfort to think so, wouldn't it?"

Her eyes went wet. "I kept checking her bank account for withdrawals, and I looked at her last phone bill to see if any calls were made after July sixth. But there's no indication that she was alive past that date. We put posters up all over Johnson City, asking for information about her. There's been no response."

"Of course, the police are doing what they can," I said.

"It's the Wake County sheriff's department, actually," she said. "But the Tennessee Bureau of Investigation is helping them. They don't have much to go on. They've questioned people who were at the river. One fellow claims to have seen a red pickup leaving the scene with a girl in it, but they haven't been able to trace it. The investigators have questioned all her college friends and her professors, but they're running out of leads. It's been three months. Pretty soon they'll quit trying altogether." Her voice shook. "You see, Mr.—Rattler—they all think she's dead."

"So you came to me?"

She nodded. "I didn't know what else to do. Amy's father is no help. He says to let the police handle it. We're divorced, and he's remarried and has a two-year-old son. But Amy is all I've got. I can't let her go!" She set down the paper cup, and covered her face with her hands.

"Could I see that picture of Amy, Mrs.—Johnson?"

"It's Albright," she said softly, handing me the photograph. "Our real last name is Albright. I just felt foolish before, so I didn't tell you my real name."

"It happens," I said, but I wasn't really listening to her apology. I had closed my eyes, and I was trying to make the edges of the snapshot curl around me, so that I would be standing next to the smiling girl, and get some sense of how she was. But the photograph stayed cold and flat in my hand, and no matter how hard I tried to think my way into it, the picture shut me out. There was nothing.

I opened my eyes, and she was looking at me, scared, but waiting, too, for what I could tell her. I handed back the picture. "I could be wrong," I said. "I told you I'm no miracle worker."

"She's dead, isn't she?"

"Oh, yes. Since the first day, I do believe."

She straightened up, and those slanting lines deepened around her mouth. "I've felt it, too," she said. "I'd reach out to her with my thoughts, and I'd feel nothing. Even when she was away at school, I could always sense her somehow. Sometimes I'd call, and she'd say, 'Mom, I was just thinking about you.' But now I reach out to her and I feel empty. She's just—gone."

"Finding mortal remains is a sorrowful business," I said. "And I don't know that I'll be able to help you."

Evelyn Albright shook her head. "I didn't come here about finding Amy's body, Rattler," she said. "I came to find her killer."

I spent three more Dixie cups of herb tea trying to bring back her faith in the Tennessee legal system. Now, I never was much bothered with the process of the law, but, like I told her, in this case I did know that pulling a live coal from an iron pot-bellied stove was a mighty puny miracle compared to finding the one guilty sinner with the mark of Cain in all this world, when there are so many evildoers to choose from. It seemed to me that for all their frailty, the law had the manpower and the system to sort through a thousand possible killers, and to find the one fingerprint or the exact bloodstain that would lay the matter of Amy Albright to rest.

"But you knew she was dead when you touched her picture!" she said. "Can't you tell from that who did it? Can't you see where she is?"

I shook my head. "My grandma might could have done it, rest her soul. She had a wonderful gift of prophecy, but I wasn't trained to it the way she was. *Her* grandmother was a Cherokee medicine woman, and she could read the signs like yesterday's newspaper. I only have the little flicker of Sight I was born with. Some things I know, but I can't see it happening like she could have done."

"What did you see?"

"Nothing. I just felt that the person I was trying to reach in that photograph was gone. And I think the lawmen are the ones you should be trusting to hunt down the killer."

Evelyn didn't see it that way. "They aren't getting anywhere," she kept telling me. "They've questioned all of Amy's friends, and asked the public to call in for information, and now they're at a standstill."

"I hear tell they're sly, these hunters of humans. He could be miles away by now," I said, but she was shaking her head no.

"The sheriff's department thinks it was someone who knew the area. First of all, because that section of the river isn't a tourist spot, and secondly, because he apparently knew where to take Amy so that he wouldn't be seen by anyone with her in the car, and he has managed to keep her from being found. Besides"—she looked away, and her eyes were wet again—"they won't say much about this, but apparently Amy isn't the first. There was a high school girl who disappeared around here two years ago. Some hunters found her body in an abandoned well. I heard one of the sheriff's deputies say that he thought the same person might be responsible for both crimes."

"Then he's like a dog killing sheep. He's doing it for the fun of it, and he must be stopped, because a sheep killer never stops of his own accord."

"People told me you could do marvelous things— find water with a forked stick; heal the sick. I was hoping that you would be able to tell me something about what happened to Amy. I thought you might be able to see who killed her. Because I want him to suffer."

I shook my head. "A dishonest man would string you along," I told her. "A well-meaning one might tell you what you want to hear just to make you feel better. But all I can offer you is the truth: when I touched that photograph, I felt her death, but I saw nothing."

"I had hoped for more." She twisted the rings on her hands. "Do you think you could find her body?"

"I have done something like that, once. When I was twelve, an old man wandered away from his home in December. He was my best friend's grandfather, and they lived on the next farm, so I knew him, you see. I went out with the searchers on that cold, dark afternoon, with the wind baying like a hound through the hollers. As I walked along by myself, I looked up at the clouds, and I had a sudden vision of that old man sitting down next to a broken rail fence. He looked like he was asleep, but I reckoned I knew better. Anyhow, I thought on it as I walked, and I reckoned that the nearest rail fence to his farm was at an abandoned homestead at the back of our land. It was in one of our pastures. I hollered for the others to follow me, and I led them out there to the back pasture."

"Was he there?"

"He was there. He'd wandered off—his mind was going—and when he got lost, he sat down to rest a spell, and he'd dozed off where he sat. Another couple of hours would have finished him, but we got him home to a hot bath and scalding coffee, and he lived till spring."

"He was alive, though."

"Well, that's it. The life in him might have been a beacon. It might not work when the life is gone."

"I'd like you to try, though. If we can find Amy, there might be some clue that will help us find the man who did this."

"I tell you what: you send the sheriff to see me,

and I'll have a talk with him. If it suits him, I'll do my
level best to find her. But I have to speak to him first."

"Why?"

"Professional courtesy," I said, which was partly
true, but, also, because I wanted to be sure she was
who she claimed to be. City people usually do give
me a fake name out of embarrassment, but I didn't
want to chance her being a reporter on the Amy Albright case, or, worse, someone on the killer's side.
Besides, I wanted to stay on good terms with Sheriff
Spencer Arrowood. We go back a long way. He used
to ride out this way on his bike when he was a kid,
and he'd sit and listen to tales about the Indian times--
stories I'd heard from my grandma—or I'd take him
fishing at the trout pool in Broom Creek. One year,
his older brother Cal talked me into taking the two
of them out owling, since they were too young to hunt.
I walked them across every ridge over the holler, and
taught them to look for the sweep of wings above the
tall grass in the field, and to listen for the sound of
the waking owl, ready to track his prey by the slightest
sound, the shade of movement. I taught them how to
make owl calls, to where we couldn't tell if it was an
owl calling out from the woods or one of us. Look
out, I told them. When the owl calls your name, it
means death.

Later on, they became owls, I reckon. Cal
Arrowood went to Vietnam, and died in a dark jungle
full of screeching birds. I felt him go. And Spencer
grew up to be sheriff, so I reckon he hunts prey of
his own by the slightest sound, and by one false move.
A lot of people had heard him call their name.

I hadn't seen much of Spencer since he grew up,
but I hoped we were still buddies. Now that he was
sheriff, I knew he could make trouble for me if he
wanted to, and so far he never has. I wanted to keep
things cordial.

"All right," said Evelyn. "I can't promise they'll
come out here, but I will tell them what you said. Will
you call and tell me what you're going to do?"

"No phone," I said, jerking my thumb back toward the shack. "Send the sheriff out here. He'll let you know."

She must have gone to the sheriff's office, straight-away after leaving my place. I thought she would. I wasn't surprised at that, because I could see that she wasn't doing much else right now besides brood about her loss. She needed an ending so that she could go on. I had tried to make her take a milk jug of herb tea, because I never saw anybody so much in need of a night's sleep, but she wouldn't have it. "Just find my girl for me," she'd said. "Help us find the man who did it, and put him away. Then I'll sleep."

When the brown sheriff's car rolled up my dirt road about noon the next day, I was expecting it. I was sitting in my cane chair on the porch whittling a face onto a hickory broom handle when I saw the flash of the gold star on the side of the car door, and the sheriff himself got out. I waved, and he touched his hat, like they used to do in cowboy movies. I reckon little boys who grow up to be sheriff watch a lot of cowboy movies in their day. I didn't mind Spencer Arrowood, though. He hadn't changed all that much from when I knew him. There were gray flecks in his fair hair, but they didn't show much, and he never did make it to six feet, but he'd managed to keep his weight down, so he looked all right. He was kin to the Pigeon Roost Arrowoods, and like them he was smart and honest without being a glad-hander. He seemed a little young to be the high sheriff to an old-timer like me, but that's never a permanent problem for anybody, is it? Anyhow, I trusted him, and that's worth a lot in these sorry times.

I made him sit down in the other cane chair, because I hate people hovering over me while I whittle. He asked did I remember him.

"Spencer," I said, "I'd have to be drinking something a lot stronger than chamomile tea to forget you."

He grinned, but then he seemed to remember what

sad errand had brought him out here, and the faint
lines came back around his eyes. "I guess you've heard
about this case I'm on."

"I was told. It sounds to me like we've got a human
sheep killer in the fold. I hate to hear that. Killing for
pleasure is an unclean act. I said I'd help the law any
way I could to dispose of the killer, if it was all right
with you."

"That's what I heard," the sheriff said. "For what
it's worth, the TBI agrees with you about the sort of
person we're after, although they didn't liken it to
sheep killing. They meant the same thing, though."

"So Mrs. Albright did come to see you?" I asked
him, keeping my eyes fixed on the curl of the beard
of that hickory face.

"Sure did, Rattler," said the sheriff. "She tells me
that you've agreed to try to locate Amy's body."

"It can't do no harm to try," I said. "Unless you
mind too awful much. I don't reckon you believe in
such like."

He smiled. "It doesn't matter what I believe if it
works, does it, Rattler? You're welcome to try. But,
actually, I've thought of another way that you might
be useful in this case."

"What's that?"

"You heard about the other murdered girl, didn't
you? They found her body in an abandoned well up
on Locust Ridge."

"Whose land?"

"National forest now. The homestead has been in
ruins for at least a century. But that's a remote area
of the county. It's a couple of miles from the Appalachian Trail, and just as far from the river, so I
wouldn't expect an outsider to know about it. The
only way up there is on an old county road. The TBI
psychologist thinks the killer has dumped Amy Albright's body somewhere in the vicinity of the other
burial. He says they do that. Serial killers, I mean.
They establish territories."

"Painters do that," I said, and the sheriff remembered his roots well enough to know that I meant a mountain lion, not a fellow with an easel. We called them painters in the old days, when there were more of them in the mountains than just a scream and a shadow every couple of years. City people think I'm crazy to live on the mountain where the wild creatures are, and then they shut themselves up in cities with the most pitiless killers ever put on this earth: each other. I marvel at the logic.

"Since you reckon he's leaving his victims in one area, why haven't you searched it?"

"Oh, we have," said the sheriff, looking weary. "I've had volunteers combing that mountain, and they haven't turned up a thing. There's a lot of square miles of forest to cover up there. Besides, I think our man has been more careful about concealment this time. What we need is more help. Not more searchers, but a more precise location."

"Where do I come in? You said you wanted me to do more than just find the body. Not that I can even promise to do that."

"I want to get your permission to try something that may help us catch this individual," Spencer Arrowood was saying.

"What's that?"

"I want you to give some newspaper interviews. Local TV, even, if we can talk them into it. I want to publicize the fact that you are going to search for Amy Albright on Locust Ridge. Give them your background as a psychic and healer. I want a lot of coverage on this."

I shuddered. You didn't have to be psychic to foresee the outcome of that. A stream of city people in colorless cars, wanting babies and diet tonics.

"When were you planning to search for the body, Rattler?"

"I was waiting on you. Any day will suit me, as long as it isn't raining. Rain distracts me."

"Okay, let's announce that you're conducting the psychic search of Locust Ridge next Tuesday. I'll send some reporters out here to interview you. Give them the full treatment."

"How does all this harassment help you catch the killer, Spencer?"

"This is not for publication, Rattler, but I think we can smoke him out," said the sheriff. "We announce in all the media that you're going to be dowsing for bones on Tuesday. We insist that you can work wonders, and that we're confident you'll find Amy. If the killer is a local man, he'll see the notices, and get nervous. I'm betting that he'll go up there Monday night, just to make sure the body is still well-hidden. There's only one road into that area. If we can keep the killer from spotting us, I think he'll lead us to Amy's body."

"That's fine, Sheriff, but how are you going to track this fellow in the dark?"

Spencer Arrowood smiled. "Why, Rattler," he said, "I've got the Sight."

You have to do what you can to keep a sheep killer out of your fold, even if it means talking to a bunch of reporters who don't know ass from aardvark. I put up with all their fool questions, and dispensed about a dozen jugs of comfrey and chamomile tea, and I even told that blond lady on Channel 7 that she didn't need any herbs for getting pregnant, because she already was, which surprised her so much that she almost dropped her microphone, but I reckon my hospitality worked to Spencer Arrowood's satisfaction, because he came along Monday afternoon to show me a stack of newspapers with my picture looking out of the page, and he thanked me for being helpful.

"Don't thank me," I said. "Just let me go with you tonight. You'll need all the watchers you can get to cover that ridge."

He saw the sense of that, and agreed without too much argument. I wanted to see what he meant about "having the Sight," because I'd known him since he was knee-high to a grasshopper, and he didn't have so much as a flicker of the power. None of the Arrowoods did. But he was smart enough in regular ways, and I knew he had some kind of ace up his sleeve.

An hour past sunset that night I was standing in a clearing on Locust Ridge, surrounded by law enforcement people from three counties. There were nine of us. We were so far from town that there seemed to be twice as many stars, so dark was that October sky without the haze of street lights to bleed out the fainter ones. The sheriff was talking one notch above a whisper, in case the suspect had come early. He opened a big cardboard box, and started passing out yellow and black binoculars.

"These are called ITT Night Mariners," he told us. "I borrowed ten pair from a dealer at Watauga Lake, so take care of them. They run about $2500 apiece."

"Are they infrared?" somebody asked him.

"No. But they collect available light and magnify it up to 20,000 times, so they will allow you excellent night vision. The full moon will give us all the light we need. You'll be able to walk around without a flashlight, and you'll be able to see obstacles, terrain features, and anything that's out there moving around."

"The military developed this technology in Desert Storm," said Deputy LeDonne.

"Well, let's hope it works for us tonight," said the sheriff. "Try looking through them."

I held them up to my eyes. They didn't weigh much—about the same as two apples, I reckoned. Around me, everybody was muttering surprise, tickled pink over this new gadget. I looked through mine, and I could see the dark shapes of trees up on the hill—not in a clump, the way they look at night, but one by one, with spaces between them. The sheriff walked away from us, and I could see him go, but when I took the Night Mariners down from my eyes, he was gone. I put them back on, and there he was again.

"I reckon you do have the *Sight,* Sheriff," I told

him. "Your man won't know we're watching him with these babies."

"I wonder if they're legal for hunting," said a Unicoi County man. "This sure beats spotlighting deer."

"They're illegal for deer," Spencer told him. "But they're perfect for catching sheep killers." He smiled over at me. "Now that we've tested the equipment, y'all split up. I've given you your patrol areas. Don't use your walkie-talkies unless it's absolutely necessary. Rattler, you just go where you please, but try not to let the suspect catch you at it. Are you going to do your stuff?"

"I'm going to try to let it happen," I said. It's a gift. I don't control it. I just receive.

We went our separate ways. I walked a while, enjoying the new magic of seeing the night woods same as a possum would, but when I tried to clear my mind and summon up that other kind of seeing, I found I couldn't do it, so, instead of helping, the Night Mariners were blinding me. I slipped the fancy goggles into the pocket of my jacket, and stood there under an oak tree for a minute or two, trying to open my heart for guidance. I whispered a verse from Psalm 27: *Teach me thy way, O Lord, and lead me in a plain path, because of mine enemies.* Then I looked up at the stars and tried to think of nothing. After a while I started walking, trying to keep my mind clear and go where I was led.

Maybe five minutes later, maybe an hour, I was walking across an abandoned field, overgrown with scrub cedars. The moonlight glowed in the long grass, and the cold air made my ears and fingers tingle. When I touched a post of the broken split-rail fence, it happened. I saw the field in daylight. I saw brown grass, drying up in the summer heat, and flies making lazy circles around my head. When I looked down at the fence rail at my feet, I saw her. She was wearing a watermelon-colored T-shirt and jean shorts. Her brown hair spilled across her shoulders and twined with the chicory weeds. Her eyes were closed. I could see a smear of blood at one corner of her mouth, and I knew. I looked up at the moon, and when I looked back, the grass was dead, and the darkness had closed in again. I crouched behind a cedar tree before I heard the footsteps.

They weren't footsteps, really. Just the swish sound of boots and trouser legs brushing against tall, dry grass. I could see his shape in the moonlight, and he wasn't one of the searchers. He was here to keep his secrets. He stepped over the fence rail, and walked toward the one big tree in the clearing—a twisted old maple, big around as two men. He knelt down beside that tree, and I saw him moving his hands on the ground, picking up a dead branch, and brushing leaves away. He looked, rocked back on his heels, leaned forward, and started pushing the leaves back again.

They hadn't given me a walkie-talkie, and I didn't hold with guns, though I knew he might have one. I wasn't really part of the posse. Old Rattler with his Twinkies and his root tea and his prophecies. I was just bait. But I couldn't risk letting the sheep killer slip away. Finding the grave might catch him; might not. None of my visions would help Spencer in a court of law, which is why I mostly stick to dispensing tonics and leave evil alone.

I cupped my hands to my mouth and gave an owl cry, loud as I could. Just one. The dark shape jumped up, took a couple of steps up and back, moving its head from side to side.

Far off in the woods, I heard an owl reply. I pulled out the Night Mariners then, and started scanning the hillsides around that meadow, and in less than a minute, I could make out the sheriff, with that badge pinned to his coat, standing at the edge of the trees with his field glasses on, scanning the clearing. I started waving and pointing.

The sheep killer was hurrying away now, but he was headed in my direction, and I thought, _Risk it. What called your name, Rattler, wasn't an owl._ So just as he's about to pass by, I stepped out at him, and said, "Hush now. You'll scare the deer."

He was startled into screaming, and he swung out at me with something that flashed silver in the moonlight. As I went down, he broke into a run, crashing through weeds, noisy enough to scare the deer across the state line—but the moonlight wasn't bright enough for him to get far. He covered maybe twenty yards before his foot caught on a fieldstone, and he went down. I saw the sheriff closing distance, and I went to help, but I felt light-headed all of a sudden, and my shirt was wet. I was glad it wasn't light enough to see colors in that field. Red was never my favorite.

I opened my eyes and shut them again, because the flashing orange light of the rescue squad van was too bright for the ache in my head. When I looked away, I saw cold and dark, and knew I was still on Locust Ridge. "Where's Spencer Arrowood?" I asked a blue jacket bending near me.

"Sheriff! He's coming around."

Spencer Arrowood was bending over me then, with that worried look he used to have when a big one hit his fishing line. "We got him," he said. "You've got a puncture in your lung that will need more than herbal tea to fix, but you're going to be all right, Rattler."

"Since when did you get the Sight?" I asked him. But he was right. I needed to get off that mountain and get well, because the last thing I saw before I went down was the same scene that came to me when I first saw her get out of her car and walk toward my cabin. I saw what Evelyn Albright was going to do at the trial, with that flash of silver half hidden in her hand, and I didn't want it to end that way.

A Matter of Character
Michael Collins

Michael Collins, aka Dennis Lynds, William Arden, John Crowe, Carl Dekker, and Mark Sadler. No matter what name he uses, his quality of writing has garnered him an Edgar, Shamus nominations, a special Edgar, the prestigious West German *Arbeitsgemeinschaft Kriminalliterature* Commendation for his entire body of work, and a Lifetime Achievement Award from the Private Eye Writers of America.

He's also an accomplished short-story writer with a list of credentials that is staggering. You can sample his work in *Deadly Allies II* and *I, P.I.*, as well as this taut thriller featuring Dan Fortune of *Cassandra in Red* fame.

When Santa Barbara PI, Dan Fortune, is asked to investigate a murder in New York City, he calls on his old partner, Joe Harris, for help. Together they team up to find the answers to a crime that spans both coasts and a shocking "Matter of Character" . . .

He wore a suit and tie, sat alone at a table in the rear of the cocktail lounge working on some ledgers. When he looked up, he smiled. "Hello, Dan."

"How are you, Joe?" I said.

The lounge was a long room on Forty-eighth Street between Eighth Avenue and Broadway. It had booths, tables, indirect lighting, and a small bar at the front where the bartender wore a red-and-gold jacket. I sat across the table.

"Classy place," I said. "How about a double Irish? On the cuff."

"You don't drink the hard stuff anymore, and I own the joint. Cash on the line. Everything changes."

"Give some people power and they turn into Hitler."

We grew up together, Daniel Tadeusz Fortune, who had once been Fortunowski, and Joseph Francis Harris. Down in Chelsea near the old docks, and he knows how I lost my left arm. He was there the night two seventeen-year-old thieves were looting a freighter and one fell into the hold, shattering his arm. Two juveniles, one whose cop father had run away and whose mother brought home too many cops who hadn't run away, and the other whose father and mother were both too drunk most of the time to stand much less run anywhere.

"Nothing's free when you own the game," he said. "Especially for tourists from cloud-cuckoo-land. I'll bet you ask for lemon slices and paper umbrellas on your beer."

"Only the best now, Joe. Stuff you don't get back here."

"Like what?"

"Sierra Nevada, Red Tail."

People get busy, drift apart, move away, and it had been five years since I'd seen Joe. Longer. But there are some people who, when there's no one else, will always be there for you and you for them.

"I need some help, Joe."

"I told you that twenty years ago."

"Not mental this time, physical. I need knowledge, expertise, contacts. I need names, faces, and the word on the street. I've been away too long."

"Let's go back to my office." He called to the bartender, "Reuben, two Red Tails in the back." And grinned at me.

It started in Santa Barbara when Samuel Armbruster came to my office, and I sent for the official New York Police Department record of the killing.

On the night of October 5, 1994, at 1:06 A.M., Roger Berenger, of 140 E. Pedregosa Street in Santa Barbara, California, was attacked in the corridor of the Emerson Hotel on West 41st Street, between Ninth and Tenth Avenue, while in the company of Ricky Franklin, 14, a male prostitute Berenger had picked up on Ninth Avenue, and was pronounced dead at the scene. Injured in the same attack, Franklin could not identify the assailants when questioned later in the hospital. There were no other witnesses. Gondolfo Godoy, hotel manager, found the victims and called the police. Autopsy by the medical examiner's office showed that Roger Berenger had died of multiple blows to the face and head. His money, watch, rings, and shoes were missing.

"Roger did not employ prostitutes, Mr. Fortune," Samuel Armbruster said. "He had neither the interest nor the need."

He was a tall man with thick gray hair and green eyes as fierce and determined as a hungry eagle.

"The evidence tells the New York police a different story," I said. "I'm afraid it tells me the same thing, Mr. Armbruster."

"Then either the evidence is wrong, or the New York police have the wrong evidence."

We sat in my office in the back room of the red-tile-roofed Summerland hacienda I share with my lady Kay Michaels. Or I sat. Samuel Armbruster stood ramrod straight, legs slightly apart as if balancing on the deck of a rolling destroyer like the naval officer he had been. ("That was a long time ago, Mr. Fortune. During wars when they needed trained officers and didn't ask irrelevant questions," he'd told me the first time he'd come to the office. "They would probably toss me out of the service today.")

"It's not complicated evidence, Mr. Armbruster. There isn't much to question."

His friend Roger Berenger had been killed on a trip to a convention of violin teachers at the Sheraton Hotel in New York. As next of kin, Armbruster had gone to New York to identify the body, bring it back to Santa Barbara, and express his strong doubts. The

New York police had been polite, but the case was open and shut, there was nothing they could do. Armbruster came to me. I still had good contacts among the NYPD, especially now that I was 3,000 miles away. Captain Pearce sent me a copy of the case file.

"It could not have happened as they say it did. Roger would never have been with such a boy or in such a place."

He still stood like Farragut on his flagship at Mobile Bay. Damn the torpedoes, full speed ahead.

"You're saying Roger wasn't gay?"

He dismissed that with a wave. "Of course he was gay, we've been together for years. But Roger would not have gone near that area, such places disgusted him. He was far too fastidious, had far too much character."

"People can change," I said as gently as I could. "Sometimes we don't know everything about—"

"Spare me the homilies, Mr. Fortune. I am well aware of the possibilities and the psychology involved, probably far more than you in respect to the gay world, and I know what Roger would and wouldn't do."

He stood there like some tough old redwood that had survived a thousand years. We don't make life easy in this country for the different who want to stand tall and live like everyone else, and do whatever anyone else can do. He was tough and strong and determined, but his life's companion had died, and he was trying to be all those things and somehow find out why. I wished he would sit down, not make me feel flabby and self-indulgent, but standing tall was part of what held him together. It probably always had been.

"Just how many years were you and Roger together, Mr. Armbruster?"

He didn't answer for a few seconds, probably looking for some hidden attack behind the question. We do that to the different in this country, too. He looked into my eyes, and looked at my empty sleeve, and whatever he saw in one or the other, he suddenly sat in my one armchair, his face no longer looking as tough or as hard.

"Twenty-six years." His voice was low, each word slow and distinct. "For twenty of those twenty-six years, we've lived in the same house. We each had a studio at the front of the house, we both composed and taught violin in those studios. We went to the same church, sang in the same choir, became deacons in that church. Twenty-six years sharing our work, our pleasures, and our troubles. Sharing our sex lives and our happiness. Now he's gone and I'm alone. My life essentially over as well as empty. But I will not let Roger's memory be a lie."

Not as tough or hard, but just as determined.

"He was found dead in the corridor of that hotel, a fourteen-year-old male prostitute he had picked up injured beside him. If he didn't go there with the boy, how did he get there?"

"That, Mr. Fortune, is what I'm hiring you to find out, isn't it?"

"You're saying that someone took him there and killed him? Someone hired the boy to lie, beat him up, and somehow made him continue to lie in the hospital?"

"I don't know what I'm saying. I only know that Roger could not have died as the New York police say he did, because he could not have been with such a boy in such a place."

"You have an idea what a motive could be?"

"If I had, I wouldn't be here, Mr. Fortune."

His green eyes didn't flinch, but they did flicker. He might not know a specific motive for a specific person to murder Roger Berenger, but he knew a general motive for too many people to murder any man like Roger. Everyone in our country who dances to a different beat knows that motive.

Over dinner, Kay watched me. "Are you going to help him?"

It was Saturday, one of our wine dinners. They're important, our wine dinners. The sharing of more than a house or a bed or even a career. She has her career and I have mine. Together we have the house and the bed. But on every Saturday we can manage we have more. A bottle of a good wine, a fine dinner, and time only for us.

"Do I have a devastated man groping for how to deal with the loss of the most important person in his life, a man who's come to a rational conclusion based on fact, or someone who knows more than he's telling me?"

"Does it matter, Dan?"

She knows me. I liked Samuel Armbruster, and when I like someone I tend to believe them, or at least go along with them until they prove they can't be believed. Most police departments wouldn't consider that a good character trait in a detective. It was one of the many ways I differed from most police officers, and most private investigators too, for that matter.

"You liked him too, Kay?"

"I like anyone who stands up for who and what he is," she said. "Mr. Armbruster is doing that. For his dead friend, and for himself."

"I'll probably have to go to New York."

"I'll live," Kay said.

"The woman of ice."

"You take good care of me. I can manage for a week or so."

I wasn't sure I could, and before I plunged back into the swamp of New York, I decided to find out a little more about my client and Roger Berenger.

In a city and county as small as Santa Barbara you work with the same police, get to know some of them well, for better or worse. Sergeant Gus Chavalas, SBPD's favorite Latino detective, is for the better. He's actually Greek, but unless he is asked directly he keeps that information to himself in a city that is twenty percent Latino. Over the years we've come to trust each other, and he'll bend a few rules if no one will get hurt.

"I checked on your two old boys. All the way back to when they came to town. We've had some crank calls and a few inquiries from nervous parents thinking of sending their kids to them for violin lessons, but both Berenger and Armbruster always came out cleaner than the cranks. Not a whisper of trouble, sex or anything else, child or adult. They're both deacons in their church, serve on the board of the symphony society, volunteer one day a week for United Way. They're active, open, and popular in the community."

"No gay bars, no cruising, no prostitutes?"

"Not on the record. No sheets on either of them, no arrests."

"They are gay?"

"Yeah, sure they're gay. They don't hide it, but they don't advertise it, if you know what I mean. You couldn't tell by how they look or how they act. At least not in public."

"So I noticed. Armbruster looks like a tough old guy."

"So was Berenger."

I heard the tone in his voice. We've gotten to know each other that well.

"You don't think Berenger died like that either?"

"Let's say from what I know about him it's out of character," Chavalas said, then shrugged. "But who knows what goes on inside someone who lives a kind of life you don't know anything about?"

"Someone different."

"Yeah. Someone different."

You can be away from New York for a few months or too many years and still know where the streets are, but not what and who are on those streets. Especially not what and who are invisible behind those streets, hidden in the back rooms and the shadows, lurking in the sewers. For that only contacts could help, and after three years in California I had damn few. In the world of the permanent underclass that now populates those shadows and sewers, a month is a year, and a year is a century.

"There were two of them," Captain Pearce said. "No names, no faces, the meat-market kid never saw them before."

"You believe that?"

"Every word, and not a syllable."

He's a college man, Captain Pearce. In ten years he's aged thirty, and he stopped expecting to rise into the ranks of the brass long ago. Or even wanting to. Whenever I come back to the city now he stares at me as if wondering how I had escaped and he hadn't, and his face tells me he knows he never will.

"You've been out in paradise too long, Fortune. You know that down there you believe everything and you don't believe anything. Truth and fact are irrelevant."

"If they took his wallet, how did you identify him or know where he was staying?"

"They left his business card case, and a hotel bill."

"Convenient. You can sell a good leather card case."

Pearce looked at me as if I'd lost my mind. I was asking for logic from two grade-school dropouts, probably stoned, battering a man to death in the dim corridor of a flophouse populated by a steady stream of hookers and nervous johns of all sexes. Maybe I had lost my mind.

"You never traced any of the loot?"

Pearce didn't even bother to answer that. The money would have been spent in an hour, the watch and rings would have been sold for ten cents on the dollar and be for sale in a flea market in Peru. Only the shoes might turn up someday—on the body of an overdose in an alley somewhere.

"Armbruster says he would never have been with that kid."

"He was."

"He had a hotel. Why the Emerson?"

"Ricky Franklin is fourteen and looks twelve. He's usually stoned and smells bad. He has purple spiked hair, pants he needs novocaine to put on. The pants are so thin his cock and ass might as well be purple too. He wouldn't get one foot inside a real hotel like the Sheraton if he was with Mother Teresa."

I watched him. "So it's open and shut. On the word of a fourteen-year-old drug addict male hooker."

"It's open and shut on probability. On where Berenger was and who he was with."

"And what he was," I said.

Pearce didn't flinch. "And what he was." He leaned forward. "Look, Dan, Berenger was a homosexual in a strange city. The boy was a male hooker, the hotel was a hooker hangout. You know how many muggings under exactly those conditions we get a year?"

"Have you talked to Samuel Armbruster?"

Pearce sat back. "I've talked to him."

"Can you see him with that boy in that hotel?"

"I never talked to Roger Berenger, not alive. And I can see anyone with anyone anywhere under the right pressure."

"If Armbruster were straight, and the hooker a fourteen-year-old girl, could you see him with her in a hotel like that? Would the pressure be right?"

As I said, Pearce is a college man.

"Probably not."

"Thanks," I said.

"But I still never met Roger Berenger."

"Neither did I, but, you know, Captain, I'm beginning to take Armbruster's word for it."

I had checked into the same Sheraton where the violin teachers' convention was held. This week it had a local association of security guards, and a national convention of police chiefs. I felt safe and secure. The hotel staff felt harried. None of the people on the desk, day or night shift, had any memory of Roger Berenger. The photograph Samuel Armbruster had given me drew nothing but blank stares from the desk clerks and the rest of the staff. If he had ever asked for his key, they had no recollection of it. In fact, no one remembered him asking for anything.

No bellman recalled going to his room, the maids didn't remember ever seeing him, and the doorman swore he had never seen a man of his description leave the hotel.

The general consensus was that Roger Berenger had never done anything in his room and had never left the hotel. Which wasn't unusual for academic convention attendees. They never caroused, ate in the coffee shop, and tipped badly.

Using a list supplied by Armbruster, I called other violin teachers who would have been at the convention. They had all shared coffee-shop meals with Berenger, had seen him often in the hotel. They all said he had attended every session until the night he was killed, played in many chamber music groups, been generally busy. He had been in good spirits, and had never mentioned going anywhere outside the hotel.

The manager, who talked to me only because Captain Pearce told him to be nice, looked at his watch more often than a drunk in a bar with a half hour to go before the last train home.

"You don't remember anything about Roger Berenger?"

"Mr. Fortune, really. A few thousand people pass through this hotel every week. I only became aware of Mr. Berenger as a guest when the police came to talk to me about his murder. I had nothing to tell them; and, I have nothing to tell you."

"Hang with me. I could have some different questions."

He sighed and looked at his watch while I asked all my questions, some of them maybe actually different. He looked at the watch with increasing frequency until I came to: "Did anything very special or unusual happen while Berenger was here? Something that involved him, or even that didn't?"

"My God, unusual things happen every minute in a hotel this size! Especially when we have conventions, and we *always* have conventions."

Hotel owners like conventions, hotel managers don't. For the managers, conventions are a headache.

"I mean so unusual even you might have taken particular notice and remembered."

He shook his head. "No, there was ..." His face went as blank as a computer screen reviewing its files while you sat and "Please Waited." "Wait ... Yes ... One of the bellmen ... Some kind of argument, an actual fight in the changing lockers. Our security people had to be called. But I don't recall—"

The head of hotel security, Chief Mazzoni, was a large man whose collar and tie were so tight they looked like a medieval neck iron. He wasn't someone who'd spent a great deal of his life behind a desk.

"Manager says Pearce sent word to help you out," Mazzoni said. "You an ex-cop like me?"

"My father was on the force. I lost the arm too young, so had to go private."

He nodded sympathetically. "So what can I do for you?"

"The manager says there was some kind of problem with a bellman. A fight?"

Mazzoni began to laugh. "Well, more like a mini-Latin riot, you know? Not exactly a fight. But what's it got to do with this Berenger guy you're interested in?"

"Probably nothing. I'm grabbing straws."

He knew about grabbing at straws. "Well, it's the new kid we took on. Another damn Latino. Eighty percent of the staff is Latino now, a hundred percent in housekeeping, and it's getting bigger 'cause they all bring their cousins when a job opens up, you know? Anyway, this part-time kid was showering in the staff rooms to go off early because we were slow, and when he comes out all his clothes are gone! Street clothes, uniform, everything. There he was buck naked, in a hurry, no one else in the staff room. He's too scared we'll get mad to go out in a towel, so he waits until the regular shift comes off, accuses one of them of swiping his clothes to get him in trouble. They all deny it, but they laugh like all hell.

"Someone calls the bell captain who reads them the riot act about practical jokes, but they swear none of them did it. That's when the last guy on the shift shows up carrying the kid's uniform. He says he found it in a fourth-floor stairwell, but no one believes him and the kid starts a fight with the guy. The bell captain breaks it up, tells the kid to calm down, lectures everyone again on practical jokes, and sends them home. The kid has to go home in the uniform. A maid finally finds his street clothes in the laundry room next day. And that was it. No one ever did find who the joker was."

"Maybe there wasn't any joker," I said. "What floor was Roger Berenger on?"

Mazzoni picked up the phone, dialed three numbers. "What room did Roger Berenger have, Pete? The queer that was killed the cops came asking about. Yeah, that one. Four-twenty-one? You're sure? How close is that room to a stairwell? Okay, thanks." He hung up, swiveled back to me. "Three rooms from the right stairwell."

"The one where the clothes were found?"

"Yeah."

We both thought for a time in the quiet office. I spoke first. "You have all your street exits and entrances under video surveillance?"

"Sure."

"You keep the tapes?"

He nodded. "Maybe a week, two."

It was a week and a half since the night Roger Berenger died.

"Have the police looked at them?"

"They never asked."

We started with the time between when the bellman's clothes disappeared and when they were "found" in the stairwell. It was on the tape from the camera that monitored a small side exit. There were two of them. One was a skinny Latino in a black western hat, black suit that looked like silk, gray shirt, and narrow yellow tie. The other was a short, muscular Anglo with a heavy macho mustache, ill-fitting sport jacket, and brown slacks.

The man who walked between them was Roger Berenger.

He did not walk well on the flickering, grainy video. His arms weren't free, his whole body resisted, and his feet seemed to drag. He wasn't leaving the hotel because he wanted to.

"Can I get some stills of those two men? Good full faces?"

"We can try."

The still photos were blurred, but recognizable. My contacts on the Strip had no reason to talk to me. After three years I had no favors to give and no markers to call in. All I saw were a lot of blank faces, closed doors, shadows on dark streets, and eyes watching me.

That was when I went to Joe Harris.

In his office we drank the Red Tail ales, Joe looked at the still photos, and I told the story of Roger Berenger and Samuel Armbruster. Joe had moved across Eighth Avenue into the higher-rent district, owned a lounge that catered to people who expected boutique beers from California, but he was still a saloon keeper, and still on the Strip if only at the edge.

"You know how many times a year a guy like Roger Berenger comes to New York looking for what he can't get at home and ends up dead in a bed in one of those hotels with a Ricky Franklin? You ain't been away that long or that far, Dan."

"Captain Pearce already reminded me," I said. "Except Roger Berenger wasn't looking. He had all he needed at home. And if he had been looking, he could have found a reasonable facsimile of Ricky Franklin ten blocks from where he lived. Everything's up to date in Santa Barbara."

"He wasn't in Santa Barbara, and he was alone."

"He wasn't alone when he left the hotel that night."

Joe stared at the photographs spread out on his desk. "You think it was a setup?"

"As Sam Armbruster said, I don't know what I think. What I know so far is, Berenger doesn't sound like a man who would be in that hotel with that boy. He didn't leave the Sheraton alone, and my hunch is he didn't leave voluntarily. I know if he hadn't been homosexual more questions would have been asked, and I'm wondering if someone counted on that."

Joe still stared down at the photos. Then he looked up, leaned back, and drank his ale. "What do you want me to do?"

"I need names, faces, connections, motives, clues. Anything I can get to help me convince the police it wasn't what it looks like, and maybe even lead me to the real killer. At least one fact to raise some doubt."

"I can give you one fact right now. What doubt it raises, I'm not so sure."

"What fact?"

"The cool Latin dude in the photo." Joe pointed to the skinny Latino in the silky black suit on one side of Roger Berenger.

"What about him?"

"His name's Belmonte. He's a pimp, lives in the Emerson, and specializes in boys."

"You think Ricky Franklin is one of his stable?"

"I don't know. But let's say it wouldn't astound me."

"I guess we better find out."

I said "we," but it was Joe who did the work.

I spent a day cruising Ninth, Tenth, and Eleventh avenues all the way from Gansevoort Street to Forty-fourth, asking questions on all the hooker tracks, drinking too much beer, and getting the same closed doors and blank stares. Our theory was I would at least stir up the mud and maybe make the carrion eaters nervous enough to come closer to the surface.

Joe sat in his office and made calls. He asked questions and listened to answers. He sent out the radar and waited for the echoes. The first ones started to come in the second day.

"Ricky Franklin's in Belmonte's stable all right, and word on the street is that since little Ricky got out of the hospital he's been scoring the good white a lot bigger than usual."

"He's found some money?"

"That's how it reads, and Ricky wouldn't have money if Belmonte didn't have more, so I dug a lot deeper, called in some very big markers. You're gonna owe me for life, Dan boy."

"I already did," I said. "Tell me more about Belmonte?"

"It appears that Mr. Belmonte paid off a big bundle of debt he'd owed a certain party for a long time. The party isn't all that pleased. The loss of the vig Belmonte was carrying cuts into his weekly take, so he didn't mind talking some in the hope someone could dry up the pimp's source of sudden cash and he could get him back on the weekly rolls. Even offered to lean on little Ricky if we need help."

"No word on the source of all this cash Belmonte and Franklin are throwing around?"

"Not yet. But I got the name of the other guy in your still photos, and that may help."

"How?"

"He's a two-bit repo man and skip tracer named Zack Murfree. He did a couple of months on a misdemeanor with Belmonte a few years ago. Word is that since then he's supplied Belmonte with fresh meat from time to time. Sort of a recruiter of street boys he meets on his travels."

"How does that help us find the source of the cash?"

"Murfree works out of L.A."

Los Angeles was close to home. Roger Berenger's home.

Ricky Franklin sneered. Cocaine courage. He sat on the filthy bed in his basement pad off Tenth Avenue, nothing on but his purple spiked hair and a sequined shirt dirtier than the bed, his legs splayed to display his wares.

"We know it was a setup, Ricky," Joe said. "Tomorrow the cops know. Dan here's a real good friend of Captain Pearce. You want the cops to know? You know how long you'll be inside? You know what happens to you inside?"

"Nothing ain't happened already out here." He rotated his hips and fluttered his fake eyelashes at Joe. "You want a taste, Mr. Harris? Maybe your friend?"

I said, "Who paid Belmonte to kill Berenger, Ricky?"

The sneer. "Who's Belmonte?"

"When the cops go looking for Mr. Belmonte," Joe said, "you won't live long enough to go to jail."

Ricky giggled. "No way, Jose. He likes my little ass too good."

I said, "He can get all the little asses he wants, Ricky. They're a dime a dozen down here."

"Screw you," the boy said, suddenly sullen.

He was still pouting when Joe's secret weapons came through the door. The friendly neighborhood loan shark and two of his larger collectors. The boy's pout turned into a grimace of horror, his sullen eyes wide with bottomless fear. A fear so strong the happy dust instantly boiled out of his veins. All the way down from his high, he cowered on the bed with his back trying to go through the wall, his skinny arms hugging his legs to his hollow chest. The loan shark enjoyed the effect he and his helpers had.

He smiled. "Tell the nice men what they want to know, boy."

Ricky shook and cowered, but he didn't speak.

"Maury."

One of the big collectors slapped Ricky across the face. Lightly. Just enough to split his lip. Ricky whimpered, wiped blood from his chin, said nothing.

"A tourist gets hurt, it's trouble," the loan shark said. "Trouble is bad for business."

"I don' know nothin'," the boy pleaded.

"Maury," the loan shark said.

Ricky screamed, covered his face, cowered. The big collector grinned, pulled the boy's hand away. He raised his fist. I caught his wrist with my lone hand. The big man scowled, pulled his arm away. Or tried to. My one arm is a lot stronger than I look.

I said, "Ricky, you want to get out of here? Off the streets? Stop peddling your ass?"

The big collector got his hand free, forgot about Ricky. He looked at me as if I were a cockroach, and he knew what to do to cockroaches. Only not this time. His boss had the picture.

"Maury," the loan shark said.

I said, "Home, Ricky. Off the shit."

The boy stared. I was a man out of his mind.

"You get detoxed, a stake, a ticket to anywhere you say," Joe said.

Ricky looked at Joe. He knew Joe had money. Joe owned a cocktail lounge. Joe was a boss. The boy blinked, looked at the loan shark and his collectors with the big fists.

"Monte he kill me," he croaked through his bloody lip.

"Belmonte does nothin'," the loan shark said. "Take the man's deal, boy."

Ricky thought it over. Maybe somewhere inside he really wanted to get out, get off the white dreams, go home. Maybe. At least he knew the alternatives, and none of them were good. He knew what Maury and the silent collector could do to him. If the cops did come after Belmonte, he knew what the pimp would do. Nubile boys *were* a dime a dozen on Tenth Avenue.

"Monte got paid to set the john up. Him 'n Zack

grab the mark over at his hotel, knock him aroun' in the Emerson, knock me aroun' so it looks good. We was s'posed to get picked up in the hall, you know? Only Monte and Zack hit the stupid fucking john too hard 'n he croaks. Jesus, we's scared, but the cops don' even ask no questions." He smirked. "I gets a thousand bucks."

"How much did Belmonte get?" I asked.

"I don' know. Ten grand maybe. Him 'n Zack splits it."

"Who hired Belmonte?"

"Zack."

"Who hired Zack?"

The boy shrugged. "I don' know."

The loan shark said, "Maury."

"I swear!" Ricky shrieked, cowered again. "I don' know! I tell you all I know! Monte goddamn kill me! You get me out o' here like you say!"

I said, "Put your pants and shoes on."

The loan shark and his collectors left. They'd done what Joe asked, given Belmonte some trouble. All in a day's work. Ricky Franklin perked up the instant they were gone, looked like he was having second thoughts about going home.

"We'll get to Belmonte," I said. "And he has friends."

Ricky put on his pants and shoes. In the pants he might as well have been still naked. Joe would have to foot the bill for a new wardrobe too.

I landed at LAX three hours later by clock time, and arrived at Zack Murfree's office an hour after that. It was in Hollywood, a three-floor walkup from the twenties. The new Hollywood. Where buildings were trashed and the streets dirty, traffic moved through at a brisk pace from somewhere else to somewhere else, and teenage hookers worked the doorways and streets. A Hollywood where the dreams had been trashed even more than the buildings.

Murfree's office had one of those old-fashioned half

glass doors with his name stenciled on it in black with gold borders. The gold was flaking off. I went in expecting to see an outer room with a blonde in a perm behind a battered wooden desk. But there was only the single large room. The battered desk was there, but no blonde. A filing cabinet, sagging sofa, two wooden chairs, and Zack Murfree. Dead.

He had been shot in the shabby desk chair that creaked and squealed for oil when I moved it, fallen forward against the desk, and slid off to the floor, his head at a grotesque angle against a bottom drawer. There was too much blood, the exit wounds too big, to tell how many bullets he'd taken, but I saw two holes in the back of the desk chair. A big handgun.

I spent an hour going through his pockets, the drawers, and the files. There wasn't much to go through. Half of one drawer in the filing cabinet (the other drawers held his laundry and junk food); nothing but paper clips and rubber bands in the desk, not even a bottle; small change and keys in his pockets. I found even less. If there had been anything about Roger Berenger, it was gone. If Zack Murfree'd had a wallet or any other personal effects, they were gone.

I called Joe. The time difference put it early evening in New York. I told him.

"You think it's someone who hired Murfree?"

"I don't know what I think. What I know is we've lost our only lead. Unless Belmonte knows more than Ricky thinks he knows."

"He knows something," Joe said. "Word is he's gone to ground. No one's seen him for twenty-four hours."

"That's me asking questions."

"Or he knew someone was after Murfree, and maybe him."

"So maybe he does know more."

"That wouldn't shock me either."

"How's Ricky?"

"Scared shitless, but safe and in detox."

"I don't suppose he's remembered anything more?"

"I think he's trying to forget what he does remember."

Which left me with no leads at all to who had hired Zack Murfree. And probably killed him.

Samuel Armbruster waved me to a high-backed wing chair in his small, neat living room. The house was on a quiet upper east street of big and small houses with front yards, trees, and flowering bushes. It wasn't one of the smaller houses, but the downstairs front had been renovated into two studios, and that made the rear rooms smaller.

"I've just made a pot of tea. Roger and I always tried to have tea at four. People should take more time to simply sit and relax, enjoy the small things. Or would you rather have a beer? I have some good micro-brewery beers. Thomas Kemper."

Thomas Kemper Pale Lager or Pilsner are good beers. Over his tea and my beer I told him what had happened in New York and Los Angeles. He listened without comment or interruption in the comfortable room of the house he had shared with Roger Berenger. When I got to the video of Berenger leaving the hotel with Belmonte and Murfree, he leaned forward over his cup of tea and his eyes glittered with anger. When I finished he sat back, placed his teacup on the coffee table, his face a mixture of rage and sorrow.

"Someone did murder Roger."

"Someone set him up, took him to the hotel. I'm not sure it was murder."

"What was it then?"

"I think an accident. They meant to beat him up, not kill him."

He leaned forward, poured milk from its small pitcher into his teacup, placed a silver strainer in the cup, took the cozy from his teapot and poured a fresh cup. He put in a sugar cube, stirred for a time before he sat back and sipped from the steaming cup.

"You're telling me they wanted Roger found by the

police in that hotel with that boy so a public record would be made. They planned to beat him but not kill him. To compromise him, discredit him, but not to kill him?"

"That's how I read it. Who would want to discredit Roger that much? Probably both of you. Give you a bad name in the community? Someone who lives here. Murfree was too close to home to be a coincidence. Someone wanted to give you a bad name in this town in a very specific way."

"As faggot users of male prostitutes, the corrupters of little boys, frequenters of the slimy underbelly."

I nodded. "Any ideas now?"

I watched him as he sat there in his neat, comfortable living room, sipped his tea and appeared to think. But he wasn't really thinking. He wasn't a man who would think that ill of anyone. Certainly not anyone he associated with.

"No one I know would sink that low."

"That isn't what Sergeant Chavalas tells me. He says there have been crank calls and inquiries from parents before they sent their children to you for violin lessons. How recent were some crank calls? Inquiries by parents?"

"There are always some parents who question, and there are always cranks."

"That's not answering my question, Sam."

He smiled. "That's the first time you've called me anything but Mr. Armbruster."

"Don't read anything into it. Tell me about the recent crank."

He shrugged. "We have a sad woman who rooms across the street. She is incapable of harm."

"Parents?"

"I don't know which parents might have been concerned about us, Mr. Fortune. They rarely tell us if they are."

"Dan," I said.

"Roger had twelve different pupils over the last

year, Dan, and I had ten. I suppose you can check on all of them."

"Who else could have had a motive to discredit you and Roger?"

"I know of no one."

"No enemies?"

"None."

"Professional rivals?"

"Violin teachers don't kill each other."

"Sour business deals?"

"We had no business deals."

"A jealous lover?"

He snorted. "We were both too old for that kind of nonsense."

"Anyone at the church or the United Way?"

There was a momentary hesitation before he said, "No."

"Where was it, Sam? The church?"

He finished his second cup of tea, placed it carefully on the coffee table. "There were some rumblings when we were made deacons. It came to nothing."

His voice was angry. Not at the questioners or the rumblings, but at a society that made him have to talk about them, even think about them.

"How come Roger went alone to New York? You're both violin teachers."

"Normally we would have gone together and made a vacation of the trip, but this year an old friend of mine died of AIDS. I had to attend the funeral and memorial service in San Francisco."

"Who would have known that?"

He shrugged. "Almost anyone. The church, United Way, parents of the pupils. The neighbors who saw Roger leave with his bags."

I left the biggest question for last. "Is there anyone you know who's capable of murder, Sam?"

"You said it wasn't murder."

"It is now. Someone didn't want Zack Murfree to talk."

* * *

None of the twelve families who had sent their students to Roger Berenger over the last year had made inquiries to the police. Two of Samuel Armbruster's had. One family had left town six months ago, the other had only good things to say about Armbruster and Berenger, and was, as near as I could tell, genuinely shocked and saddened by the murder. Only one person in the last year had called the police to demand the arrest of the two dangerous criminals who lived in her decent neighborhood and lured small children into their house. The lady in rooms across the street. Mrs. Bithia Petit.

She peered at me around a door still on its chain. "The police won't do anything about those terrible men, but I see what goes on. Those children always going in and out. All the screaming and the crying, the parents dragging them in, and the police do nothing! It's so horrible."

"They give violin lessons to children, ma'am. The parents are only—"

"They may fool you and everyone else, but they don't fool me, not for a second. I know evil when I see it and hear it."

"Have you ever been to New York, Ms. Petit? Maybe recently? Hired anyone to go there? Maybe—"

"I don't dare leave this house until I know they're gone. And I must be back before they return or they'll catch me too. The devil never sleeps, young man."

"Tell me about what they do, Mrs. Petit. Tell me—"

The pale face in the narrow opening became terrified. "I know who you are! You're with them! You're the evil!"

The door slammed shut, and I was left alone on the front steps. I listened but heard nothing more inside. No movement, no sound at all, as if Mrs. Bithia Petit were standing motionless inside, hardly breathing, until the evil in the world walked away from her door.

The Reverend Anthony Cartwright nodded me to a chair in the small sitting room of his rectory. "A tragedy, Mr. Fortune. I still find it almost impossible to believe."

"What?" I said. "That Berenger was killed, or that he was where he was killed?"

His blue eyes were steady. "Both."

"Armbruster tells me not all of your congregation would be that surprised."

The minister smiled. "I'm sure Samuel *didn't* tell you that, Mr. Fortune. He isn't a man to believe bad of anyone, to dwell on the past, or to harbor ill will. If he mentioned our problems, it was you who wormed it out of him. Am I right?"

I nodded. "Tell me about the 'problems.' "

The pastor tented his fingers and looked ministerial. "Roger and Samuel made no secret of their lifestyle, and some parishioners weren't pleased. Not that they should have hidden anything, of course, and they certainly didn't flaunt ... Still—" Reverend Cartwright hesitated, frowned, then, when I made no comment, hurried on. "It was really nothing. A few people asked questions about the compatibility of Christian belief and homosexuality, but we talked it out in an open and honest discussion led by Roger and Samuel themselves. They are fine men. Then, one would expect that from a naval hero, of course."

He tried to smile, but it didn't come out right. He wasn't convincing himself about how "nothing" it had been any more than he was convincing me.

"It wasn't all that pleasant, was it, Reverend?"

He squirmed in his chair behind his desk, then sighed. "I'm afraid I may have made a mistake. I should have realized people can be pushed too far, moved too fast." He sighed again, rested his chin on his tented fingers.

"When you made them deacons?"

He nodded. "Those who had questioned them being with us at all became ugly, and many in the flock saw it as going beyond Christian toleration to approval, and they weren't ready for that."

"Became ugly how?"

His voice was a shade bitter. "They would have no 'homo' deacons. It was an 'affront to Jesus.' All Christian leaders must be 'pure,' 'normal.' The worst declared it an outrage, even a sacrilege. Words like disgusting and filthy were used. Some said it turned their stomachs every time Samuel and Roger passed the plate." He shook his head with a kind of horror. "It was unbelievable to me. Perhaps I've been too sheltered in my small world. But I was shocked by the vehemence, the flood of anger."

"But you didn't back down?"

He spread his hands with a kind of despair. "How could I? I believe in Christian love, in equality before God. I liked Roger and Samuel, even admired them. I couldn't give in to bigotry. Not in the church. Never."

"Where does it stand now?"

"I'm glad to say, while perhaps all the congregation isn't completely reconciled, the crisis has passed. Some people left, but most have returned, and the most violent objections have faded away. We're not home yet, but the violence has vanished."

Or had it simply taken a more deadly direction?

On the phone Joe said, "Belmonte's a ghost, Dan. It's like he's dropped off the planet. Little Ricky's so scared of Belmonte he won't leave the detox center to go to the airport and fly home until he knows where Belmonte is."

"Belmonte's got to know more than Ricky says," I said from my office.

"And as scared of someone as Ricky is of him." Joe stopped as if to listen to the distant sirens at his end. The sounds of New York. "You figure it's someone at that church?"

"That's what I think."

"How would they know enough to arrange it all back here, Dan?"

"Maybe they hired it done."

"You have any leads about who?"

"With Murfree dead and Belmonte missing, not even a hope."

The sirens sounded again in the distance at the other end of the line. "Maybe we can find out. Smoke Belmonte into the open. Make him think we know more than we do and make a move."

"How do we do that?"

"Bring your Mr. Armbruster to New York, send him around the hooker walks asking questions. Make him act like Berenger told him more than he's told the cops."

"Who's going to believe that?"

"Belmonte, for one. And maybe the guy who hired Belmonte and Murfree."

"Why the hell would they believe it, Joe?"

"Because they couldn't afford not to," Joe said. "And maybe the guy who started it all might decide to try for your client too. Get rid of another queer."

"You want me to be the bait in a trap," Samuel Armbruster said.

"You don't have to, Sam. It could be damned dangerous."

We were in his neat living room again. There was no tea or beer this time. I'd come to the point the moment he opened the door. Now he sat facing me across the coffee table.

"Yes, I do," he said. "If I want to know what really happened to Roger and why. That's what you're saying."

"There could be other ways. Someone will crack, Belmonte will show up, they'll trace the gun that killed Murfree."

"You don't believe that, Dan."

I said nothing.

"When?" Armbruster said.

"The sooner the better."

"Tomorrow then. Go and get the tickets."

"All right."

"Now tell me what I have to do."

* * *

For three days, Sam Armbruster talked to the young boys on Ninth, Tenth, and Eleventh avenues, walked below Houston and along the dark water of the river with Joe wandering around him like a wino digging in garbage cans, and me staked and out of sight so my arm wouldn't show. Sam asked questions about Belmonte, implied far more knowledge of the death of Roger Berenger than any of us had. Until the scrawny, frightened, and lost children fled when he came near them, those who hadn't vanished the moment he appeared on the street.

The twelve-year-old who didn't run or hide picked Armbruster up at 9:10 P.M. on Eleventh Avenue in the thirties. Joe lifted his head out of a garbage can and went after them. I waited until Sam and the kid turned the corner toward Tenth Avenue, then ran for Joe's car. When I caught up with them, they were headed north on Tenth: the boy, Armbruster, and Joe staggering along far behind them. I pulled ahead, parked, and watched until they appeared in the rearview mirror. When they all passed and were a block ahead, I pulled out and repeated the maneuver until the boy reached home.

This time home was a flophouse hotel on West 40th Street between Ninth and Tenth avenues. Criminals and pimps have no imagination. The narrow, seedy lobby was empty when I went in. The face of the night clerk was equally narrow and seedy. He looked shocked to see a man alone in his lobby.

"Three people just came in: a tall older man, a skinny kid you knew, and a short guy with dark hair. What room did you tell the short guy you gave the kid?"

"I didn't tell no one nothin'. Never saw no one like that."

"Yes, you did, and I'm meaner than he is."

I smiled.

"Number fourteen, third floor."

"Which room's Belmonte in? And don't waste my time."

"Fifteen."

"Across the hall?"

He nodded.

I went up. The door to fifteen was open, and Belmonte wasn't inside. He was in fourteen. With a gun. I took it away from him. I didn't take the gun away from the big man with the beard.

The clerk had told me about Belmonte in fifteen, but not about the man in twelve. He came through the connecting door between twelve and fourteen with a 10mm Glock in his massive hand. Six-feet-four, 250 pounds, he had a trimmed full beard, a western hat, and cold eyes. He didn't say a word or waste a second. His first shot caught Joe, slammed him back against the wall. His second shot would be for me.

I knew, in one long, slow split second, that this man had killed Roger Berenger and Zack Murfree, and that he wasn't going to face a murder charge if there was any way out at all. He had no choice and neither did I. Both shots from my little Sig-Sauer took him through his left eye, so close together you could have covered the small black holes with a quarter. I'm a good shot, I have to be, and with one arm I can't afford to wing a man twice my size who has his own gun and nothing to lose.

He hit the floor on his back before his Glock did. He didn't move again.

"Damn and damn," I said, my face feeling as pale as it could get, and ran to bend over Joe. There was more frustration in his eyes than pain.

"Shit," he said. He knew what I knew. "How do we get the goddamn guy who hired him now?"

"How do you feel?"

"Like I'd rather be dead," Joe said. "I'm okay. Those Glocks're too big for fast action, he only winged me. Nothing a week in the hospital won't fix."

On the bed, Sam Armbruster was staring down at

the big dead man, and the boy sat in a kind of trance. Nothing that had happened had reached him. He lived in some invisible world of his own where there wasn't any pain. Belmonte looked at the big man, at the blood oozing from under his head now. The pimp's face was so white it was green.

"What was his name?" I said to Belmonte. "The whole goddamn story."

Belmonte doubled over in a corner and threw up. When he finally stopped retching, he sat on the floor against the wall and couldn't stop staring at the big man dead on the floor. And he couldn't stop talking. The dead man was Matt Brunner. A bounty hunter who worked out of Santa Barbara. Someone there had hired him to discredit Roger Berenger. When he'd learned Berenger was coming to New York alone, he got Zack Murfree to hire Belmonte and frame Berenger with little Ricky. They beat Berenger up so the police would come and it would be on public record, and the client could reveal it and ruin both Roger and Sam Armbruster.

"The old guy don' got to go die, you know? We don' mean the old faggot got to croak!"

"Who in Santa Barbara?"

Belmonte looked like he would throw up again. "I don' know! I swear! Zack and Brunner they never done tol' me. I swear!"

On the bed, Sam Armbruster said, "Then we'll never find out."

"We'll find out," I said.

We did.

It took some work by the NYPD, the SBPD, and me, but two weeks later we faced all seven of them in the rectory of the Reverend Anthony Cartwright. Five men and two women. All over forty. All angry and outraged. One of them, Mr. Frederick Zackheim, demanded, "Who are these men, Cartwright? What is this nonsense all about?"

"My name is Sergeant Chavalas," Gus Chavalas

said. "Santa Barbara Police. Mr. Fortune and Mr. Harris there are private investigators hired by Mr. Samuel Armbruster. That mean anything to you?"

They said nothing.

"It should," Chavalas said. "Since you all hired Matt Brunner to set Roger Berenger up with a New York prostitute he'd never have been anywhere near on his own."

There were seven explosions of protest. Or six. Mr. Fred Zackheim said only, "I know no one named Brunner. I'm not—"

I said, "Yes, you do. He was a professional, Matt Brunner. Organized. He kept records. Even the Nazis kept records of all they did."

"None of our names would have been in his records," Fred Zackheim said.

"True, Mr. Zackheim, and the transaction was in cash, of course. However, unfortunately for you fine people, Brunner's records named where his client lived, what the deal was, and the fee: $25,000 in advance. None of you are rich, so I doubted anyone came up with the full twenty-five grand. That's—"

"That's where we came in." Chavalas said. "Only one of you had dealt with Brunner, and that had been in cash. But Dan figured the rest of you would have paid the spokesman by check. I mean, who would ever know? Reverend Cartwright told us which members of his congregation had objected most to Berenger and Armbruster being deacons, and we got a court order to open your bank records."

"And there you were," I said. "Six people who paid large chunks of money to the same man on the same day two days before Brunner was hired. Isn't that right, Mr. Zackheim?"

Fred Zackheim stood up. "That proves nothing. No court—"

"With Belmonte, Ricky Franklin, Brunner's records, and Dan and Joe's work," Chavalas said, "I think it does. And I think a court will too, Mr. Zackheim."

The gray-haired man's eyes flashed, "No court will blame us for trying to purify our church of that filth."

The silence was like an enormous weight on the small rectory room. Until one of the women began to talk. Her voice shook. With anger, but with fear too now. "He called a meeting, Fred did. He asked when were we going to stop talking about those perverts and do something. When would we show the Reverend, the whole city, what they really were? Expose them. We asked how we could do that? How could we know what they did and when? He told us he knew a man who would make sure. We told him he was crazy. He told us to put our money where our mouths were. If he could arrange to get those two out of the church, would we pay for it? We were scared, but we wanted that evil out of our church. We wanted them to be exposed so no decent person would associate with such ... such ... obscene perverts."

A man looked at the floor. "We never knew what he was going to do."

"No," Joe said. "You just knew he was going to destroy two people you hated because they weren't like you." He walked out of the room past the two uniformed policemen outside the door.

I said, "Brunner learned of Roger's trip alone to New York. He knew Zack Murfree had plenty of contacts in New York of the kind he needed, and made his plan. Roger Berenger died. You didn't plan that, but it was okay as long as you weren't suspected. It wasn't okay with Sam Armbruster. He came to me. He knew Roger wouldn't have done what it looked like he had. It was a matter of character. Something none of you would understand."

They all glared at me. Anger and hate mixed with fear. Fear for themselves.

"I want my lawyer," Frederick Zackheim said.

On the next Sunday the church held a memorial service for Roger Berenger. The Reverend Cartwright delivered the eulogy himself. Joe and I stood at the back and watched Samuel Armbruster walk down the aisle to the altar rail to receive communion before passing the collection plate. Today he would pass it alone, no matter how long that took.

He walked slowly, with great dignity, a black armband on the sleeve of his impeccable dark gray suit.

The church was only three-quarters full, and some people left during the eulogy. More left when Armbruster passed the collection plate alone. Few shook his hand where he stood on the steps with the reverend after the service.

Joe and I stood beside him in the morning sun, wondering.

An Almost Perfect Heist
Carolyn G. Hart

Carolyn G. Hart's mystery novels have won her international acclaim as well as the Agatha, the Anthony and the Macavity awards. She has more than twenty-two novels, including five juvenile mysteries, to her credit.

She's well known for her *Death on Demand* series featuring Annie Laurance and Max Darling. Their latest adventure is *Southern Ghost.* She recently launched a new mystery series featuring retired reporter Henrietta O'Dwyer Collins with the publication of *Dead Man's Island.*

Meet Henrie O' for yourself. It was just another day at college, but when her favorite student failed to show, Henrie just knew there had to be a reason.

Her investigation turned up a surprise that could prove deadly. Needing some help, she turned to her favorite partner, Homicide Lt. Don Brown. Would they be able to foil "An Almost Perfect Heist"? . . .

I won't claim I was immediately suspicious.

My involvement began very simply. I was uneasy.

You see, I believe in character.

I'm not saying people are predictable—not quite. I am saying that character tells. When a student—even a serious, responsible student—fails to show up for a critically important class, well, in the university world, that student has blown it. End of chapter because faculty isn't responsible for student attendance.

I could have left it at that.

Sure.

And I could leave a lost puppy on the shoulder of a superhighway, too.

The latter situation is pretty clear-cut. You see the dog, you see the cars, you take action.

This situation involved a leap. But when uneasiness crystallized into foreboding, I knew I couldn't ignore it. Nor is foreboding, given the circumstances, too strong a word.

My young friend at Homicide, Lt. Don Brown, insists that I have an instinct for malfeasance bordering on the uncanny and that only I would have taken action.

I shrug modestly when Don waxes hyperbolic. This simply reinforces Don's conviction that I, Henrietta O'Dwyer Collins, am a human divining rod for evil. That suits my purposes. I like having a buddy in Homicide. Occasionally he'll drop by and pose questions, always hypothetically, and I know I'm having a chance to use my wits to aid justice, a pursuit I enjoy.

But there was no second sight involved in the affair last week. Rather it was simply responding to the accumulated experience of almost a half century as a reporter. If I've learned one truth, it is this: Character tells.

That day, Wednesday, was going as expected. Since I've retired from newspapering, I've enjoyed a second career as a professor in a journalism department quite unlike most others. The journalism faculty at Derry Hills College is made up of former professionals—real admen and women, real reporters and editors, real TV newscasters and writers and producers, real publicists, people who worked in the world and worked well.

In common with the celebrated school in Columbia, the Derry Hills journalism department edits the town newspaper, *The Clarion,* with students serving as reporters. The unlikelihood of two professionally staffed college journalism departments occurring in the same state is proof that the "Show Me" reputation of Missouri is well deserved.

I wear a number of hats in this community of old pros, teaching at one time or another basic and advanced reporting, feature writing, investigative reporting, and magazine writing. This semester I was handling the op-ed page and teaching two three-hour courses. I also had two independent study students.

One of the great pleasures in teaching is getting to know people who are eager and curious and involved in life, the basic motivations of those drawn to journalism.

This semester I was especially enjoying one of my independent study students, Eleanor Vickery. In the parlance of academia, Eleanor was a nontraditional student. In her late thirties, she was back in school, working on the undergraduate degree she'd not completed when she dropped out of school to marry.

In the course of our twice-weekly, hour-long conferences (Journalism 4732, Advanced Magazine Articles), I'd learned a good deal about Eleanor and her husband Ray, president of the Derry Hills National Bank. They were the parents of three boys, Sean, Richard, and Riley. They loved to camp, ski, and sail. Ray was a Scoutmaster. Sean had just achieved the rank of Eagle Scout. Eleanor taught the junior high Sunday school class at St. Mark's.

Eleanor radiated good humor, and her infectious smile lightened whatever room she entered. With her unpretentious manner and willingness to work, she fit right into the school milieu even though she drove a Lexus and wore designer clothes. I'd met her husband at the faculty's fall open house for students. Ray Vickery was a chunky, ex-football star with bright, thoughtful eyes and a pleasant manner.

As a student, Eleanor displayed a quick, lively mind and a fine concern for doing everything right. She frequently peppered me with questions:

Shouldn't a direct quote be absolutely accurate?

Although government publications aren't copyrighted, wouldn't an honorable journalist attribute any material quoted?

How could anyone defend using an anonymous source?

Why don't newspapers mount a campaign against the government for the price support of tobacco?

What did I think of a famous magazine's practice of presenting information obtained from several interviews as if the material had been produced in a single interview scene?

And Eleanor was always on time for our conferences.

Always.

Wednesday morning was our last session for the semester. It was also the deadline for Eleanor to turn in her three-part series on local nursing homes. If there is one absolute in my classroom as in my life, it is meeting deadlines.

I am not an unreasonable woman. An emergency appendectomy, a blizzard, a train wreck, these are acceptable excuses. But don't knock on my door a day late and say you overslept. Or the dog ate it. Or your computer crashed.

So at six minutes after nine A.M. on Wednesday, I looked up at my clock, puzzled and concerned. I knew, without question, that Eleanor Vickery would have called if there were a serious domestic problem, and only something serious would have kept her away. After all, the series was fifty percent of her grade and this morning was the deadline.

At nine-fifteen, I stared at my telephone, willing it to ring.

It didn't.

At nine-twenty-five, I placed my hand on the telephone.

In my head, the debate raged:

Coming to class is Eleanor's responsibility.

Something's wrong, something's terribly wrong.

There's a name for people who poke their noses uninvited into other peoples' lives: busybody.

I'd bet my life on Eleanor.

At nine-thirty, I called the Vickery house. Four rings, the recorded message, "We can't come to the phone ..."

I didn't leave a message.

Why should I? It wasn't part of my job description to discover why an excellent and heretofore absolutely responsible student was apparently self-destructing. Failure to turn in the series would result in an F for the course.

That weighed on the one hand.

On the other, I have confidence in my own judgment, and in my judgment, Eleanor Vickery was rock-solid dependable.

I went down the hall to *The Clarion* newsroom and checked the emergency call scanner. No car accidents. No ambulance runs. No reports from the northside police patrol car.

On the one hand ...

Back in my office, I jabbed the buttons on the phone.

The recorded message ...

Slowly, I replaced the receiver.

I walked to my window and looked out at the brilliant redbuds and the daffodils swaying in the light breeze.

A gorgeous spring day.

Car trouble?

Eleanor could have walked to the campus by now.

A sick child?

But, once again, whip quick, I knew Eleanor would call if that were the case. Unless it was life threatening and nothing mattered—nothing—but the life of her child.

There are so many advantages to living in a small town.

I'd met Mae Reno last fall when I gave a talk on famous women foreign correspondents to a local women's group. Mae was the program chair; she was also chief nurse at the Derry Hills Hospital emergency ward.

It took me less than five minutes to track Mae down. She rang me back within three minutes. No Vickery patient at the Derry Hills Hospital.

I walked back to the window, watched two laughing coeds slip off their shoes and dangle their feet in a cold pool. Spring madness.

This was Eleanor's senior spring. She was, damn it, graduating in three weeks. I could see her sitting in the chair in front of my desk—her eyes shining, smiling that shy, eager smile—and telling me about the grand celebration Ray had planned. "He just won't listen. He's invited everyone we've ever known and all of my family to a picnic and I'm so embarrassed." And so thrilled. So happy and proud and thrilled.

She wouldn't graduate with three hours of F.

I walked down the hall, stuck a Post-It note to my classroom door, giving my ten o'clock class a free cut, and headed for the parking lot.

I left a trail of dust as my MG bolted out of the lot.

The Vickerys live on Derry Hill's well-to-do north side in a rambling two-story frame house. Very nice indeed but not flashy. They aren't that kind of family.

I drove slowly past.

Eleanor's Lexus was parked in the drive. The front drapes were drawn. Lights glowed in the living room. Mail poked up from the letter box on the porch.

And the morning paper rested midway up the curving drive.

That was the real tipoff—the morning paper in the drive.

People in the news business, including students, get the paper even before they pour their coffee.

I drove around the block, cruised slowly past one more time.

And the newspaper, still sheathed in its shiny pale green plastic wrap—there'd been a forty percent chance of showers today—lay there so innocently.

It wouldn't mean a thing to anyone else that the newspaper had not been brought in yet. Lazy morning, perhaps.

I was almost to the end of the block.

My paper had been propped up on my breakfast

table at shortly after six A.M. I'd especially enjoyed seeing a feature by Eleanor in the Life section.

No matter how many years you write and whether a writer admits it or not, a reporter always gets a thrill out of a byline and quickly scans any article the day it comes out.

I turned at the end of the block, braked beneath an oak midway down the block. This was an older part of town, the homes built in the early nineteen hundreds. This neighborhood had sidewalks and alleys. I hesitated, then switched off the motor. It might be better to go on foot.

I like alleys. They remind me of a childhood in Cairo where my father was a correspondent for INS and later, when I was a young teenager and Dad was transferred, of dark and dank alleys in Paris. I always remember those gray stones glistening with rain. This was a distinctly small-town Missouri alley, narrow, yes, but dusty, with metal trash cans lined next to frame garages.

A deep bark exploded next to a chain-link fence. A schnauzer quivered with hostility.

A marmalade cat stared at me unblinkingly from a perch in a sycamore.

I reached the Vickery backyard.

A dark blue coupe was parked next to the Vickery garages. The small car faced out into the alley.

Not too remarkable, after all. The kind of car a housemaid might drive.

I walked along the car, stepped behind it. There was a rental-car insignia on the rear window. Dried mud obscured the license plate.

But there were no traces of mud on the rest of the car.

I looked toward the back of the house. It was so still, so quiet.

Ominously quiet.

But that welling up of unease came from within me, of course. I knew that. The house itself exuded charm and loving care, the paint fresh and white, the window glasses sparkling in the spring sunlight, the comfortable tan wicker furniture on the wide verandas as inviting as the offer of lemonade garnished with a sprig of backyard mint.

I was looking at a perfect example of small-town America at its best. But I wasn't reassured.

This house was too quiet, too drawn in, too lifeless on a gorgeous spring morning. This was a morning made for open doors and bustling activity.

And the morning newspaper lay in its plastic wrap on the front drive.

I glanced again at the rental car with its muddied plate.

My best advice to young reporters: Don't just stand there. *Find out.*

I moved quietly alongside the drive, stepping soundlessly on the thick spring grass, slipping behind spirea bushes until I reached the steps to the back veranda.

I paused on the top step.

Midway between the steps and the back door, a high school letter jacket—maroon trimmed with silver—lay in a crumpled heap next to a shiny green backpack.

Dropped there?

Thrown there?

Whatever, they shouldn't have been there.

I reached the back door, hesitated, then quietly pulled open the screen.

I turned the knob, again so quietly, so delicately.

The door was locked.

And that was odd, too.

This wasn't a city. This was Derry Hills, a little Missouri town. I know the mores. I'd have bet my MG that nine out of ten back doors on this block were unlocked at this very minute.

I slipped along the back porch, went around the corner of the house.

The curtains were drawn at every window I passed. Yet the windows were open, up an inch or two from the sills. That's what I would expect on a spring morning. But I would also have expected the curtains to be open.

I paused at each window, bent my head, listened.

A bus rumbled past in the street. Somewhere in the distance a dove cooed. Across the street a lawnmower clattered. But the open windows yielded no sound.

I reached the front porch and a bay window.

These drapes were also drawn, yet all three windows were open.

It made no sense.

Why open windows for the light, silky spring breeze, then pull the drapes?

Again, I bent down to listen.

". . . taking him so long? He should be there. I don't like this." The man's voice was uncommonly high—and ragged with tension.

"Traffic backs up on Springstead. The construction." Eleanor spoke rapidly, her tone an odd mixture of reassurance—and fear. "Please, he'll be there—oh, listen, listen, there's the car door now."

Car door? I glanced toward the driveway. Sun glinted on the gray Lexus.

Car door?

"You see, it's going to be all right. Just like Ray said. He promised. You'll see," Eleanor chattered. "Please, just be patient."

"That better be him. If he wants to see you and the kid again, by God, it better be him."

I stared at the drawn curtains in frustration, then eased open my purse. My fingers scrabbled against the soft leather bottom. Dammit, where—finally, I found the nail file.

I knelt by the middle window and wedged the slender metal file into the screen, jimmied it to make room, until the tip reached the edge of the curtain.

Carefully, I eased the curtain back just a hairbreadth.

I had a narrow field of vision, a central portion of the living room including an old-fashioned fireplace framed by black marble and a comfortable-looking couch with bright chintz cushions.

But the teenage boy sitting stiffly on the sofa looked far from comfortable, his body rigid, his eyes enormous, his face carefully devoid of expression. He was an attractive kid, dark haired and green eyed. His broad forehead and generous mouth were a masculine replica of his mother's face. He wore a red-and-white striped rugby shirt, neatly ironed blue jeans, white socks, and penny loafers. And he stared unwaveringly across the room.

I couldn't see what he was looking toward.

Here's where I had to make some choices.

Something odd was occurring in Eleanor Vickery's living room. Eleanor had pled for patience. Why?

I didn't know.

Should I slip back alongside the house, try to edge open the curtain in another window? The best I could manage from any window was a narrow slice of the room.

Would I find out more?

Or would I attract the attention of the man with the high voice?

Sometimes you have to go on instinct.

My instinct told me to go for help.

I didn't have a lot to tell Don Brown.

Maybe to a cop who didn't know me, a cop in a big city, Eleanor missing a deadline, the newspaper lying untouched in the front drive, the odd exchange I'd overhead, maybe that wouldn't be enough to act.

But Don is my friend.

And instinct clamored now.

Fortunately, I wear rubber-soled flats. I consider high heels to be exactly on a par with the old, barbaric Chinese custom of binding women's feet—and approved by male society for much the same reasons.

So I was able to slip quietly, so quietly around the corner of the house and down the side porch.

I had to get away without being seen.

I took only one chance.

I assumed since no alarm had yet been raised about my presence that the man in the room with Eleanor was operating on his own, that there was no lookout.

I forgot to allow for one thing. I wasn't in a big city. I was in a small town.

The rattle of magnolia leaves alerted me.

I looked to my left, directly into bulging, shocked eyes. I had only a swift glimpse of a pink-cheeked face and dyed blond hair before the low branches of the magnolia snapped behind her.

Oh, Christ!

I didn't have time—but I had to take time.

I ran to a side gate, opened it, and plunged into a glorious garden bright with jonquils and flowering dogwood and magnificent royal purple iris. I almost took a header into a stone-rimmed pond.

I veered away at the last moment and stumbled over a garden trowel.

She glanced back over her shoulder, her eyes huge, her cheeks flaming from her unexpected flight.

"Wait. Please!" I called out softly.

She hesitated for just an instant, then clattered up the back steps, slamming the door behind her.

Oh God, nosy neighbors can be wonderful. But not this time.

If the police arrived, sirens wailing—I whirled around and thudded to the alley gate behind this house, running as fast as I could down the alley, hoping the man in Eleanor's house wouldn't be spooked by the sudden eruption of barks.

I'm an old jogger, yes, but an old and slow one. Now my chest ached and my right knee threatened to buckle.

The schnauzer lunged against his fence. A German shepherd leaped like a ballerina. I kept on running. I had to contact the police before Eleanor's neighbor brought them with sirens screaming.

I'd left the MG unlocked, perhaps the greatest distinction between a little town and a city. So I had my mobile phone in hand without a pause, though I was trying to draw breath into my lungs even when the dispatcher answered.

"Lieutenant Brown. This is an emergency. Henrietta Collins calling."

In less than a second, Don was on the line.

"Henrie O?" His voice was tight with concern.

It was my late husband Richard who gave me that nickname, saying I put more surprises into a single day than O. Henry ever put in a short story. At one point early in our acquaintance (when I'd decoyed a killer to my apartment), Don said fervently that Richard sure as hell got it right the first time.

Gasping for breath, the words came out in spurts. "Don, thank God you're there. A call has just been made from 317 Ninth Street, reporting a trespasser at the Vickery residence at 319 Ninth Street. Make sure no patrol car comes to the front of the house. Do that first. Tell them to come to the alley between Ninth and Tenth on Crawford."

"Right."

The line clicked.

I waited.

"Done. Now, what's wrong?"

I like having Don's respect. I like even more that I can respect him. He listens. Even when it's a tough tale to take in. Quickly, I told him why I'd come to the Vickery house and what I'd seen and heard.

"You saw only a teenager? One of the sons? Nobody else?"

"Right. He looked about seventeen. But he was looking at someone. Or something. And he was—I won't overstate it—but something was terribly wrong. The way he was sitting. The look on his face."

"You didn't see the man?"

"No. I heard him. And I didn't like it, Don. He sounded ... jumpy. He was threatening Eleanor Vickery."

"Is he armed?"

"I don't know. I didn't see him. I didn't see a weapon," I said carefully. "But he must have one. Or he has an accomplice with one. Don, Eleanor and her son are prisoners. I'm positive."

Don took a deep breath.

I could imagine him seated at his desk, his wiry shoulders hunched, his blue eyes intent. Don Brown looks like such an average thirtyish guy, nondescript sandy hair, an almost slight build, a studiedly vacuous face. It takes a perceptive viewer to note the lively intelligence in his eyes, the stubborn jut of his chin, the compact muscles of a long-distance runner.

"No weapon?" That troubled him. If he rousted out the special weapons and tactical team and it turned out Eleanor and her son were quarreling with good old uncle Frank, Don would be in big trouble.

Big trouble.

"Don, I'm sure she's a hostage—and she's the wife of Ray Vickery."

I didn't have to tell him who Ray Vickery was.

"Eleanor told this man that Ray would do—something."

"Okay." Don didn't say a word about his job, how he'd lose it in a flash if this turned into a fiasco.

One reason I never visit him at the station is because Don's chief appears pathologically hostile to older women who don't sit with their hands folded and their faces molded in halo-sweet submissiveness. Not my style.

"I'll—"

I interrupted. I already had a plan.

He said nothing for two seconds after I'd finished. Another deep breath. "Yeah."

Because once he thought about it, Don knew I was right. He didn't complain. He didn't object. He didn't tell me it was dangerous. He just said, "Yeah."

Much as he didn't like it.

At fifteen minutes after ten, I walked up on the front veranda of the Vickery house.

If all had gone on schedule, Don was even now slipping onto the back porch of the Vickery house.

Next door a crew of painters pulled up and began to unload scaffolding, paint cans, brushes—they were more backup. I couldn't see the alley from here but I was sure it was well populated with Derry Hills's finest.

I wondered if the pudgy blond woman was watching through the slats of her venetian blinds.

Now to find out what made Eleanor's teenage son stare fixedly across his own living room.

This wasn't the first time I'd worn a body transmitter. The unit rode on a belt hidden beneath my bulky cotton sweater. The antenna ran vertically up my right side, again, of course, beneath the sweater. The microphone was clever, slickly embedded in an old-fashioned-looking brooch snugly pinned on my right lapel.

In my right hand, I carried a slender tool that makes opening a door, especially an old-fashioned lock, easier than punching time on a microwave. I also carried a keyring with assorted keys.

With every step, the heavy stun gun in my left sweater pocket thumped gently against my hip.

I piped a shrill greeting as I pattered across the porch. "Ellie, it's Aunt Henrietta! So sorry I'm late. Such a mess!" I was at the door, opening the screen, and shoving the slender length of ridged metal in the keyhole. As I twisted and turned it, I increased the volume. "The jam boiled over and the stove is just stickier than flypaper in August." The lock clicked, the door swung open. I banged inside. "Ellie, Ellie, where are you? I can't believe you aren't ready to go. I'm a good hour late and then you didn't even answer my call."

I'd already tucked my door opener into a pocket. Keys dangled innocently from my hand. "Ellie?"

I reached the archway that opened into the living room.

"Oh my goodness," I said loudly—to be sure Don heard every word—"Young man, why do you have a shotgun? And why are you wearing that rubber mask? Oh my goodness, Ellie, who tied you to that chair?"

Eleanor Vickery was tied to a straight chair with cord wound round and round her. Her hair was straight, her face wore no makeup. A damp dark stain—coffee?—marked the front of her pale peach silk robe. After the first hopeful jerk of her head toward me, the light in her eyes died, replaced by stark fear as she looked up at the huge man standing beside her. His face was hidden by a Halloween mask of Ronald Reagan.

I felt the flicker of fear myself.

Because the shotgun he held in trembling hands was pointed straight at me. And I couldn't make contact with that rubberized, inhuman face. It was like staring into a cold sea or a dark pit.

For an instant, we were a frozen tableau, I poised in the archway, Eleanor imprisoned in the chair, her son perched tensely on the edge of the sofa, their huge captor—God, six-foot-four, 250 pounds—aiming the shotgun at my head.

And weaving through the stillness among us was an odd crumpling sound, like someone crushing tissue.

"Who the hell are you?" The high voice came out almost in a squeal. But the lips of the Halloween mask didn't move.

I felt a prickle move down my spine. I understood now why Eleanor had tried so hard to reassure him. He was teetering on the edge of panic—with a vicious, dangerous weapon in shaking hands.

"Why, I'm Ellie's aunt. Who are you? What's going on here, Ellie tied up and you with that shotgun!" Out of the corner of my eye, I could see Eleanor's son tensing.

Oh God, no!

I clasped a hand to my chest. "Oh, dear. I think I'd better sit down. I feel all faint," and I tottered toward the couch.

The shotgun followed me.

The teenager's shoulders slumped. Just a little.

I dropped onto the sofa. "Oh, this is dreadful, just dreadful!"

"Shut up." The shotgun wavered between me and the boy.

Eleanor drew her breath in sharply. She strained against the ropes. "Don't point it at Sean, don't!"

All the while that peculiar sound continued, a shuffling with an occasional crackle or pop.

There was the squeak of an opening door.

The rubberized mask turned a little to the left.

Eleanor, too, looked toward the rosewood table near the window.

Beside me, Sean tensed again.

Unobtrusively, I gripped his arm, gave it a tiny yank.

His eyes jerked toward me.

"No." I mouthed it, tilted my head briefly, so briefly, toward the hall behind me.

Sean frowned.

Then, I, too, looked toward the rosewood table and saw a radio transmitter sitting there.

Footsteps sounded.

Electronic surveillance is no secret to criminals. Now I knew where the sounds were coming from.

A woman spoke.

We all looked at the transmitter, leaned forward to listen. Static interrupted her words. ". . . Mr. Vick . . . boxes look heavy . . . all right?"

Strain thinned Ray Vickery's voice to a husky whisper. "Fine, just . . . Special proj—" The shuffling sounds resumed amid the crackle of static.

I knew what I'd heard, Ray Vickery speaking in a bugged room. I had no doubt the bug was in Ray's office at the First National Bank.

The shuffling, crackling sound that filled the room suddenly stopped. Footsteps sounded again amid the crackle of static. A door slammed. Now the only sound from the bugged office of the bank president was a flat, lifeless buzz.

The big man abruptly began to pace. His masked face moved from the couch to Eleanor and back again, and the shotgun swung from us to her, from her to us.

"Okay, okay. Twenty-five seconds. That's what he's got. Twenty-five seconds to get to his car." He turned heavily and lumbered toward us. "Or we'll take a little trip, kid. You and me." And the shotgun was inches from Sean's head.

A car door opened, shut. Ray Vickery's frightened, desperate voice sounded so clearly in the room where his family was held hostage. "I'm in the car. I'm coming. Don't hurt them, please, don't. I've got the money, just like you want." The ignition turned, the motor roared, tires squealed. "As much as I could carry. At least five hundred thousand. Please ..."

The robber's huge chest heaved. I could see beads of sweat sliding down his neck.

The shotgun went back and forth, from us to Eleanor, from Eleanor to us.

The roar of the car motor filled the room. Ray Vickery talked in a harsh monotone, "I'm coming ... for Christ's sake, I'm coming ..."

And I had to make my move.

Soon.

Because Don should be in the house now. And my job was to decoy the robber's attention away from the archway that opened into the hall.

But first I looked toward Eleanor. "Where are Richard and Riley?" I spoke quite clearly. Don needed to know how many of us were in the house.

"They'd already left for school," she said dully. "They catch their bus at seven-thirty."

"Yeah, yeah." The cheery, pink-cheeked Reagan mask nodded. "I knew that." Pride sounded in the high voice. "I planned it down to the last second."

Sean's hands tightened into fists. "He was waiting for me, outside the back door."

The dropped letter jacket and backpack.

Ray's voice blared from the transmitter. "I'm at Crawford and Pike. Two more blocks. I'm coming ..."

"Okay, kid. Now, when your dad gets here, we'll let him come inside and I'll tie him up, then you'll move the cash to my car. Then we leave. Together.

I'll be safe as long as you're with me." The mask turned toward Eleanor. "Don't try and get loose and call the cops. Don't do it—not if you ever want to see the kid again."

Eleanor shuddered. "No. Oh, no, no, no."

An old cop once told me never to get in an abductor's car. "You're dead if you go. Make him shoot you there." If the robber walked out with Sean, we'd never see him alive again. I could feel death in that lovely room.

I figured I had maybe two more minutes before Ray Vickery arrived. I had to make my move before then.

I had to be quick and I had to be good.

"Stand up, kid."

But even as Sean leaned forward, I gave a wrenching cry and gripped his arm.

"My heart. Oh, my heart." I clung to Sean. With my face turned away from the robber, I whispered. "Police in the hall. Help me across the room, close to him." And I began to struggle to my feet.

Sean took just a second, then he moved, too, putting an arm protectively around me.

"Air. Sean, I've got to have air. The window . . ."

We veered toward the front windows.

Five feet from the robber.

Four.

I put my left hand into the deep cardigan pocket, gripped the stun gun.

"Oh, dear," I moaned. "Pain. Oh, Ellie. My angina. Oh dear, so sick. Air. I need air." I wavered unsteadily, Sean supported me.

Three feet.

The robber backed away. "Hey, stay where you are, auntie."

Two feet.

One foot.

I was even with him.

The robber turned to face me.

And now his back was to the archway.

My hand came out of the pocket, gripping the TV

remote-sized oblong plastic case. I pressed the button and lunged toward him, jamming the gun into his chest.

"Help!" I yelled.

Sean, God, yes, he was quick and smart.

Sean grabbed the robber's arm, struggled for the shotgun.

Behind me I heard the thudding footsteps, but I kept on pressing, pressing and now it was five seconds and the huge man, screaming, began to topple.

The stun gun hissed and spluttered.

Glass crashed as the nearest windows were breached.

The front door crashed open.

A firm voice yelled, "Hands up. You're under arrest."

And Don was pulling me away. "He's out, Henrie O. That's enough. We've got him."

I do enjoy awards ceremonies.

Chief Holzer handed the commendation medal to my favorite homicide detective. "The entire Derry Hills police department is proud of your extraordinary role in saving the Vickery family last month." He reached out and pumped Don's hand. "Congratulations, Lieutenant."

He didn't even look my way.

Not that I minded.

Later, as I sipped tea at the reception immediately following, cosponsored by the First National Bank of Derry Hills, I gave Eleanor Vickery a hug.

She stood, holding tightly to her husband's arm.

"I'm looking forward to the picnic, Eleanor."

"I don't know . . ." Her face was somber.

"Of course, we're going to have it, Ellie." Ray Vickery looked down at her, a worried frown tight between his eyes.

She was still having trouble.

I knew that. Understood it.

It's hard to recapture the joy of innocence—and Eleanor's world had been an innocent one. She'd never known fear.

I touched her arm gently. "I'm counting on that picnic. Don't disappoint me."

"If it weren't for you—"

"And Don. And a great police force. And Sean."

Her eyes lightened. She looked across the room where Sean stood, deep in conversation with Don.

"And you, Eleanor."

"Me? I didn't do anything."

"You," I said firmly. "You've always done your best, Eleanor. That's why I came to your house. I knew you would never let me down or yourself—or your family."

She stared deep into my eyes.

I knew what she saw, a lean and angular woman with dark hair silvered at the temples, a Roman coin profile, and dark eyes that have seen much and re-membered much—and, at this moment, were both stern and admiring.

"Really?" she asked faintly.

"Really."

She looked at me, then back across the room at Don and her son, the center of an admiring crowd.

Some of the old spark touched her eyes. "But you're the one who really saved us." Her voice rose with a journalist's outrage at a half-told story.

I welcome a teaching point wherever I find it. "It's all right. Especially this time. But take it from me, Eleanor. Never trust official sources."

She stood very straight. "No, it's not all right. I want everyone to know what really happened. I'll do the true story for *The Clarion.*"

That put me in a pickle. I don't like to compromise facts, but I didn't want to embarrass my only buddy in the Derry Hills police department.

So, I had to share another journalistic truth with Eleanor. "Sometimes, my dear, it's very important to maintain confidentiality because you need access to those sources in the future."

I should have known better, of course. Character always tells.

Eleanor wrote her story. It won first in the intercollegiate press association contest for investigative reporting.

Don was pleased even though he couldn't admit that publicly. He'd wanted me to have co-billing all along.

Chief Holzer wasn't pleased.

But so what else is new?

Seasons of the Heart

Ed Gorman

for Charlotte MacLeod

Ed Gorman is the author of seven crime novels, including *The Autumn Dead* **and** *The Night Remembers.* His short-story collection *Prisoners* was called "distinguished" by *Ellery Queen Magazine* and "consistently excellent" by *Booklist.*

His stories have won the Shamus and the Spur awards and have been nominated for both the Edgar and the Anthony. His work has appeared in magazines as diverse as *Redbook, The Magazine of Fantasy and Science Fiction,* and the British version of *Penthouse.* He is copublisher of *Mystery Scene Magazine.*

Ed brings his evocative yet taut style to this next story. Meet Robert Wilson, his daughter Emmy and granddaughter Lisa. As partners, they run an Iowa farm. But their tranquil lives are shattered, when an enemy from Robert's past stalks him in "Seasons of the Heart" . . .

In the mornings now, the fog didn't burn off till much before eight, and the dew stayed silver past nine, and the deeper shadows stayed all morning long in the fine red barn I'd helped build last year. The summer was fleeing.

But that wasn't how I knew autumn was coming.

No, for that all I had to do was look at the freckled face of my granddaughter Lisa, who would be entering eighth grade this year at the consolidated school ten miles west.

For as much as she read, and when she wasn't doing chores she was always reading something, even when she sat in front of the TV, she hated school. I don't think she'd had her first serious crush yet, and the girlfriends available to her struck her as a little frivolous. They were town girls and they didn't have Lisa's responsibilities.

This particular morning went pretty much as usual.

We had a couple cups of coffee, Lisa and I, and then we hiked down to the barn. It was still dark. You could hear the horses in the hills waking with the dawn, and closer by the chickens. Turnover day was coming, a frantic day in the life of a farmer. You take the birds to market and then have twenty-four hours to clean out the chicken house before the new shipment of baby chicks arrives. First time I ever did it, I was worn out for three days. That's when my daughter Emmy read me the Booker T. Washington quote I'd come to savor: "No race can prosper till it learns that there is as much dignity in tilling a field as writing a poem." Those particular words work just as well as Ben-Gay on sore muscles. For me, anyway.

The barn smelled summer sweet of fresh milk. Lisa liked to lead the animals into the stalls, she had her own reassuring way of talking to them in a language understood only by cows and folk under fourteen years of age. She also liked to hook them up.

The actual milking, I usually did. Lisa always helped me pour the fresh milk into dumping stations. We tried to get a lot of milk per day. We had big payments to make on this barn. The Douglas fir we'd used for the wood hadn't come cheap. Nor had the electricity, the milking machines, or the insulation. You've got to take damned good care of dairy cattle.

I worked straight through till Lisa finished cleaning up the east end of the barn. This was one of those days when she wanted to do some of the milking herself. I was happy to let her do it.

Everything went fine till I stepped outside the barn to have a few puffs on my pipe.

Funny thing was, I'd given up both cigarettes and pipe years before. But after Dr. Wharton, back in Chicago when I was still flying commuter planes, told me about the cancer, I found an old briar pipe of mine and took it up again. I brought it to the farm with me when I came to live with Emmy. I never smoked it in an enclosed area. I didn't want Lisa to pick up any secondhand smoke.

The chestnut mare was on the far hill. She was a beauty and seemed to know it, always prancing about to music no one else seemed to hear, or bucking against the sundown sky when she looked all mythic and ethereal in the darkening day.

And that's just what I was doing, getting my pipe fired up and looking at the roan, when the rifle shot ripped away a large chunk of wood from the door frame no more than three inches to my right.

I wasn't sure what it was. In movies, the would-be target always pitches himself left or right but I just stood there for several long seconds before the echo of the bullet whining past me made me realize what happened.

Only then did I move, running into the barn to warn Lisa but she already knew that something had happened.

Lisa is a tall, slender girl with the dignified appeal of her mother. You wouldn't call either of them beauties, but in their fine blond hair and their melancholy brown eyes and their quick and sometimes sad grins, you see the stuff of true heartbreakers. It was a tradition they inherited from my wife, who broke my heart by leaving me for an advertising man when Emmy was nine years old.

"God, that was a gunshot, wasn't it?"

"I'm afraid it was."

"You think it was accidental, Grandad?"

"I don't know. Not yet, anyway. But for now, let's stay in the barn."

"I wonder if Mom heard it."

I smiled. "Not the way she sleeps."

She put her arms around me and gave me a hug. "I was really scared. For you, I mean. I was afraid somebody might have— Well, you know."

I hugged her back. "I'm fine, honey. But I'll tell

you what. I want you to go stand in that corner over there while I go up in the loft and see if I can spot anybody."

"It's so weird. Nobody knows you out here."

"Nobody that I know of, anyway."

She broke our hug and looked up at me with those magnificent and often mischievous eyes. "Grandad?"

She always used a certain tone when she was about to ask me something she wasn't sure about.

"Here it is. You've got that tone."

Her bony shoulders shrugged beneath her T-shirt, which depicted a rock-and-roll band I'd never heard of. They were called The Flesh Eaters and she played their tapes a lot.

"I was just wondering if you'd be mad if I wrote it up."

"Wrote what up?"

"You know. Somebody shooting at you."

"Oh."

"Mrs. Price'll make us do one of those dorky how-I-spent-my-summer-vacation deals. It'd be cool if I could write about how a killer was stalking my grandad."

"Yeah," I said, "that sure sounds cool all right."

She grinned the grin and I saw both her mother and her grandmother in it. "I mean, I might 'enhance' it a little bit. But not a lot."

"Fine by me, pumpkin," I said, leading her over to the corner of the barn where several bales of hay would absorb a gunshot. "I'll be right back."

I figured that the shooter was most likely gone, long gone probably, but I wanted to make sure before I let Lisa stroll back into the barnyard.

I went up the ladder to the hayloft, sneezing all the way. My sinuses act up whenever I get even close to the loft. I used to think it was the hay but then I read a *Farm Bulletin* item saying it could be the rat droppings. For someone who grew up in the Hyde Park area of Chicago, rat droppings are not something you often consider as a sinus irritant. Farm life was different. I loved it.

I eased the loft door open a few inches. Then stopped.

I waited a full two minutes. No rifle fire.

I pushed the door open several more inches and looked outside. Miles of dark green corn and soybeans and alfalfa. On the hill just about where the mare was, I saw a tree the gunman might have fired from. Gnarly old oak with branches stout enough for a hanging.

"Grandad?" Lisa called up from below.

"Yeah, hon?"

"Are you all right?"

"I'm fine, hon. How about you?"

"God, I shouldn't have asked you if I could write about this for my class."

"Oh, why not?"

"Because this could be real serious. I mean, maybe it wasn't accidental."

"Now you sound like your grandmother."

"Huh?"

"She'd always do something and then get guilty and start apologizing." I didn't add that despite her apologies, her grandmother generally went right back to doing whatever she'd apologized for in the first place.

"I'm sorry if I hurt your feelings, Grandad."

Lisa never used to treat me like this. So dutifully. Nor did her mother. To them, I was just the biggest kid in the family and was so treated. But the cancer changed all that. Now they'd do something spontaneous and then right away they'd start worrying it. There's a grim decorum that goes along with the disease. You become this big sad frail guy who, they seem to think, just can't deal with any of life's daily wear and tear.

That's one of the nice things about my support group. We get to laugh a lot about the delicate way our loved ones treat us sometimes. It's not mean laughter. Hell, we understand that they wouldn't treat us this way if they didn't love us, and love us a lot.

But sometimes their dutifulness can be kind of funny in an endearing way.

"You 'enhance' it any way you want to, pumpkin," I said, and started to look around at fields sprawling out in front of me.

I also started sneezing pretty bad again, too.

I spent ten more minutes in the loft, finally deciding it was safe for us to venture out as soon as we finished with the milking for the day.

On the way out of the barn, I said, "Don't tell your mom. You know, about the gunshot."

"How come?"

"You must be crazy, kid. You know how she worries about me."

Lisa smiled. "How about making a bargain?"

"Oh-oh. Here it comes."

"I won't tell Mom and you let me drive the tractor."

Lots of farm kids die in tractor accidents every year. I didn't want Lisa to be one of them. "I'll think about it, how's that?"

"Then I guess I'll just have to think about it, too." But she laughed.

I pulled her closer, my arm around her shoulder. "You think I'm wrong? About not telling your mom?"

She thought for a while. "Nah, I guess not. I mean, Mom really does worry about you a lot already."

We were halfway to the house, a ranch-style home of blond brick with an evergreen windbreak and a white dish antenna east of the trees.

Just as we reached the walk leading to the house, I heard a heavy car come rumbling up the driveway, raising dust and setting both collies to barking. The car was a new baby-blue Pontiac with an official police insignia decaled on the side.

I stopped, turned around, grinned at Lisa. "Remember now, you've got Friday."

"Yeah, I wish I had Saturday, the way you do."

We'd been betting the last two weeks when Chief of Police Nick Bingham was going to ask Emmy to marry him. They'd been going out for three years, and two weeks ago Nick had said, "I've never said this to you before, Emmy, but you know when I turned forty last year? Well, ever since, I've had this loneliness right in here. A burning." And of course my wiseass daughter had said, "Maybe it's gas." She told this to Lisa and me at breakfast next morning, relishing the punchline.

Because Nick had never said anything like this at all in his three years of courting her, Emmy figured he was just about to pop the question.

So Lisa and I started this little pool. Last week I bet he'd ask her on Friday night and she'd bet he'd ask her on Saturday. But he hadn't asked her either night. Now the weekend was approaching again.

Nick got out of the car in sections. In high school, he'd played basketball on a team that had gone three times to the state finals and had finished second twice. Nick had played center. He was just over six-five. He went to college for three years but dropped out to finish the harvest when his father died of a heart attack. He never got the degree. But he did become a good lawman.

"Morning," he said.

"Pink glazed?" Lisa said when she saw the white sack dangling from his left hand.

"Two of 'em are, kiddo."

"Can I have one?"

"No," he said, pulling her to him and giving her a kind of affectionate Dutch rub. "You can have both of 'em."

He wasn't what you'd call handsome but there was a quiet manliness to the broken nose and the intelligent blue eyes that local ladies, including my own daughter, seemed to find attractive, especially when he was in his khaki uniform. They didn't seem to mind that he was balding fast.

Emmy greeted us at the door in a blue sweatshirt and jeans and the kind of white Keds she'd worn ever since she was a tot. No high-priced running shoes for her. With her earnest little face and tortoiseshell glasses, she always reminded me of those quiet, pretty girls I never got to know in my high school class. Her blond hair was cinched in a ponytail that bobbed as she walked.

"Coffee's on," she said, taking the hug Nick offered as he came through the door.

We did this three, four times a week, Nick finishing up his morning meeting with his eight officers, then stopping by Donut Dan's and coming out here for breakfast.

Strictly speaking, I was supposed to be eating food a little more nutritional than doughnuts but this morning I decided to indulge.

The conversation ran its usual course. Lisa and Nick joked with each other, Emmy reminded me about all the vitamins and pills I was supposed to take every morning, and I told them about how hard a time I was having finding a few good extra hands for harvest.

Lisa sounded subdued this morning, which caused Emmy to say, "You feeling all right, hon? You seem sort of quiet."

Lisa faked a grin. "Just all that hard work Grandad made me do. Wore me out."

Lisa was still thinking about the rifle shot. So was I. Several times my eyes strayed to Nick's holster and gun.

Just as we were all starting on our second cup of coffee, Lisa included, a car horn sounded at the far end of our driveway. The mail was here.

Wanting a little time to myself, I said I'd get the mail. Sometimes Lisa walked down to the mailbox with me, but this morning she was still working on the second pink glazed doughnut. The rifle shot had apparently not affected her appetite.

After the surgery and the recuperation, I decided to spend whatever time I had left—months maybe or years, the doctors just weren't very sure—living out my Chicago-boy fantasy of being a farmer. Hell, hadn't my daughter become a farmer? I inhaled relatively pure fresh air and less than two miles away was a fast-running river where, with the right spoon and plug and sippner, you could catch trout all day long.

I tried to think of that now as I walked down the rutted road to the mailbox. I was lucky. Few people ever have their fantasies come true. I lived with those I loved, I got to see things grow, and I had for my restive pleasure the sights of beautiful land. And there was a good chance that I was going to kick the cancer I'd been fighting the past two years.

So why did somebody want to go and spoil it for me by shooting at me?

As I neared the mailbox, I admitted to myself that the shot hadn't been accidental. Nor had it been meant to kill me. The shooter was good enough to put a bullet close to my head without doing me any damage. For whatever reason, he'd simply wanted to scare me.

The mailbox held all the usual goodies, circulars from True-Value, Younkers Department Store, Hy-Vee supermarkets, Drugtown, and the Ford dealer where I'd bought my prize blue pickup.

The number ten white envelope, the one addressed to me, was the last thing I took from the mailbox.

I knew immediately that the envelope had something to do with the rifle shot this morning. Some kind of telepathic insight allowed me to understand this fact.

There was neither note nor letter inside, simply a photograph, a photo far more expressive than words could ever have been.

I looked away from it at first, then slowly came back to it, the edge of it pincered between my thumb and forefinger.

I looked at it for a very long time. I felt hot, sweaty, though it was still early morning. I felt scared and ashamed and sick as I stared at it. So many years ago it had been, something done by a man with my name, but not the same man who bore that name today.

I tucked picture into envelope and went back to the house.

When I was back at the table, a cup of coffee in my hand, I noticed that Emmy was staring at me. "You all right, Dad?"

"I'm fine. Maybe just getting a touch of the flu or something."

While that would normally be a good excuse for looking gray and shaken, to the daughter of a cancer patient those are terrifying words. As if the patient himself doesn't worry about every little ache and pain. But to tell someone who loves you that you suddenly feel sick . . .

I reached across the table and said to Nick, "You mind if I hold hands with your girl?"

Nick smiled. "Not as long as you don't make a habit of it."

I took her hand for perhaps the millionth time in my life, holding in memory all the things this hand had been, child, girl, wife, mother.

"I'm fine, honey. Really."

All she wanted me to see was the love in those blue eyes. But I also saw the fear. I wanted to sit her on my lap as I once had, and rock her on my knees, and tell her that everything was going to be just fine.

"Okay?" I said.

"Okay," she half-whispered.

Nick went back to telling Lisa why her school should have an especially good basketball team this year.

On the wall to the right of the kitchen table, Emmy had hung several framed advertisements from turn-of-the-century magazines, sweet little girls in bonnets and braids, and freckled boys with dogs even cuter than they were, all the faces and poses leading you to believe that theirs was a far more innocent era than ours. But the older I got, the more I realized that the human predicament had always been the same. It had just dressed up in different clothes.

There was one photograph up there. A grimy man in military fatigues standing with a cigarette dangling from his lips and an M16 leaning against him. Trying to look tough when all he was was scared. That man was me.

"Well," Nick said about ten minutes later.

Emmy and Lisa giggled.

No matter how many times they kidded Nick about saying "Well" each time he was about to announce his imminent departure, he kept right on saying it.

Emmy walked him out to the car.

I filled the sink with hot soapy water. Lisa piled the breakfast dishes in.

"Grandad?"

"Yes, hon?"

"You sure you don't want to tell Mom about the gunshot?"

"No, hon, I don't. I know it's tempting but she's got enough to worry about." Emmy had had a long and miserable first marriage to a man who had treated adultery like the national pastime. Now, on the small amount of money she got from the farm and from me paying room and board, Emmy had to raise a daughter. She didn't need any more anxiety.

"I'm going into town," I said, as I started to wash the dishes and hand them one by one to Lisa, who was drying.

"How come?"

"Oh, a little business."

"What kind of business?"

"I just want to check out the downtown area."

"For what?"

I laughed. "I'll fill out a written report when I get back."

"I'll go with you."

"Oh, no, hon. This is something I have to do alone."

"Detectives usually have partners."

"I think that's just on TV."

"Huh-uh. In *Weekly Reader* last year there was this article on Chicago police and it said that they usually worked in teams. Team means two. You and me, Grandad."

I guessed I really wasn't going to do much more

than nose around. Probably wouldn't hurt for her to ride along.

By the time Emmy got back to the kitchen, looking every bit as happy as I wanted her to be, Lisa and I had finished the dishes and were ready for town.

"When will you be back?"

"Oh, hour or two."

Emmy was suspicious. "Is there something you're not telling me?"

"Nothing, sweetheart," I said, leaning over and kissing her on the cheek. "Honest."

We went out and got in the truck, passing the old cedar chest Lisa had converted into a giant tool box and placed in the back of the pickup. She had fastened it with strong twine so it wouldn't shift around. It looked kind of funny sitting there like that, but Lisa had worked hard at it so I wasn't about to take it out.

Twenty years ago there was hope that the interstate being discussed would run just east of our little town. Unfortunately, it ran north, and twenty miles away. Today the downtown is four two-block streets consisting of dusty red brick buildings all built before 1930. The post office and the two supermarkets and the five taverns are the busiest places.

I started at the post office, asking for Ev Meader, the man who runs it.

"Gettin' ready for school, Lisa?" Ev said when we came into his office.

She made a face. Ev laughed. "So what can I do for ya today?"

"Wondering if you heard of anybody new moving in around here?" I said. "You know, filling out a new address card."

He scratched his bald head. "Not in the past couple weeks. Least I don't think so. But let me check." He left the office.

I looked down at Lisa. "You going to ask me?"

"Ask you what, Grandad?"

"Ask me how come I'm asking Ev about new people moving into town."

She grinned. "Figured I'd wait till we got back in the truck."

"No new address cards," Ev said when he came back. "I'll keep an eye out for you if you want."

"I'd appreciate it."

In the truck, Lisa said, "Is it all right if I ask you now?"

"I'm wondering if that shot this morning didn't coincide with somebody moving here. Somebody who came here just so they could deal with me."

"You mean, like somebody's after you or something like that?"

"Uh-huh."

"But who'd be after you?"

"I don't know."

The man at the first motel had a potbelly and merry red suspenders. "Asian, you say?"

"Right."

"Nope. No Asians that I signed in, anyway."

"How about at night?"

"I can check the book."

"I'd appreciate it."

"Two weeks back be all right?"

"That'd be fine."

But two weeks back revealed no Asians. "Sorry," he said, hooking his thumbs in his suspenders.

"How come Asians?" Lisa said after we were back in the truck.

"Just because of something that happened to me once."

We rode in silence for a time.

"Grandad?"

"Yeah."

"You going to tell me? About what happened to you once?"

"Not right now, hon."

"How come?"

"Too hard for me to talk about." And it was. Every

time I thought about it for longer than a minute, I could feel my eyes tear up.

The woman at the second motel wore a black T-shirt with a yellow hawk on it. Beneath it said, "I'll do anything for the Hawkeyes." Anything was underlined. The Hawkeyes were the U of Iowa.

"Couple black guys, some kind of salesmen I guess, but no Asians," she said.

"How about at night?"

She laughed. "Bob works at night. He doesn't much like people who aren't white. We had an Asian guy, I'd hear about it, believe me."

The man at the third motel, a hearty man with a farmer's tan and a cheap pair of false teeth said, "No Asian."

"Maybe he came at night?"

"The boy, he works the night shift. Those robberies we had a few months back—that convenience store where that girl got shot?—ever since, he keeps a sharp eye out. Usually tells me all about the guests. He didn't mention any Asian."

"Thanks."

"Sure."

"I'll be happy to ask around," he said.

"Cochran, right?"

"Henry Cochran. Right."

"Thanks for your help, Henry."

"You bet."

"You going to tell me yet?" Lisa said when we were in the pickup and headed back to the farm.

"Not yet."

"Am I bugging you, Grandad?"

I smiled at her. "Maybe a little."

"Then I won't ask you any more."

She leaned over and gave me a kiss on the cheek, after which she settled back on her side of the seat.

"You know what I forgot to do today?" she said after a while.

"What?"

"Tell you I loved you."

"Well, I guess you'd better hurry up and do it then."

"I love you, Grandad."

The funny thing was, I'd never been able to cry much till the cancer, which was a few years ago when I turned fifty-two. Not even when my two best soldier friends got killed in Nam did I cry. Not even when my wife left me did I cry. But these days all sorts of things made me cry. And not just about sad things, either. Seeing a horse run free could make me cry; and certain old songs; and my granddaughter's face when she was telling me she loved me.

"I love you, too, Lisa," I said, and gave her hand a squeeze.

That afternoon Lisa and I spent three hours raking corn in a wagon next to the silo, stopping only when the milk truck came. As usual Ken, the driver, took a sample out of the cooling vat where the milk had been stored. He wanted to get a reading on the butter-fat content of the milk. When the truck was just rolling brown dust on the distant road, Lisa and I went back to raking the corn. At five we knocked off. Lisa rode her bike down the road to the creek where she was trying to catch a milk snake for her science class this fall.

I was in scrubbing up for dinner when Emmy called me to the phone. "There's a woman on the line for you, Dad. She's got some kind of accent."

"I'll take it in the TV room," I said.

"This is Mr. Wilson?"

"Yes."

"Mr. Wilson, my name is Nguyn Mai. I am from Vietnam here visiting."

"I see."

"I would like to meet you tonight. I am staying in Iowa City but I would meet you at the Fireplace restaurant. You know where is?"

"Yes, the Fireplace is downtown here."

"Yes. Would seven o'clock be reasonable for you?"

"I have to say eight. There's a meeting I need to go to first."

"I would appreciate it, Mr. Wilson."

She sounded intelligent and probably middle-aged. I got no sense of her mood.

"Eight o'clock," I said.

After dinner, I took a shower and climbed into a newly washed pair of chinos and a white button-down shirt and a blue windbreaker.

In town, I parked in the Elks lot. Across the cinder alley was the meeting room we used for our support group.

The hour went quickly. There was a new woman there tonight, shy and fresh with fear after her recent operation for breast cancer. At one point, telling us how she was sometimes scared to sleep, she started crying. She was sitting next to me so I put my arm around her and held her till she felt all right again. That was another thing I'd never been too good at till the cancer, showing tenderness.

There were seven of us tonight. We described our respective weeks since the last meeting, exchanged a few low-fat recipes and listened to one of the men discuss some of the problems he was having with his chemotherapy treatments. We finished off with a prayer and then everybody else headed for the coffee-pot and the low-fat kolaches one of the women had baked especially for this meeting.

At eight I walked through the door of the Fireplace and got my first look at Nguyn Mai. She was small and fiftyish and pretty in the way of her people. She wore an American dress, dark and simple, a white sweater draped over her shoulders. Her eyes were friendly and sad.

After I ordered my coffee, she said, "I'm sorry I must trouble you, Mr. Wilson."

"Robert is what most people call me."

"Robert, then." She paused, looked down, looked up again. "My brother Nguyn Dang plans to kill you."

I told her about the rifle shot this morning, and the envelope later.

"He was never the same," she said, "after it happened. I am his oldest sister. There was one sister younger, Hong. This is the one who died. She was six years old. Dang, who was twelve at the time, took care of the funeral all by himself, would not even let my parents see her until after he had put her in her casket. Dang always believed in the old religious ways. He buried Hong in our backyard, according to ancient custom. The old ways teach that the head of a virgin girl is very valuable and can be used as a very powerful talisman to bring luck to the family members. Dang was certainly lucky. When he was fourteen, he left our home and went to Saigon. Within ten years, he was a millionaire. He deals in imports. He spent his fortune tracking you down. It was not easy."

"Were you there that day?"

"Yes."

"Did you see what happened?"

She nodded.

"I didn't kill her intentionally. If you saw what happened, you know that's the truth."

"The truth is in the mind's eye, Robert. In my eye, I know you were frightened by a Cong soldier at the other end of our backyard. You turned and fired and accidentally shot Hong. But this is not what my brother saw."

"He saw me kill her in cold blood?"

"Yes."

"But why would I shoot a little girl?"

"It was done, you know, by both sides. Maybe not by you but by others."

"And so now he's here."

"To kill you."

During my second cup of coffee, she said, "I am afraid for him. I do not wish to see you killed, but even more I do not wish to see my brother killed. I know that is selfish, but those are my feelings."

"I'd have the same feelings." I paused and said, "Do you know where he is?"

"No."

"I looked for him today, after the envelope came."

"And you didn't find him?"

I shook my head. "For what it's worth, Mai, I never forgot what happened that day."

"No?"

"When I got back to the States, I started having nightmares about it. And very bad migraine headaches. I even went to a psychologist for a year or so. Everybody said I shouldn't feel guilty, that those accidents happen in war. Got so bad, it started to take its toll on my marriage. I wasn't much of a husband—or a father, for that matter—and eventually my wife left me. I'd look around at the other guys I'd served with. They'd done ugly things, too, but if it bothered them, they didn't let on. I was even going to go back to Nam and look up your family and tell them I was sorry, but my daughter wouldn't let me. At that point she was ready to put me in a mental hospital. She said that if I seriously tried to go, she'd put me away for sure. I knew she meant it."

"Did you talk to the police today, about his taking a shot at you?"

"You've got to understand something here, Mai. I don't want your brother arrested. I want to find him and talk to him and help him if I can. There hasn't been a day in my life since then I haven't wanted to pick up the phone and talk to your family and tell them how sorry I am."

"If only we could find Dang."

"I'll start looking again tomorrow."

"I feel hopeful for the first time in many years."

I stayed up past midnight because I knew I wouldn't sleep well. There was a Charles Bronson movie on TV, in the course of which he killed four or five people. Before that day in Nam, when I'd been so scared that I'd mistaken a little girl for a VC, I had been all enamored of violence. But no longer. After the war I gave away all my guns and nearly all my pretensions to machismo. I knew too well where machismo sometimes led.

Ten hours later, coming in from morning chores, I heard the phone ringing. Emmy said it was for me.

It was the motel man with the merry red suspenders. "I heard something you might be interested in."

"Oh?"

"You know where the old Sheldon farm is?"

"I don't think so."

"Well, there's a lime quarry due west of the power station. You know where that would be?"

"I can find it."

"There's a house trailer somewhere back in there. Hippie couple lived there for years, but they moved to New Mexico last year. Guy in town who owns a tavern—Shelby, maybe you know him—he bought their trailer from them and rents it out sort of like an apartment. Or thought he would, anyway. Hasn't had much luck. Till last week. That's when this Asian guy rented it from him."

The day was ridiculously beautiful, the sweet smoky breath of autumn on the air, the horses in the hills shining the color of saddle leather.

The lime quarry had been closed for years. Some of the equipment had been left behind. Everything was rusted now. The whining wind gave the place the sound of desolation.

I pointed the pickup into the hills where oak and hickory and basswood bloomed, and elm and ash and ironwood leaves caught the bright bouncing beams of the sun.

The trailer was in a grassy valley, buffalo grass knee-deep and waving in the wind, a silver S of creek winding behind the rusted old Airstream.

I pulled off the road in the dusty hills and walked the rest of the way down.

There was a lightning-dead elm thirty yards from

the trailer. When I reached it, I got behind it so I could get a better look at the Airstream.

No noise came from the open windows, no smoke from the tin chimney.

I went up to the trailer. Every few feet I expected to hear a bullet cracking from a rifle.

The window screens were badly torn, the three steps tilted rightward, and the two propane tanks to the right of the door leaned forward as if they might fall at any moment.

I reached the steps, tried the door. Locked. Dang was gone. Picking the lock encased in the doorknob was no great trouble.

The interior was a mess. Apparently Dang existed on Godfather's pizza. I counted nine different cartons, all grease-stained, on the kitchen counter. The thrumming little refrigerator smelled vaguely unclean. It contained three sixteen-ounce bottles of Pepsi.

In the back, next to the bed on the wobbly nightstand, I found the framed photos of the little girl. She had been quite pretty, solemn and mischievous at the same time.

The photo Dang had sent me was very different. The girl lay on a table, her bloody clothes wrapped around her. Her chest was a dark and massive hole.

I thought I heard a car coming.

Soon enough I was behind the elm again. But the road was empty. All I'd heard was my own nerves.

During chores two hours later, Lisa said, "You find him?"

"Find who?"

"Find who? Come on, Grandad."

"Yeah, I found him. Or found his trailer, anyway."

"How come you didn't take me with you? I'm supposed to be your partner."

I leaned on my pitchfork. "Hon, from here on out I'll have to handle this alone."

"Oh, darn it, Grandad. I want to help."

There was a sweet afternoon breeze through the barn door, carrying the scents of clover and sunshine.

"All that's going to happen is I'm going to talk to him."

"Gosh, Grandad, he tried to kill you."

"I don't think so."

"But he shot at you."

"He tried to scare me."

"You sure?"

"Pretty sure."

After washing up for the day, I went into the TV room and called Mai and told her that I'd found where her brother was staying.

"You should not go out there," she said. "In my land we say that there are seasons of the heart. The season of my brother's heart is very hot and angry now."

"I just want to talk to him and tell him that I'm sorry. Maybe that will calm him down."

"I will talk to him. You can direct me to this trailer?"

"If you meet me at the restaurant again, I'll lead you out there."

"Then you will go back home?"

"If that's what you want."

She was there right at eight. The full moon, an autumn moon that painted all the pines silver, guided us to the power station and the quarry and finally to the hill above the trailer.

I got out of the car and walked back to hers. "You follow that road straight down."

"Did you see the windows? The lights?"

He was home. Or somebody was.

"I appreciate this, Robert. Perhaps I can reason with my brother."

"I hope so."

She paused, looked around. "It is so beautiful and peaceful here. You are fortunate to live here."

There were owls and jays in the forest trees, and the fast creek silver in the moonlight, and the distant song of a windmill in the breeze. She was right. I was lucky to live here.

She drove on.

I watched her till she reached the trailer, got out, went to the door, and knocked.

Even from here, I could see that the man-silhouette held a handgun when he opened the door for her. Mai and I had both assumed we could reason with her brother. Maybe not.

"You up for a game of hearts?" Lisa asked awhile later.

"Sure," I said.

"Good. Because I'm going to beat you tonight."

"You sure of that?"

"Uh-huh."

As usual I won. I thought of letting her win but then realized that she wouldn't want that. She was too smart and too honorable for that kind of charity.

When she was in her cotton nightie, her mouth cold and minty from brushing her teeth, she came down and gave me my good-night kiss.

When Lisa was creaking her way up the stairs, Emmy looked into the TV room and said, "Wondered if I could ask you a question?"

"Sure."

"Are you, uh, all right?"

"Aw, honey. My last tests were fine and I feel great. You've really got to stop worrying."

"I don't mean physically. I mean, you seem preoccupied."

"Everything's fine."

"God, Dad, I love you so much. And I can't help worrying about you."

The full-grown woman in the doorway became my quick little daughter again, rushing to me and sitting on my lap and burying her tear-hot face in my neck so I couldn't see her cry.

We sat that way for a long time and then I started bouncing her on my knee.

She laughed. "I weigh a little more than I used to."

"Not much."

"My bottom's starting to spread a little."

"Nick seems to like it fine."

With her arms still around me, she kissed me on the cheek and then gave me another hug. A few minutes later, she left to finish up in the kitchen.

The call came ten minutes after I fell into a fitful sleep. I'd been expecting Mai. I got Nick.

"Robert, I wondered if you could come down to the station."

"Now? After midnight?"

"I'm afraid so."

"What's up?"

"A Vietnamese woman came into the emergency room over at the hospital tonight. Her arm had been broken. The doc got suspicious and gave me a call. I went over and talked to her. She wouldn't tell me anything at all. Then all of a sudden, she asked if she could see a man named Robert Wilson. You know her, Robert?"

"Yes."

"Who is she?"

"Her name is Nguyn Mai. She's visiting people in the area."

"Which people?"

I hesitated. "Nick, I can't tell you anything more than Mai has."

For the first time in our relationship, Nick sounded cold. "I need you to come down here, Robert. Right away."

Our small town is fortunate enough to have a full-time hospital that doubles as an emergency room.

Mai sat at the end of the long hallway, her arm in a white sling. I sat next to her in a yellow form-curved plastic chair.

"What happened?"

"I was foolish," she said. "We argued and I tried to take one of his guns from him. We struggled and I fell into the wall and I heard my arm snap."

"I don't think Nick believes you."

"He says he knows you."

"He goes out with my daughter."

"Is he a prejudiced man, this Nick?"

"I don't think so. He's just a cop who senses that he's not getting the whole story. Plus you made him very curious when you asked him to call me."

"I knew no one else."

"I understand, Mai. I'm just trying to explain Nick's attitude."

Nick showed up a few minutes later.

"How's the arm? Ready for tennis yet?"

Mai obviously appreciated the way Nick was trying to lighten things up. "Not yet," she said, and smiled like a small shy girl.

"Mind if I borrow your friend a few minutes, Mai?"

She smiled again and shook her head. But there was apprehension in her dark eyes. Would I tell Nick that her brother had taken a shot at me?

In the staff coffee room, I put a lot of sugar and Creamora into my paper cup of coffee. I badly needed to kill the taste.

"You know her in Nam, Robert?"

"No."

"She just showed up?"

"Pretty much."

"Any special reason?"

"Not that I know of."

"Robert, I don't appreciate lies. Especially from my future father-in-law."

"She phoned me last night and we talked. Turns out we knew some of the same people in Nam. That's about all there is to it."

"Right."

"Nick, I can handle this. It doesn't have to involve the law."

"She got her arm broken."

"It was an accident."

"That's what she says."

"She's telling the truth, Nick."

"The same way you're telling the truth, Robert?"

In the hall, Nick said, "She seems like a nice woman."

"She is a nice woman."

When we reached Mai, Nick said, "Robert here tells me you're a nice woman. I'm sorry if my questions upset you."

Mai gave a little half bow of appreciation and good-bye.

In the truck, I turned the heat on. It was two o'clock on a late August night and it was shivering late-October cold.

"Where's your car?"

"The other side of the building," Mai said.

"You'd better not drive back to Iowa City tonight."

"There is a motel?"

After I got her checked in, I pulled the pickup right to her door, Number 17.

Inside, I got the lights on and turned the thermostat up to eighty so it would warm up fast. The room was small and dark. You could hear the ghosts of it crying down the years, a chorus of smiling salesmen and weary vacationers and frantic adulterers.

"I wish I had had better luck with my brother tonight," Mai said. "For everybody's sake."

"Maybe he'll think about it tonight and be more reasonable in the morning."

In the glove compartment I found the old .38 Emmy bought when she moved to the farm. Bucolic as rural Iowa was, it was not without its moments of violence, particularly when drug deals were involved. She kept it in the kitchen cabinet, on the top shelf. I had taken it with me when I left tonight.

In the valley, the trailer was a silhouette outlined in moon silver. I approached in a crouch, the .38 in my right hand. A white-tailed fawn pranced away to my left; and a raccoon or possum rattled reeds in a long waving patch of bluestem grass.

When I reached the elm, I stopped and listened. No sound whatsoever from the Airstream. The propane tanks stood like sentries.

The doorknob was no more difficult to unlock tonight than it had been earlier.

Tonight the trailer smelled of sleep and wine and rust and cigarette smoke. I stood perfectly still listening to the refrigerator vibrate. From the rear of the trailer came the sounds of Dang snoring.

When I stood directly above him, I raised the .38 and pushed it to within two inches of his forehead.

I spoke his name in the stillness.

His eyes opened but at first they seemed to see nothing. He seemed to be in a half-waking state.

But then he grunted and something like a sob exploded in his throat and I said, "If I wanted to, I could kill you right now, but I don't want to. I want you to listen to me."

In the chill prairie night, the coffee Dang put on smelled very good. We sat at a small table, each drinking from a different 7-Eleven mug.

He was probably ten years younger than me, slender, with graying hair and a long, intelligent face. He wore good American clothes and good American glasses. Whenever he looked at me directly, his eyes narrowed with anger. He was likely flashing back to the frail bloody dead girl in the photo he'd sent me.

"My sister told you why I came here?"

"Yes."

"You came to talk me out of it, that is why you're here?"

"Something like that. The first thing is, I want to tell you how sorry I am that it happened."

"Words."

"Pardon?"

"Words. In my land there is a saying, 'Words only delay the inevitable.' If you do not kill me, Mr. Wilson, I will kill you. No matter how many words you speak."

"It was an accident."

"I am a believer in Hoa Hao, Mr. Wilson. We do not believe in accidents. All behavior is willful."

"I willfully murdered a six-year-old girl?"

"In war, there are many atrocities."

Anger came and went in his eyes. When it was gone, he looked old and sad. Rage seemed to give him a kind of fevered youth.

"You were there, Dang. You saw it happen. I wasn't firing at her. I was firing at a VC. She got in the way."

He stared at me a long time. "Words, Mr. Wilson, words."

I wanted to tell him about my years following the killing, how it shaped and in many respects destroyed my life. I even thought of telling him about my cancer and how the disease had taught me so many important lessons. But I would only sound as if I were begging his pity.

I stood up. "Why don't you leave tomorrow? Your sister is worried about you."

"I'll leave after I've killed you."

"What I did, Dang, I know you can't forgive me for. Maybe I'd be the same way you are. But if you kill me, the police will arrest you. And that will kill Mai. You'll have killed her just as I killed your other sister."

For a time he kept his head down and said nothing. When he raised his eyes to me, I saw that they were wet with tears. "Before I sleep each night, I play in my head her voice, like a tape. Even at six she had a beautiful voice. I play it over and over again."

He surprised me by putting his head down on the table and weeping.

In bed that night, I thought of how long we'd carried our respective burdens, Dang his hatred of me, and my remorse over Hong's death. I fell asleep thinking of what Dang had said about Hong's voice. I wished I could have heard her sing.

When I got down to the barn in the morning, Lisa was already bottle-feeding the three new calves. I set about the milking operations.

Half an hour later, the calves, the rabbits, and the barn cats taken care of, Lisa joined me.

"Mom was worried about you."

"Figured she would be," I said. "You didn't tell her anything, did you?"

"No, but Nick did."

"Nick?"

"Uh-huh. He told her about the Vietnamese woman."

"Oh."

"So Mom asked me if I knew anything about it."

"What'd you say?"

"Said I didn't know anything at all. But I felt kinda weird, Grandad, lying to Mom, I mean."

"I'm sorry, sweetheart."

At lunch, baloney sandwiches and creamed corn and an apple, Emmy said, "Dad, could I talk to you?"

"Sure."

"Lisa, why don't you go on ahead with your chores? Grandad'll be down real soon."

Lisa looked at me. I nodded.

When the screen door slapped shut, Emmy said, "Nick thinks you're in some kind of trouble, Dad."

"You know how much I like Nick, honey. I also happen to respect him." I held her hand. "But I'm not in any kind of trouble."

"Who's the Vietnamese woman?"

"Nguyn Mai."

"That doesn't tell me much."

"I don't mean for it to tell you much."

"You getting mad?"

"No. Sad, if anything. Sad that I can't have a life of my own without answering a lot of questions."

"Dad, if Nick wasn't concerned, I wouldn't be concerned. But Nick has good instincts about things like this."

"He does indeed."

"So why not tell us the truth?"

I got up from the table, picked up my dishes, and carried them over to the sink. "Let me think about it a little while, all right?"

She watched me for a long time, looking both wan

and a little bit peeved, and finally said, "Think about it a little while, then."

She got up and left the room.

There were two carts that needed filling with silage. Lisa and I opened the trapdoor in the silo and started digging the silage out. Then we took the first of the carts over and started feeding the cows.

When that was done, I told Lisa to take the rest of the afternoon off. She kept talking about all the school supplies she needed. She'd never find time for them if she was always working.

During the last rain, we'd noticed a few drops plopping down from the area of the living room. The roof was a good ten years old. I put the ladder against the back of the house and went up and looked around. There were some real bad spots.

I called the lumber store and got some prices on roofing materials. I told them what I wanted. They'd have them ready tomorrow afternoon.

There was still some work to do, so after a cup of coffee, I headed for the barn. I hadn't quite reached it before the phone rang.

"For you, Dad," Emmy called.

"Robert?"

"I thought maybe you'd be gone by now, Mai. I went out and visited your brother last night. I don't know if he told you about it. I also don't know if it did any good. But at least I got to tell him I was sorry."

"I need to meet you at the hill above his trailer. Right away, please. Something terrible has happened."

"What're you talking about, Mai?"

"Please. The hill. As soon as possible."

"Can you drive?"

"Yes. I drove a little this morning."

"What's happened, Mai?"

"Your granddaughter. Dang has taken her."

As I was grabbing my jacket, and remembering that I'd left the .38 in the glove compartment, Emmy came into the room.

"I need to go out for a little while."

She touched my arm. "Dad, I don't know what just happened, but why don't you get Nick to help you?"

I'd thought about that, too. "Maybe I will."

I drove straight and hard to the hill. All the way there I thought of Dang. One granddaughter for one little sister. Even up. I should have thought of that and protected Lisa.

Mai stood by the dusty rental car.

"How do you know she's down there?"

"An hour ago, I sneaked down there and peeked in the window. She is sitting in a chair in the kitchen."

"But she's still alive? You're sure?"

"Yes."

"Did you see if she's bleeding or anything?"

"I don't think he has hurt her. Not yet, anyway."

"I'm going in to get her."

She nodded at the .38 stuffed into my belt. "I am afraid for all of us now. For Dang and for your granddaughter and for you. And for me."

She fell against me, crying. I was tender as I could be, but all I could think of was Lisa.

"I tried to talk him into giving her up. He says that he is only doing the honorable thing." More tears. "Talking won't help, Robert."

I went east, in a wide arc, coming down behind the trailer in a stand of windbreak firs. The back side of the Airstream had only one window. I didn't see anybody watching me.

I belly-crawled from the trees to the front of the trailer. By now I could hear him shouting in Vietnamese at Lisa. All his anger and all his pain was in those words. The exact meaning made no difference. It was the sounds he made that mattered.

I went to the door and knocked. His words stopped immediately. For a time there was just the soughing silence of the prairie.

"Dang, you let Lisa go and I'll come in and take her place."

"Don't come in, Grandad. He wants to kill you."

"Dang, did you hear me? You let Lisa go and I'll

come in. I have a gun now, but I'll drop it if you agree."

His first bullet ripped through the glass and screening of the front door.

I pitched left, rolling on the ground to escape the second and third shots.

Lisa yelled at Dang to stop firing, her words echoing inside the trailer.

Prairie silence again, a hawk gliding down the sunbeams.

I scanned the trailer, looking for some way to get closer without getting shot. There wasn't enough room to hide next to the three stairs; or behind the two silver propane tanks; or even around the corner. The bedroom window was too high to peek in comfortably.

"He's picking up his rifle, Grandad!" Lisa called.

Two more shots, these more explosive and taking larger chunks of the front door, burst into the afternoon air. I rolled away from them as best I could.

"Grandad, watch out!"

And then a cry came, one so shrill and aggrieved I wasn't sure what it was at first, and then the front door was thrown open and there was Dang, rifle fire coming in bursts as he came out on the front steps, shooting directly at me.

This time I rolled to the right. He was still sobbing out words in Vietnamese and these had the power to mesmerize me. They spoke exactly of how deep his grief ran.

Another burst of rifle fire, Dang standing on the steps of the trailer and having an easy time finding me with his rifle.

There was a long and curious delay before my brain realized that my chest had been wounded. It was as if all time stopped for a long moment, the universe holding its breath, and then came blood and raging blinding pain. Then I felt a bone in my arm crack as a bullet smashed into it.

Lisa screamed again. "Grandad!"

As I lay there, I realized I had only moments to do

what I needed to. Dang was coming down from the steps, moving in to kill me. I raised the .38 and fired.

The explosion was instant and could probably be heard for miles. I'd been forced to shoot at him at an angle. The bullet had missed and torn into one of the propane tanks. The entire trailer had vanished inside tumbling gritty black smoke and fire at least three different shades of red and yellow. The air reeked of propane and the burning trailer.

I called out for Lisa, but I knew I could never get to my feet to help her. I was losing consciousness too fast.

And then Dang was standing over me, rifle pointed directly down at my head.

I knew I didn't have long. "Save her, Dang. She's innocent just the way your sister was. Save her, please. I'm begging you."

The darkness was swift and cold and black, and the sounds of Lisa screaming and fire roaring faded, faded.

The room was small and white and held but one bed and it was mine.

Lisa and Emmy and Nick stood on the left side of the bed while Mai stood on the right.

"I guess I'll have to do some of your chores for a while, Grandad."

"I guess you will, hon."

"That means driving the tractor."

I looked at Emmy, who said, "We'll hire a couple of hands, sweetheart. No tractor for you until Grandad gets back."

Nick looked at his watch. "How about if I take these two beautiful ladies downstairs for some lunch? This is one of the few hospitals that actually serves good food."

But it wasn't just lunch he was suggesting. He wanted to give Mai a chance to speak with me alone.

Lisa and Emmy kissed me then went downstairs with Nick.

I was already developing stiffness from being in bed

so long. After being operated on, I'd slept through the night and into this morning.

Mai leaned over and took my hand. "I'm glad you're all right, Mr. Wilson."

"I'm sorry, Mai. How things turned out."

"In the end, he was an honorable man."

"He certainly was, Mai. He certainly was."

After I'd passed out, Dang had rushed back into the trailer and rescued Lisa, who had been remarkably unscathed.

Then Dang had run back inside, knowing he would die in the smoke and the flames.

"Tomorrow would have been our little sister's birthday," Mai said. "I do not think he wanted to face that."

She cried for a long time cradled in my good left arm, my right being in a sling like hers.

"He was not a bad man."

"No, he wasn't, Mai. He was a good man."

"I am sorry for your grief."

"And I'm sorry for yours."

She smiled tearily. "Seasons of the heart, Mr. Wilson. Perhaps the seasons will change now."

"Perhaps they will," I said, and watched her as she leaned over to kiss me on the forehead.

As she was leaving, I pointed to my arm sling and then to hers. "Twins," I said.

"Yes," she said. "Perhaps we are, Robert."

For the farm details, I drew on memory and a fine book entitled *The American Family Farm,* Ancona/Anderson, Harcourt Brace Jovanovich, 1989.

What's a Friend For?

Margaret Maron and
Susan Dunlap

Susan Dunlap has been a social worker in Baltimore, upper Harlem, the South Bronx, and in Richmond, California, as well as a hatha yoga teacher. She also created three best-selling mystery protagonists: Private Eye Kiernan O'Shaughnessy (*High Fall*), police detective Jill Smith (*Time Expired*), and amateur sleuth Vejay Haskell (*The Last Annual Slugfest*).

Margaret Maron is the author of two mystery series: Lt. Sigrid Harald, NYPD (*Past Imperfect*), and Judge Deborah Knott, of Colleton County, North Carolina (*Shooting at Loons*). In 1993, Margaret's *Bootlegger's Daughter* won the Agatha, Edgar, Anthony, and Macavity awards. Her short stories have also won an Agatha and Macavity awards.

Sue and Margaret partnered up to create a truly unique short story. When Deborah Knott needed some West Coast sleuthing, she called on her college roommate Kiernan O'Shaughnessy for help, after all "What's a Friend For?" . . .

My elderly cousin Lunette got off the plane apologizing from the moment she spotted me waiting at the tinsel-draped gate at our Raleigh-Durham airport. "Oh, Deborah, honey, I'm so frigging sorry."

Even though I was now a duly sworn district court judge, Aunt Zell still thought I had plenty of time to pick up some of the aunts, uncles, and cousins coming in for Christmas from Ohio, Florida, New Orleans, or, in Lunette's case, Shady Palms, California.

Her hair was Icy Peach, her elegantly slouchy green

sweatshirt had an appliquéd Rudolph with a red nose that really did light up, and her skintight stretch pants seemed to be fashioned from silver latex. Nevertheless, for all the holiday joy in her twice-lifted face you'd have thought it was the first day of Lent instead of the day before Christmas Eve.

Lunette's of my mother's generation. We're first cousins once removed, which, if you're into genealogy, means that she and Mother shared a set of grandparents on our Carroll side.

But whereas most of the Carrolls have stuck right here in Colleton County ever since our branch got booted out of Virginia and wound up in North Carolina in the early 1800s, Lunette was born without a dab of tar on her heels. She became an airline stewardess in the early fifties, married a Jewish sales exec from California, and crisscrossed the country with him for twenty years till he took early retirement. Then they became semi-rooted in Shady Palms, where Lunette's continued to live since his death six years ago.

The family's tried to get Lunette to come home, but she says all her friends are there, the gaming tables of Las Vegas are just a short drive away, and anyhow, she's too old to exchange blue language for blue hair or give up the Hadassah and join the Women's Missionary Union.

But she does come back for Christmas now that Jules is gone. They never had children, and Lunette says, "If I'm going to have to listen to foolish old women burble on about their blippity-blip grandchildren, it might as well be kids I'm kin to. Besides, you can't get decent sweet potato pie out in California."

We made our way downstairs through the holiday throng to the baggage claim area and while we waited for the carousel to start turning, I finally grasped that Lunette was half-crying, half-cursing because her condo had been ripped off less than a week ago.

Through Aunt Zell, I'd heard most of the details when she called two days earlier to confirm what time her flight was due. Over the phone, Aunt Zell said

Lunette had sounded almost matter-of-fact: Half her friends have been robbed, she guessed she was over-due; she was sorry to lose Jules's wedding ring, but she'd been wearing most of the jewelry she cared about and she wasn't all that sad to be rid of the ugly pieces she'd inherited from Jules's mother. "Everybody coos over marcasite these days, but when I was a girl, it was old-lady stuff. Yuck!"

The stereo and color TV were brand new, but insurance would replace them, too. Mostly she'd seemed annoyed because the thief had left such a mess and because the local police didn't seem all that concerned.

She was still blueing the air around us with her views on the boys in blue—a prissy young mother glared at Lunette and made a point of leading her child away—when a loud bell sounded and the carousel rumbled into motion. Soon everyone was grabbing for luggage, and Lunette wasn't the only passenger with several shopping bags of brightly wrapped presents.

"Oh, is this young lady your cousin?" asked a middle-aged black woman when she and Lunette reached for the same shiny red shopping bag. They had been seat-mates on the plane. "You're a judge, I believe? Your cousin told me about your loss. Such a shame."

Loss? Loss of what? My virginity? Last year's run-off? My freedom now that I was on the bench? Or had somebody died while I wasn't looking? No time to ask Lunette because she'd trotted off after someone who'd mistaken her garment bag for his.

We finally got it all sorted out, carried everything out to my sports car, and belted ourselves in somehow without smashing anything. As I zipped through the exit lanes and pointed the car toward Raleigh, Lunette switched my radio from a country music station to one that was rapping out carols with new lyrics that gave a whole other meaning to the term "blue Christmas." I compromised by switching it off completely.

"What did that woman mean about my loss?" I asked in the ensuing silence.

"I swear, you're as hard of hearing as Jules used to be. What the hell do you think I've been trying to tell you? Last night when I was packing, I was going to wrap it up and give it to you for Christmas. And that's when I realized that that double-damned SOB had taken it, too."

"The *locket?*" I was aghast. "The Carroll locket?"

Lunette's surgically smooth face almost crumpled again. "Two hundred years it's been in our family and I was the one to lose it," she mourned tearfully. "I *meant* to get the chain mended and send it to you when you won the election, but then—"

She didn't have to finish. I'd actually lost the runoff election and getting appointed was almost anticlimactic. What with one thing and another, I had forgotten that Lunette had promised to give me the Carroll locket if I ever made it to the bench.

The heavy gold octagon-shaped locket was the only family treasure salvaged when our branch left Virginia. It had been passed down in the family from generation to generation, always going to the oldest son's bride until Lunette turned out to be her father's only child. There were two male Carroll cousins in her generation, but she hadn't liked either of their wives and steadfastly ignored all hints that the Carroll locket should go back to someone with the Carroll name.

More than its age and monetary worth, the locket was valued in our family because of the myths that had grown up around it. It had been pawned at least a dozen times, given as surety in exchange for fertilizer money or to meet a mortgage payment, and more than once it had been lost forever. Or so its then-owner thought. But always the locket came back, redeemed by bounteous crops or recovered through miracles.

In 1822, it had fallen into a deep well. Three months later, it was pulled up in a wooden bucket.

In 1862, Anne Carroll tucked it inside her husband's

uniform when he went off to Yorktown. "It'll bring you back to me," she whispered. He fell in battle, but a Yankee soldier sent the locket home to her with his condolences, one corner of the hinged lid nicked by the Minié ball that had pierced the young rebel's heart.

In 1918, while a new bride frolicked on the beach with her groom, it had slipped into the sand unnoticed. Two years later, as she helped her firstborn build a sand castle, the tot's bright red tin shovel clinked against something metallic and there was the locket, a bit pitted by the salty sand but otherwise intact.

Lunette herself had lost it last March at a movie theater. Her friends found the broken chain, but the locket had completely disappeared. Yet when she undressed that night, it fell out of her bra. "And I know I shook my clothes out thoroughly," she swore. "The bloody thing's like the monkey's paw. You couldn't throw it away if you tried."

Nevertheless, she'd stowed it in her jewelry box till she could remember to get the chain mended.

Now as we took the bypass around the south side of Raleigh, she seemed disconsolate.

"It'll never come back this time," she predicted gloomily.

"Maybe the police will get lucky." I comforted her.

My words only set her off again. Those lazy SOBs. They didn't even want to come out because her losses were less than five thousand dollars. And when they did come, they didn't bother to try to find fingerprints. "They said whoever took my things had probably already pawned them. I didn't really care till I realized the locket was gone. Hell! They didn't even question the neighbors very well. Mrs. Katzner across the street said she saw somebody loading a stereo in the back of his car, and she even took down the license number and gave it to me."

She rummaged in her silver shoulder bag and pulled out a crumpled slip of paper which she shoved under my nose. "See? A California state license."

I glanced at the digits and then pulled around a pickup with two dogs and a shabby-looking fir tree in the back.

"Did you tell the police detectives?"

"Of course I did. Know what those brother-buckers said?" Her voice dripped sarcastic venom. " 'Ma'am, the plates were probably stolen last week. Nobody rips off a house in broad daylight using his own plates.' "

She was so upset that I asked her to let me have the license number. "I'll get someone to run a check," I told her.

"Why bother? The cops are probably right, damn their eyes. Too bad Maria Vincelli died."

She lost me there. "Who?"

"Maria Vincelli. Her brother was connected. Nobody came near our building while Maria was living there. But she died four years ago and that's when we started getting ripped off."

"Connected? You mean mob connected?"

"Mob, schmob. She never really said, but he used to come once a month to visit her in one of those shiny black cars with the tinted windows so you can't ever tell how many people are inside. Everybody felt so safe."

By the time we reached Dobbs, Lunette had begun to brighten up a little. Then we turned into Aunt Zell's drive and several Carroll women appeared on the veranda to welcome her back. Lunette clasped my hand. "Promise you won't say a word about it till after Christmas," she implored. "Some of those old biddies would peck my eyes out if they knew the locket's gone for good."

Jeeter and Gloria would be sympathetic, but Lib and Mary Frances had such sharp tongues that I promised I'd hold mine. Relieved, Lunette jumped out of my car, held out her arms to the advancing cousins, and cooed, "Oh, you sweet things, I'm just so glad to *see* you!"

Nevertheless, while Aunt Zell pressed coffee and fruitcake on everybody, I slipped upstairs to my private quarters and called a friend in the highway patrol. In almost no time, she called back to say that she'd tracked it down and found it'd been issued to a certain Samuel James Watkins in San Diego. No report that it'd been stolen. She then called a friend of hers in San Diego who ran his name through files out there and discovered a long string of petty larcenies. Was it really going to be that simple?

I pulled out a Rand-McNally and traced the distance between Shady Palms and San Diego. An easy drive.

My finger continued another short distance up the map along the California coast and the name La Jolla jumped out at me. Probably wouldn't do a bit of good. She was probably busy. Or gone for the Christmas holidays.

Nevertheless, I flipped to the O's in my Rolodex and started dialing.

When the phone rang, Kiernan O'Shaughnessy was dropping into a back bend. "Damn!" she grumbled, as her hands hit the floor. She walked, crablike on all fours across to the desk and lifted up one arm to reach the receiver. Instead of the "hello" she intended, it came out "Huruhhh."

"Kiernan?"

"Yes?"

"It's Deborah Knott. Did I catch you at a bad time?"

"As a matter of fact, yes," she said, holding the back bend, but now in control of her breath. "Fortunately, I can still do two things at once. And even if I couldn't, I'd choose talking to you. So how're things in the wilds of Colleton County?"

"It's Christmas. Something you probably don't have to bother with out there, but relatives are flocking in here like homing pigeons to Capistrano."

"Swallows," Kiernan corrected.

"Whatever. Listen, I'm calling about my cousin Lunette. She's on my mother's Carroll side. I need to ask a professional favor now that you're a licensed detective. Unless you're too busy?''

Smiling at the way her former housemate's voice still went up at the end of sentences, Kiernan pushed herself erect and pulled down the hem of her T-shirt. "Gee, Deb, I'd love to help, but I'm really busy at the moment. I need to do some more back bends, then catch some sun on my beachfront deck. After that it'll be time to watch bronzed young men amble over the rocks or balance on their body boards out on the waves."

Before Deborah could laugh, she said, "Actually, what I'm doing is waiting for the one thing that will make this duplex on the beach in La Jolla perfect."

"Which is?"

"A servant. I'm running an ad for a house-keeper/cook. Someone like your cousin Lunette, who'll run the house, cook great meals, and love my dog."

Deborah laughed. "If that's your standard, forget Lunette because she's forgot every bit of raising she ever had. She hasn't lifted a mop in half a century, she uses the oven for storage, and if she took your dog out, it'd probably be to sell him."

"Then it's just as well that I've found the perfect woman. At least I think I have. Listen to this: She managed an inn for ten years, planned the menus herself, is so tidy she straightened the kitchen counter while we talked, and best of all, she speaks in mono-syllables. I'll hardly know she's here."

Kiernan's voice had not dropped at the end of her sentence. Even so, Deborah asked, "But—?"

"But I'd hoped for someone who could spell me with Ezra when I'm on a case," Kiernan admitted. "Mrs. Pritchard looks to be sixty-some years old. A very matronly sixty-some. I can't see her loping along the beach with an Irish wolfhound. Still, she likes Ezra and that's what counts in the end, isn't it?"

"So you hired her? That's nice. Now, my cousin—"

"I have one more applicant to screen," Kiernan interjected smoothly. "A man. Might be interesting to have a real butler, don't you think? Remember those old Mr. Belvedere movies they used to run on Channel 5? Who was that actor? Robert Young? David Niven?"

"I really don't remember."

"Not David Niven . . . Clifton Webb! But unless this guy's actually a gentleman's gentleman, Mrs. Pritchard will get the job."

"I'm sure she'll do just fine."

Deborah hadn't interrupted, or *said* anything to indicate impatience, but that impatience was clear to Kiernan. While finishing up some postgrad work in Chapel Hill, the two women had shared an apartment off-campus. It had taken almost half the summer for Kiernan, a Northerner from a family that made silence a life form, to discern the slight hesitation before responses, and to realize that when Deborah flattened her tones like this, she might as well be screaming, "Dammit! Stop interrupting and let me get to my point!"

Once Kiernan understood, she had taken devilish pleasure in lengthening her descriptions, slipping into circuitous conversational byways and sluggish swamps of supposition as long and drab as the Great Dismal, all the time waiting to see how long good southern manners would last. By September, Deborah's record stood at thirty-eight minutes. Kiernan went back to California without ever revealing the game, but she did wonder what Deborah made of her and those rambling half hours.

"So, Deborah," she said with a grin, "what's this favor?"

Kiernan was still listening to her friend's tale of Cousin Lunette and the Carroll locket when the doorbell rang. "Can you hang on a minute, Deb? I'll just glance over this last applicant's résumé and unless he's better than Niven or Webb, he'll be on his way before he gets as far as the sofa."

She put the phone on the table and opened the door.

"Brad Tchernak," the applicant said, extending a hand the size of Rhode Island. The man didn't fill the entire doorway, but he didn't leave room for anyone else to squeeze through. "Everyone calls me Tchernak."

"You're a chef?" she asked amazed. "I would have taken you for a linebacker."

"Line*man*. *Former* offensive lineman with the Chargers."

"A lineman rather than a cook," she said, not moving from the door.

"Not a professional cook, but a great one, and a great housekeeper."

Maybe, Kiernan thought. He might not match Mrs. Pritchard's professional qualifications, but this guy was definitely a hunk. A tall, athletic, wiry-haired, bearded honest-to-God hunk. If she were merely decorating the duplex, she'd grab him. But she didn't need a live-in hunk; she needed a housekeeper, a nice middle-aged lady with the legs of a miler.

"Don't jump to conclusions," Tchernak said. "And don't say no before you let me whip up a dinner that will answer all your questions. Where's your kitchen? Through there?"

"No. I've already—"

Toenails scratched on stairs, a furry rump hit the wall, and a moment later the Irish wolfhound clambered down the last step. Momentarily he stood nearly shoulder to shoulder with Kiernan, assessing the intruder. At this point in introductions, the other applicants had edged out the door.

Tchernak didn't move.

Ezra's mouth opened slightly. Tchernak stepped forward, a grin twitching his wiry brown beard. Ezra leaped, paws landing on Tchernak's shoulders, tongue lathering both of Tchernak's cheeks. Tchernak scratched the huge dog's stomach. "Am I hired?"

"Not so fast," she said, the haloed picture of Mrs.

Pritchard in her mind. "But go ahead and check out the kitchen."

"Kiernan!" The voice shouting from the receiver came in loud and clear and there wasn't a drop of graciousness, southern or otherwise, in it.

She picked up the phone. "Sorry, Deb. This interview's a bit more complicated than I expected."

"So I gather."

Ignoring Deborah's sarcastic tone, she said, "You were just about to ask me for a favor?"

"Damn straight. You've got a slimeball out there in California and he's got the Carroll locket. *My* locket. The one Cousin Lunette was going to give me when I won the election. You reckon you could find out where he pawned it and buy it back? I've got his name, address, and phone number."

Kiernan couldn't gracefully refuse. Not after leaving Deborah on the phone till she was actually screaming. Anyhow, how hard could it be to find a small-time thief who steals from little old ladies?

"If the locket hasn't been melted down, I'll find it," she promised.

She put down the phone and stood in the doorway that separated her flat from the large kitchen and small studio that would soon be Mrs. Pritchard's. With Ezra in there and with Tchernak opening and closing cabinets—apparently searching for some cooking paraphernalia she didn't have—the kitchen seemed smaller than a child's playhouse, and she began to comprehend fully just how big Tchernak was. Together, both craggy faces surrounded by shaggy gray brown hair, he and Ezra looked not unlike a pair of oversized werewolves whipping up a snack.

But this was no time to be pondering the physical attributes of a man who would be out of her life in an hour. The man she needed to assess was Samuel James Watkins, and she needed to get on him now if Deborah's cousin Lunette was going to have a happy Christmas.

Kiernan wasn't crazy about leaving a stranger in her

house, but she told herself that while burglars may answer ads, they don't usually offer to make dinner. And there was something she trusted about Tchernak. Maybe it was just because he resembled the world's best dog. Or maybe she was just after a free meal. Still, she asked, "How long will you be cooking, Tchernak?"

"An hour if I hurry. Why?"

"I have to run an errand. It might keep me two hours. I don't want to hold you up."

Tchernak smiled. "That's okay. I'll just take him for a run on the beach before I start dinner."

Mrs. Pritchard, she thought. *Quiet, competent Mrs. Pritchard. If I pass up a gem like her . . .*

Kiernan called the number for Samuel James Watkins twice on her way to his house and got only a noncommittal answering machine: *"This is 555-8782. Leave a message."*

A careful man who didn't want associates to know how long he'd been gone or when he'd be back?

A careful man in a distinctly downscale San Diego neighborhood, she decided as she drove past the auto repair shop at Watkins's address. His house would be in the back.

Darkness comes early in December and covers a lot of illicit activity. Nevertheless, Kiernan parked a block away and kept to the shadows. She knew that housebreaking was not the way to begin a career as a licensed private investigator, but she'd just slip in this once and she'd be careful.

And she'd never do it again.

Absolutely never.

Kiernan made her way along the tall threadbare hedge beside the auto repair shop and pushed through it into the backyard—a few square feet of hard-packed dirt with one dead jade plant in the far corner. Watkins's "house" at the rear of the lot was two stories tall and maybe twelve feet square, probably two rooms one atop the other. All the windows were closed, barred, and locked, and the door had enough locks to impress a New Yorker.

Kiernan moved into the shadows, weighing her options. Even with tools, this assemblage of locks could consume more time than was reasonable for the entire search. She couldn't afford to be caught, and certainly not before she even got inside. But the little house was hers now, asking to be entered. She was damned if she'd give up.

She circled around back, checking each window, finding each locked. Watkins was indeed a very careful man.

But even careful men can make mistakes and his was a second-floor bathroom window, opened eight inches from the top. Logic would have told him no one could get to the window without dragging a two-story ladder back past the auto repair shop. And once at the window, no one could enter without breaking the glass.

But he hadn't counted on a woman barely five feet tall, not quite a hundred pounds, who had spent her entire adolescence practicing gymnastics. For Kiernan, climbing a tree to the roof, lowering herself over the edge and into the window was nothing like the challenge of the uneven bars or the balance beam. Or even dropping back into a back bend.

On this roof, she thought as she positioned herself above the window, the main danger was loose shingles, or a rain gutter too fragile to support her. But she would have to trust it. Grasping the gutter with both hands, she lowered her feet over the edge of the roof and slid them down the side of the house till she felt the space left by the open window. She shifted to ease her legs inside. The rain gutter creaked. She caught her feet inside the window and pulled. The rain gutter snapped free of the roof. She fell back, hanging in air. Frantically she pressed with her legs, locking the muscles of her legs, her butt, her back, to keep from slamming down into the glass. She shifted her hands to the window, took a thankful breath, and slid down inside, her flashlight banging against the sill.

Best if I don't fall, she thought. *Watkins isn't likely to have insurance.*

The bathroom was so small the sink was over the toilet tank. No place to hide contraband here. In the bedroom there was barely room for the bed and the stairs. A couple of blankets were on the bare mattress, but no sign of clothing. Two stereos were piled in the corner along with three electric typewriters and a dusty computer monitor. They looked like rejects from a tag sale.

Feeling her way in the dark, she walked down the steps. The stairs creaked; the leaves of the tree scraped the windows. Headlights shone in the path from the auto repair shop. Watkins could come back anytime. With any number of nasty associates.

She froze, listening. For the first time it occurred to her she couldn't go back out the bathroom window and up onto the roof, not with no rain gutter to grab onto. If all the windows were not just locked, but dead bolted . . .

The headlights disappeared.

She eased down the remaining steps and flashed her light quickly around the tiny room, at a stove, fridge, water heater, sink, tiled counter, a door on wooden horses that passed for a desk with a worn leather swivel chair next to it, and a phone and answering machine atop it. She pressed the play button and cryptic voices whispered in the darkness: *"Mickey says yeah." "Eddie says he's got more, so call him." "That shipment from Fresno's due in on time."*

Beneath the desk, something glittered in the flashlight's narrow beam. It was a jet-and-crystal earring and Kiernan eased open a nearby carton. It held several brand-new blenders, but no records or files. And definitely no TVs, stereos, marcasite jewelry, or octagonal gold lockets.

Reluctantly, Kiernan faced the facts. This was just his accommodation address, a transfer point. His cache could be in the auto repair shop out front. Or in self-storage anywhere in San Diego County. Or Riverside, Orange, or Imperial counties. With someone this organized, Deborah's cousin's things could be scattered around the whole Southwest. The odds of getting anything back were astronomical.

A wasted trip.

And she could probably waste more time watching this place, trailing Samuel James Watkins to his real home, trying to track down all his fences, and still not come up with the locket.

She walked up the stairs, slid out through the window, and dropped to the ground—a long dismount, but not one of Olympic quality. It went with her mood. How embarrassing it was going to be to have to tell Deborah that she'd failed.

"Look, don't worry about it," I told Kiernan when she called a couple of hours later and described how she'd spent the time since I phoned her. I was horrified to think she'd actually broken and entered, yet quite touched that she would take such a risk for me.

"Too bad we can't sic Maria Vincelli's brother on him," I said lightly.

"Who?"

I repeated Cousin Lunette's speculations about her former neighbor's mob connections and heard Kiernan laugh across the miles.

"Maybe it's not too late," she said and hung up without another word.

Tchernak was pulling popovers from the oven when Kiernan got off the phone.

"And from the broiler," he said with a flourish, "shish kebobs of fresh-from-the-dock Ahi tuna, marinated green tomatoes, shiitake mushrooms, and Walla Walla onions—frozen because they're only available one month a year, but lovingly thawed. Ideally the tomatoes should be flown in fresh from Jersey, but—" He shrugged.

With his paw, Ezra tapped Tchernak's leg.

"He wants his offering," Kiernan explained.

Tchernak waited a moment, then turned, pulled an all-tuna kebob from the broiler and put it on the counter to cool.

Ezra let out a gleeful yip. She hadn't heard one of those since he was a puppy.

That did it, Kiernan thought. *Mrs. Pritchard is going to have to find other employment.*

She was halfway through the gooseberry/kiwi sorbet before she could divert her attention from the food and ask, "Tchernak, I have another brief and totally different job that I could use your help on. Tonight."

Tchernak's face seemed to freeze. He was waiting.

"Whether or not you do it will have no effect on my decision about hiring you. Really."

He nodded noncommittally.

"And it's only fair to warn you that it's slightly illegal."

Tchernak grinned. "What do I do?"

They worked out the script over espresso. Twenty-five minutes later, Tchernak was growling into Samuel James Watkins's answering machine with a very credible Chicago accent. "Listen up, scuzzbag, 'cause this is the voice of Christmas present—"

"You did what?" I asked sleepily when Kiernan's second call of the evening woke me around two A.M. Eastern Standard Time.

Incoherent with laughter (and maybe five or six glasses of California chardonnay), Kiernan O'Shaughnessy described how her new butler? houseboy? dog walker?—Californians certainly do give themselves interesting Christmas presents—had recorded a message for Watkins. As I understood it, this Tchernak person pretended to be a Mafia hit man who resented the hell out of Watkins ripping off his old Aunt Lunette in Shady Palms.

"I'm sorry I can't take a month off and track down his whole operation," Kiernan apologized, "but if it's any consolation, we've probably put the fear of the Celestial in him. With a little luck, he'll be jumping at every shadow and wondering how much longer his kneecaps will be intact."

I had to laugh. It wasn't the Carroll locket, but it certainly was a unique Christmas present.

"Have a merry," I told her.

"I plan to." She laughed and I heard Ezra barking happily in the background.

Court reconvened on the third of January, so I couldn't drive Lunette to the airport. Just as well since it was a long, exhausting session as I handed out fines and suspended sentences to those who'd celebrated the holidays not wisely, but too well. It was nearly eleven and I was ready to fall into bed when my telephone rang.

Across three thousand miles, I heard Lunette's excited voice. "It's the weirdest freaking thing you ever saw!" she cried. "I unlocked my front door and everything was piled in the middle of the living room floor—stereo, TV, my silverware, all that blinking marcasite, Jules's ring—and oh, Deborah! The locket! It's back. I'm going to send it to Dennis's son first thing tomorrow. Did I tell you? He's getting married Valentine's Day."

"Wait a minute," I protested. "You promised it to me."

"Oh, honey, I'd love to give it to you, but don't you see? The only reason it's come back is so it can go to a Carroll bride. How 'bout I send you a diamond necklace instead?"

"Diamond necklace? I didn't know you had one."

"I didn't." She giggled. "But now I have two. And a sapphire ring. And a string of pearls. Whoever brought my things back, he left a lot of extra stuff. A ruby brooch. Some silver bracelets. A—"

As my cousin rattled on like a four-year-old detailing every item in her Christmas stocking, I sighed, reached for my Rolodex, and flipped to the O's.

The Partner Track
William Bernhardt

William Bernhardt made his debut as a novelist with the national best-seller, *Primary Justice,* featuring attorney Ben Kincaid. He followed that with *The Code of Buddyhood* and two more Kincaid novels: *Blind Justice* and *Deadly Justice.* You can meet up with Kincaid in his fourth outing *Perfect Justice* plus a non-series legal thriller, *Double Jeopardy.*

Like his series character, Bill is a trial attorney at a large Tulsa law firm where he promotes legal services for the poor and elderly.

This is Bill's first anthology appearance and you will be mesmerized by the story of two attorneys: William Danforth the golden boy in style, looks, appeal, flash; Clark Dudley the hardworking drone, who was solid and competent but definitely lacking in pizazz.

It was a partnership that made for competition, anger, and—a slight derailment on "The Partner Track" . . .

It seemed as though Clark had always hated William Danforth. If not him specifically, then what he was, what he represented. Which was, in sum total, everything that Clark was not.

First and foremost, William Danforth was beautiful. Not handsome—beautiful. Not that Clark Dudley spent a lot of time admiring men—don't get the wrong idea. But it didn't take a careful eye to realize that Danforth was an Adonis, a god among men. He was tall, well over six feet, and he bore himself with impeccable posture. His wavy blond hair was immaculately styled, never a strand out of place, except on those occasions when a windblown lock might present an image of boyish dishabille. His features were strongly etched: a long proud nose, small unobtrusive ears, full inviting lips.

Second, there was the matter of Breeding. With a capital B. In fact, Clark had no idea from what family Danforth had sprung, but he knew that it was a *Family,* a well-heeled enclave with a summer home, a yacht, and an oversized Old English sheepdog. Clark could picture them all lounging on the beach or at the country club, riding polo ponies, sipping drinks from tall glasses, and posing for pictures in loose-fitting cotton tennis sweaters. Clark had never heard Danforth mention his background or family, but its presence was revealed in his every gesture, every mannerism. The way Danforth ordered food at a restaurant. The way he tipped the bellhop. The way he swung a tennis racquet. And most of all, the way he handled himself at the law firm.

Finally, of course, there was the matter of money. Danforth had it. Lots of it. Clark had no idea where it came from, but Danforth's lifestyle could only have been possible if he had access to more funds than the law firm was paying him. He drove a midnight-blue Jaguar XJ6 made in 1987, the last year they came with the elegant eyebrow hood. His suits were perfectly cut, obviously tailored. And he lived in a house that, although not large, was of better quality than the homes of many of the firm's senior partners. Popular rumor, which Clark did not doubt for a moment, had it that on a given night any number of gorgeous women in various states of disrobement could be seen tiptoeing in and out of Danforth's house.

All of these factors combined to form a composite creature Clark couldn't help but detest. There was simply something that set Danforth apart, some ineffable quality made up of a multitude of features, but which Clark finally decided could best be described as an unbearable *casualness,* an easy, indifferent approach to life. Clark had observed this before. He saw it as a child, in the well-dressed children at the private school he peered at through the chain-link fence surrounding the playground of his own third-rate grade school. He had seen it again at college, sauntering across fraternity-house lawns, swilling beer and nuzzling coeds. And now, when he had finally achieved something, a job with the finest firm in the city, he saw it again, its living embodiment in the person of William Danforth.

By contrast, Clark could only view his own life, the paltry allotment fate had given to him, as shabby and worthless. He was neither beautiful nor handsome. He was at least ten pounds overweight, with a sloped forehead and a reddish turnip of a nose. He had begun balding before he finished law school; by the time he came to the firm he had nary a hair on his head.

Neither could Clark make any claim to Family or Breeding. His father had been a sheetrocker; his mother had been nothing; and now they were both dead. He had never been on a vacation, never ridden a horse, never been on a boat. Mostly he had spent his life at a variety of menial jobs—working his way through school, then working grunt-level intern jobs, trying to learn the practice of law. He drove a Toyota, he bought off the rack, and his entire apartment would probably fit in Danforth's bathroom.

He didn't have women traipsing in and out of his apartment, either. Truth to tell, he didn't have anyone. And he never had.

Clark had met Danforth, appropriately enough, on his first day at the law firm. Clark had spent the previous five years in the legal trenches, slowly building a reputation for solid, competent work. Danforth had come straight from Harvard.

Danforth was the last member of the incoming class of associates to arrive that day. Clark gaped as he entered the lobby where they all waited. Danforth's appearance transfigured the room. Clark saw the effect first in the eyes of the receptionist, a homely dark-haired woman with her nose buried in a *Redbook* magazine. Even before Danforth spoke, she looked up. Her expression softened, her eyes glazed over.

"Can I help you?" she said. They were the same words she had spoken to Clark and each of the others, but now they were entirely different. To Clark, the words had been superficial politeness. Addressed to Danforth, they were more like an urgent plea.

Just as vividly, Clark recalled the initial meeting with their supervising partner, Monk Israel. Like the receptionist before him, Israel's attention was captivated by Danforth. What began as a general address to a group of ten soon became a private colloquium between Israel and Danforth.

Israel had begun his remarks by emphasizing the importance of the work the associates would be asked to do during their first few years with the firm, and how their performance would determine whether they were on the "partner track." In passing, Israel mentioned a large take-or-pay case he was litigating.

"That must be the Avonco case," Danforth interjected.

Clark, along with all the others, was astonished. They couldn't believe anyone had the audacity to interrupt Israel. Especially on their first day.

To everyone's surprise, Israel seemed pleased, even flattered. "You know something about the case?"

"Heard some gentlemen discussing it down at the club Saturday," Danforth said, with the casual air to which Clark subsequently became so accustomed. "Believe they were Avonco's general counsel."

"George Reynolds?" Israel asked.

"Right. With Clarence LaFave. They were having a very intense discussion."

"Must've been trying to formulate a response to our motion *in limine*. I don't suppose you ... overheard anything?"

Danforth smiled, a golden, heartwarming smile. "They're worried, Monk. Very worried."

Clark didn't know which offended him most—Danforth's audacious use of Israel's first name or his shameless sucking up. The problem was, when Danforth said it, it didn't seem like flattery. It was as if the two had known one another all their lives, as if they were two old friends sharing a confidence. Danforth had known exactly what to say, and when and how to say it.

By the end of that first week, Clark heard that Danforth had been assigned to Israel's litigation team, the flashiest, most high-profile subset of the firm. Israel flew Danforth to Hawaii that weekend to assist with some depositions in a pending environmental case. There were only three depositions, but the two remained on the islands for two weeks.

Clark was assigned to the tax team. He soon found himself buried in the stacks, putting in sixteen-hour days struggling with rules and regulations and administrative reports. He wouldn't see the light of day for years.

Clark first had the privilege of working with Danforth about six months later. One of the firm's large gas pipeline clients was protesting an assessment of severance tax on certain interstate gas production. In addition to the administrative protest, a lawsuit was filed in federal court arguing that the assessment violated the commerce clause of the U.S. Constitution. Because the case involved both litigation and tax issues, Clark and Danforth's teams were drawn together.

As the junior men on their respective teams, Clark and Danforth were given the job of sifting through all the documents produced by the parties during discovery. The quantity of documentation was immense; well over a hundred thousand pieces of paper were exchanged. The firm had to lease additional space just to house it all. Clark was told this was a standard tactic in big corporate lawsuits. The idea was that if they produced a huge quantum of paperwork, opposing counsel would never find the two or three pieces of paper that might actually make a difference.

That was the chore put to Clark and Danforth—read everything, and find the smoking guns. They also were required to draft an abstract of all documents reviewed for future use. A modern-day search for a needle in a haystack. And they had less than a week to do it. At the end of the week, the parties were scheduled to attend a pretrial conference at which, according to Monk Israel, it was critical that he know as much about the case as possible. It was made clear to Clark and Danforth that this was an important case with a lot riding on it. Their respective futures at the firm might well be determined by their performance on this critical job.

Clark worked eighteen-hour days all week. He was not a fast reader or writer, so he started immediately and worked at every possible opportunity.

Danforth, by contrast, drifted in and out of the room where the documents were kept. He would glance at a few pages, a patently bored expression plastered on his face, then shuffle on to something else. He lunched at his club; he played his usual racquetball game on Tuesdays and Thursdays. He reviewed the various drafts of Clark's abstract with a supercilious look that bordered on contempt.

Fine, Clark thought. *It's your funeral.* And he kept plugging away at it, anticipating that day at the end of the week when he would report to Monk Israel that he had completed the assignment and Danforth hadn't done a damn thing.

Unfortunately, the immensity of the project proved too much even for Clark's concerted effort. On the last night before the conference, he had reviewed more than forty-five thousand pages—less than half. It was clear he had no hope of finishing on time.

To his surprise, Danforth wandered in just after midnight. He was yawning and his eyes looked watery and tired. "Still here, old boy?"

Danforth's forced congeniality grated on Clark's shopworn nerves. "The job isn't done."

"Doesn't much look like it's going to be, either. What are you doing here at this late hour?"

"You know as well as I do that Israel wanted this project completed by tomorrow morning," Clark said bitterly.

"You did your best. Why don't you call it a night?"

"But he wanted it done tonight!"

"Yes, but that just wasn't realistic. No one can fault you for not doing the impossible. We'll take the heat together."

"Still—"

"Look, Monk hasn't even looked at this abstract you've generated. That means he's going to need someone knowledgeable about these documents at the pretrial. God knows I don't know anything about them. That means it's going to have to be you. And what good will you be to him if you've been up all night banging your head against the wall?"

Obnoxious though he was, Danforth had a point. Clark did want to be at his best tomorrow, though not precisely for the reason Danforth had espoused. He knew his far greater familiarity with the documentation would give him an opportunity to show up Danforth at the pretrial, to demonstrate once and for all his superior legal acumen. That was an event he had been savoring for days. Truth to tell, the thought of it was what had gotten him through the miserable work of the past week.

Clark went home, got six hours sleep, and woke up the next morning fresh and ready to take on the world. He arrived at the office early and met Monk Israel as he stepped off the elevator.

" 'Morning, Mr. Israel."

" 'Morning," he replied. He walked briskly to his office and draped his coat around a brass hanger. Clark realized with irritation that Israel probably couldn't recall his name. "Got that abstract for me?"

"No," Clark replied, swallowing hard. "I mean, yes. Well, what's done, that is."

"What's done?" Israel's eyes moved closer together. "You mean it isn't finished?"

"No, sir. It isn't."

Israel threw his briefcase down on the floor. "Don't you know the pretrial conference is today?"

"Yes, sir. But that's why—"

"Don't give me your excuses!" Israel's face flushed with fury. "It's absolutely critical that I know what's in the documentation *today*. Otherwise, the other side will hang me out to dry!"

"But, *sir!*" Panic flashed through Clark's body. How could he have miscalculated so horribly? "I thought that—"

At precisely that instant Danforth sauntered into Israel's office. His untied necktie was draped over his neck, his shirt was untucked, and he wasn't wearing shoes. His hair was in disarray, although Clark noted that it was a very stylish, even attractive, disarray.

"May I intrude?" Danforth said, his head tilted to one side.

"Please!" Israel shouted. "Your fellow associate tells me that the task we entrusted to you is incomplete!"

"Well . . . ," Danforth said slowly, "that's not entirely correct. It *was* incomplete. I finished it last night."

It was difficult to tell who said it more loudly, Clark or Israel. *"What?"*

"I let Clark take the lead with this project," Danforth explained, "because, as you know, Monk, I've been swamped with the Anderson litigation. I found out last night, though, that the chore was less than half finished. So I stayed up all night and completed it."

Clark stared at the man, his eyes cold. "You couldn't possibly have—"

"I enlisted help. At my expense, of course."

"I don't care how you did it," Israel said. "Just so you got it done."

"I supervised the work carefully," Danforth added. "And I made sure the abstract is accurate."

"Thank God I put you on this case." Monk stepped around Clark as if he didn't exist and slapped Danforth on the shoulder. "You really salvaged this screwup. I knew I could count on you." They walked out of the office together, without so much as a parting word to Clark.

Needless to say, Monk Israel took Danforth to the pretrial conference, not Clark. In fact, shortly thereafter Clark was taken off the case and returned to his usual tax law drudgery.

By careful scrutiny of the expense records, Clark learned that Danforth had hired a team of Kelly temporaries to review the documents that night. He acted as if this was a brilliant, spur-of-the-moment inspiration that saved the case. Clark wasn't so stupid, though. What were the chances that Danforth would be able to hire a temporary, much less fifteen of them, in the middle of the night? No, he must've planned it in advance. He must've intentionally lured Clark out of the office so he could bring in his servants and make his grandstand play.

Not that it mattered, in the end. However it happened, the result was that Danforth was permanently ensconced as Israel's right-hand man, a position that virtually guaranteed his rapid advancement in the firm. And Clark remained in the library with his rules and regulations and administrative opinions. That single incident cemented the course both men would follow for the next seven years.

Clark did manage to hold onto his position at the firm. No one thought he was a superstar, no, not a wunderkind like William Danforth. But he did capable work in a mind-numbing field that no one else was particularly interested in entering. He was a bulldog, not a peacock, but a firm that large needed its bulldogs and was happy to keep them as long as they stayed out of sight and didn't expect much.

By contrast, less than three years after he arrived, William Danforth was handling cases on his own. In five, he was considered one of the premier litigators in the firm, perhaps in the city. Although still an associate, he received assignments normally only entrusted to senior partners. And why not? He almost always won his cases, and on the rare occasions when he didn't, he still came out smelling like a rose. The judges liked him, and most important, clients liked him. In most instances, they specifically asked that he be assigned to their cases. They liked his style, his wit. They enjoyed the afternoons ostensibly spent discussing their cases on the greens at his country club. There seemed little question but that Danforth would make partner when the time came.

The status of Clark's candidacy was quite another matter. Although he was considered adequate in his field, his limitations were continually raised as a reason that he should not be made a full partner. A lawyer should be well-rounded, his opponents argued. They should be capable of providing a wide array of legal services. An ability to make sense of convoluted IRS proclamations was admirable, but a partner should have something more.

It was to this end that, after he had been with the firm almost seven years, Clark was assigned to the TelCon case. Although it had a tangential tax connection, the real reason for Clark's involvement was to give him one last opportunity to get out of the tax rut and show some facility for handling litigation. Despite the obvious pressure this test would entail, Clark embraced it eagerly. He wanted a chance to get out of the library and to prove he was capable of doing more. His enthusiasm did not wane—until he learned he would be working under William Danforth.

Working *with* Danforth, they said, in deference to the fact that both men had come to the firm at the same time. But Clark knew what they really meant. Danforth was the litigator in charge. Clark was the green tax associate tossed a snowball to see if he could run with it.

Clark was given a deposition, a chance to interview

one opposing witness in the presence of a court reporter. *TelCon* v. *Applied Sciences* was a telecommunications case involving the functionality of a computerized circuit testing and monitoring device. The facts were technical and complex, and it was essential that Clark have a firm grasp of all of them. The witness, one Dr. Chang, was a Chinese software designer, and Clark knew that if he wasn't up to speed on the facts, the man would bury him in jargon.

To prevent that result, Clark buried himself in preparation—the most detailed, most exacting work he had done in his entire life. He read every pleading in the file—and they numbered over five hundred. He read technical journals issued by AT&T, WilTel, and other leaders in the telecommunications industry. He scrutinized the blueprints and schematics for the testing system, until he thoroughly understood what the device was supposed to do, and where it fell short.

Clark did not limit his preparation to the assimilation of knowledge, however. He knew the critical element in litigation, that which separated the men from the boys, so to speak, was *strategy*. He carefully considered what he was going to do, what he would ask, how he would ask it. He analyzed all possible approaches before settling on the one that seemed most likely to guarantee success. Rather than coming on strong, like the enemy, Clark decided that his initial approach would be reserved, even deferential. He would make admiring remarks about the witness' credentials and his work. In that way, he would try to gain the man's confidence, his trust, and thus encourage him to talk openly. Especially since the man was steeped in the Asian tradition, Clark thought Chang would respond to this treatment. He might well end up telling Clark things he would never tell a straight-on hardball litigator.

On the day of the deposition, Clark took his seat with confidence. William Danforth sat beside him, and three senior partners and the client representative sat behind him. It didn't matter. He wasn't going to let it bother him. On the contrary, it was best that they were here, he told himself, so they could see with their own eyes the spectacular job he was sure he could deliver. Given half a chance.

"Have you received any degrees or citations for your work in computer-based telecommunications?" A question certain to develop goodwill; there was nothing a techie enjoyed more than rehashing his résumé.

Dr. Chang dutifully spent the next ten minutes reeling off an impressive list of commendations.

"Have you worked on any other projects similar to the LDMS you developed for TelCon?"

Another similarly lengthy list followed, as Chang established his competence to work on this project. Clark simply smiled and listened quietly. He could tell some of the partners in the back were becoming impatient, but that was all right. It would pay off in the end. Good things come to those who wait.

Clark extracted similar lists regarding professional organizations to which Chang belonged and his former employments. With each question, Chang seemed to become less hesitant, more relaxed, more open. Clark was already congratulating himself. The strategy was working perfectly.

"I understand there were some problems with the LDMS though, right?"

Chang gestured expansively. "TelCon had problems with the LDMS. I never did."

Here Clark saw an opportunity to bring his extensive technical studies to bear. "Well, isn't it true that the com-light indicator did not accurately reflect disabled circuits?"

"The com-light indicator is only as accurate as the database powering it."

"And that database, Croesus version 3.1, was supplied by your company, correct?"

"Supplied by us, yes, but installed by TelCon."

"Is that important?"

"Of course. TelCon hardwired it into the bypass

circuitry, patched through the mainframe." Out of the corner of his eye, Clark saw Danforth drum his fingers impatiently on the table. Not surprising. The man probably wasn't following a word of this.

"Your schematics show the database being installed via the Z-base hard drive," Clark continued. "That's substantially the same method, isn't it?"

"Only if the T-28 circuit is off. During peak hours, it should be installed direct to the hard disk."

More finger drumming. Clark ignored it. "Doesn't that depend on whether the terminals are handling transmission levels over 2,000 bps?"

"Not necessarily. On most days, the T-28, like the DM-42 it is linked with, will be entirely inactive. Therefore, the data stream must be channeled through the auxiliary connection—"

Danforth's fist suddenly slammed down on the conference table. "Damn it, man, the machine just didn't work! Right?"

Chang's eyes were wide as saucers. He was obviously taken aback by the sudden change in tone. "That—that depends on whether—"

"Don't give me a lot of technical mumbo-jumbo. You supervised the installation at TelCon. Did it work?"

"Work is such an indefinite term—"

"Did it test the circuits?" Danforth asked insistently.

"Well, no."

"Did it monitor activity on the circuits?"

"Not accurately."

"Aren't those the two jobs it was supposed to perform?"

Chang seemed afraid to give anything but a direct answer. "I believe so."

"Then it didn't work, did it?"

Chang swallowed hard, then looked down at the table. "No. It didn't work."

Afterward, Monk Israel and the other partners congratulated Danforth on his skillful handling of the expert. "If I heard any more of that computo-babble, I was going to scream," Israel said, laughing. "Thank goodness you were here to cut through the crap. That's what litigators are for."

It was no surprise to anyone, least of all Clark, when decisions were announced the following week and Danforth was made a full partner. Clark was offered a position as what was generously called a "limited partner." He would be held out to the rest of the world as a partner, but within the firm itself, he would receive none of the perks and privileges, and would not participate in the hefty bonus pool the partners divided at the end of the fiscal year.

In other words, they were willing to keep Clark around to do their dirty work, but they were keeping him tightly tied to their leash. He was not really a partner, and he never would be.

That was when Clark first began to contemplate the possibility of *killing* William Danforth.

Of course, thinking about murder is one thing; carrying it out is quite another. Most people fantasize about the violent elimination of an adversary at one time or another, but few actually commit the crime. Clark thought about it, because it gave him pleasure to do so, but in his heart of hearts he never really believed it would come to pass.

A few days after the decisions were announced, Clark was invited to a reception the firm threw in honor of the new partners. He almost didn't go; he was still despondent, depressed to the point of almost being suicidal. He wasn't sure which bothered him more: that the partners he had served so long and so well had shafted him, or that Danforth had risen above him once more.

Still, a few of the partners leaned on him, hinting broadly that attendance was "expected," so Clark went. The reception was held at the Pelican Club, a penthouse-level private dining room. The instant he stepped off the elevator and stared out at the Brooks

Brothers suits and the glittering long dresses, he realized he had made a mistake. He didn't belong here; he wasn't one of them. Even if the firm was able to convince outsiders that he was a true partner, a supposition of which he was quite uncertain, he would know the truth, and the truth shamed him.

He took a crystal flute of champagne and sat in the corner sulking. He knew he should attempt to mingle, to glad-hand a few clients who might have future tax problems, but he just didn't feel up to it. He might well have sat alone for the entire evening, but for the intrusion of Herbert Bloch, an elderly, semiretired partner in the real estate department. "Clark, have you met the Carmichaels?"

Clark rose to his feet and peered at the man and woman being introduced. He had not met them before. The man was a standard-issue business client—blue pinstriped suit, button-down shirt, school tie.

But the woman—! She was something else again. She was slender, though not anorexic, tall, though not taller than Clark, and beautiful. She wore her black evening gown with a simple understated elegance. Her silky blond hair rolled down to her shoulders, bouncing engagingly as she tilted her head from side to side. Her face was small, but striking; moreover, it was interesting. Gazing at her, Clark received an impression of intelligence and taste.

Clark caught himself staring and hurriedly looked away. What on earth was such a creature doing with this pinstriped exemplar of boardroom banality? He had to be thirty years older than she was. She must be his second go at it; a trophy wife.

"Clark, this is Edward Carmichael. He owns Princeton Steel." They shook hands with an appropriately sturdy grip. "And this is his daughter, Sophie."

His daughter. Of course. Clark tried to mask his enthusiasm and relief as he shook her delicate hand.

"Sophie's brother is here somewhere," Carmichael grumbled. "Or is supposed to be, anyway. Excuse me while I go hunt for him."

Carmichael walked away with Bloch in tow, leaving Clark and Sophie staring awkwardly at one another. Clark offered to fetch her champagne; she declined. He cleared his throat; she coughed.

Clark was filled with despair. For once, fate had smiled and brought this beautiful creature to him. And what was he doing with the opportunity? Nothing. Absolutely, pathetically, nothing.

"Congratulations on making partner," Sophie said. Her voice was quiet, but her eyes seemed earnest.

Clark shuffled his feet. "Oh . . . it's not what it seems."

"It's quite an accomplishment, if you ask me. There are thousands of lawyers in this city who would do almost anything to be a partner in this firm. I'm impressed."

"Well . . . thank you." Clark tried desperately to think of something clever, some engaging urbane banter, but nothing came. He was extremely awkward around women. Despite the fact that he was in his mid-thirties, he'd had precious little experience with them. He didn't know what to say, what to do, or where to stand, and these failings became all too apparent to him now, when he so wanted to make a good impression.

"Tell me about your work," Sophie said, but Clark knew the request was made out of social necessity, not out of any real desire to hear the minutiae of his boring practice. He began to describe a few cases, doing his best to make them seem glamorous, but it was a hopeless cause. Her weight shifted from leg to leg, and he knew he would soon lose her. In desperation, he mentioned his work on the TelCon case . . . with William Danforth.

Her eyes immediately brightened. "You work with William Danforth?"

Please God, no, he thought to himself. *Not her, too.* "You're a . . . friend of Danforth's?"

"I know who he is," she said, smiling. "And I know he works on the most important cases this firm handles. So if you work with him, you must be rather important, too."

It was the turning point in their relationship. Like it or not, his link with Danforth had raised him in her eyes. They ended up spending the entire evening together, talking, laughing, and enjoying one another's company.

When the party was at an end, and the last stragglers were leaving, Clark walked Sophie to the door where her father waited. She linked her arm around his; Clark momentarily thought his heart had stopped.

"Thank you for the lovely evening," she said. "I thought tonight would be a terrible bore, but it wasn't. It was the most pleasant night I've spent in ages."

Clark forced himself to speak. "Wo—Would—" God, he was *stuttering* now! "Would it be all right if I called you sometime?"

A vibrant smile spread from one end of her face to the other. "Oh, I was hoping you would ask! Of course it is. I can think of nothing more splendid. You can tell me more about your work. And perhaps"— her head tilted to one side, her hair bobbing—"perhaps we can come to know one another even better."

And so romance bloomed in Clark's heavy heart. He initially resolved not to call her for at least three days so as not to seem too eager, but ended up calling her the next day. It didn't matter. She seemed thrilled to hear from him, and agreed to go out to dinner the following Friday.

She still lived with her father, in a huge mansion near the country club. Just the sight of it put Clark on edge, but he summoned whatever fortitude he possessed and pressed on. Once inside, he chatted amiably with her father, admired Sophie's attire, and took her to a small seafood restaurant he favored. He had prepared a list of safe conversational topics, but they were soon exhausted, and she began to ask whether he was involved in any more lawsuits. He wondered that she had not become a lawyer herself; she was obviously fascinated by the litigation process. She listened to his dry little tax-practice stories, but he knew she was only being polite. Something more would be required if he was to hold her interest.

And so it was that an event Clark would previously have thought impossible occurred. The following Monday morning, Clark entered Danforth's office, waited twenty minutes while he finished a phone conversation with the country club golf pro, and then asked if he could work with Danforth on some of his litigation matters.

"I don't expect to actually take part in the discovery or trial process," Clark said. "But I could handle the research, and the drafting of pleadings and briefs. Whatever you'd be comfortable giving me. I just want to be involved."

Danforth peered across his desk, a finger thoughtfully pressed to his lips. "I must admit, Clark, this comes as rather a surprise. I didn't think you had much interest in litigation."

"I do now. I want this very much. Very, very much." He steadied himself. *"Please."*

Danforth nodded slowly, then spoke. "Well, if you're sure that's what you want. I'll have to rearrange some assignments ... but that's the least I can do for a fellow partner."

They shook hands, then Clark left his office. He thought he was going to be sick. He raced back to his own office and slammed the door. He felt as though he had sold his soul to the devil. But for such a prize, he told himself. Such a prize.

Danforth was true to his word. Over the course of the next three months, he involved Clark in no less than ten different litigation cases. In some, Clark's research and writing was essential; in others, his involvement was tangential at best. Either way, though, Clark had an opportunity to learn the details of the cases, the ins and outs, the secret strategies. And then he would regale Sophie with his anecdotes, which he practiced in front of a mirror before each date. She would laugh, or shake her head in amazement at his erstwhile legal prowess. She was entranced.

Clark was happier than he had ever been in his life. Despite the fact that his workload had nearly doubled, he saw Sophie two, sometimes three times a week. And on each meeting, they became more intimate than the time before. He knew now that he loved Sophie Carmichael. And he felt certain she loved him as well.

They were picnicking by the lake on a gorgeous, clear summer day, when Clark finally summoned the courage to ask her. He picked her up that morning in his new Chrysler LeBaron convertible. Not a Jaguar, granted, but fine enough. Sophie seemed thrilled with it. He presented her with her own set of keys, and they took turns driving, Clark watching the wind rush through her hair.

They found a private place by the side of the lake and ate the picnic lunch she had prepared. Sophie had brought her camera, and spent well over an hour photographing Clark from every angle with every possible expression. He feigned annoyance, but in fact, he was delighted. He felt his courage mounting—maybe it was the warmth of the sun, or the intimacy of the location, or the wine they had sipped with their chicken sandwiches. Or perhaps he simply knew with unavoidable certainty that the time had come.

He was surprised when, without warning, she asked, "Are you happy, Clark?"

He took her hand. "Of course I am. When I'm with you. How can you doubt it?"

She brushed a loose strand of hair from her face. "I never see you smile."

"I suppose it doesn't come naturally." He said nothing more on the subject; this wasn't what he wanted to talk about, what he had planned and rehearsed so many times. He tried to say the words, to start his prepared speech, but found he couldn't. "Got a new case yesterday with Danforth," he said instead, stalling.

"Really? I'll bet that was exciting. You must enjoy working with him."

Clark hesitated. "To be honest with you, Sophie—as I always shall be—working with Danforth can be somewhat ... trying."

To his surprise, she was immediately sympathetic. "I can imagine. He seems ... well, I can understand what it must be like for you."

Clark thought his heart might swell out of his chest. She understood! "Some of his practices are ... not entirely what I can approve of."

She nodded. "But that makes it all the more important that you continue to work with him."

Clark frowned. "I don't think I quite follow ..."

"You're a good man, Clark. A man of principle. I could tell that from the first moment I met you." She paused. "A man like William Danforth could learn from your example."

Clark felt paralyzed, unable to respond. She thought William Danforth could learn something—from him? The idea had never even occurred to Clark. He was so certain that others perceived him as Danforth's inferior that it seemed unthinkable that someone might feel otherwise.

"Sophie," he said, with newfound confidence, "I love you. Will you marry me?"

"Of course I will," she said, laughing merrily. "I thought you'd never ask."

They set an early date for the wedding, barely two weeks away. After all, they weren't children and they didn't need a big fuss. They simply wanted to be married, the sooner the better.

In the few remaining days before the wedding, Clark attacked his work with unprecedented enthusiasm and vigor. Even his partners commented on his increased productivity, and the improved quality of his work. For the first time, Clark found he could hold up his end of a conversation, could tell a joke in the boardroom, could laugh heartily at the jokes of others. He felt he had the confidence not just to survive, but to excel.

He was particularly aggressive about his work with Danforth. After all, he no longer had anything to fear from the man, no reason to worry about falling short of his standard. Although this improved the quality of his work, it greatly diminished the quality of their relationship. Clark found himself bristling at each instruction, and even making sharp retorts in response to Danforth's insufferable comments. This was perhaps the most significant change in the new improved Clark; for the first time, he felt free to be openly contemptuous of the contemptible.

A few days before the wedding was scheduled to take place, after they had spent the entire day together sewing up the last threads of a particularly difficult labor case, Danforth invited Clark to join him for dinner at his home. Clark was amazed; he had been nothing but rude to Danforth all day long. It wasn't intentional, but now that Clark felt free to be honest about his feelings, his resentment of Danforth swelled almost out of control. Why was Danforth a full partner, and Clark not? Why did he get the best work, the best of everything, and Clark not? The old daydreams returned, but this time with a startling vividness and urgency.

Clark had a date with Sophie for later that night, but at last he consented to meet with Danforth beforehand. Clark had been astonished to receive Danforth's invitation; he was even more astonished when he arrived and learned he was the only person Danforth had asked. He found Danforth in his den, sitting before the fire, a brandy snifter cradled in his hands.

"Ah, Clark. Glad you could come." He gestured expansively at the overstuffed chair opposite him.

Clark sat in the chair and Danforth poured him a brandy. "Is no one else coming?"

"Didn't I make that clear to you?" Danforth said with seeming innocence. "I didn't invite anyone else.

It's a tradition of mine. After a large case is concluded, I like to relax with the partner with whom I've worked on the case most closely. I thought you understood."

"No," Clark said. He sniffed at his drink. It was strong, far more potent than anything to which he was accustomed. Probably aged—some rare expensive vintage.

"You did excellent work on this case," Danforth commented. "Put in a lot of hard hours."

"Well," Clark said hesitantly, "you put in some eighteen-hour days yourself."

"I learned the value of hard work some time ago." Danforth peered into his drink reflectively. "I got into a spot of trouble when I was younger, had a hard time working my way out of it. Had to take several extraordinarily unpleasant jobs before I started law school. Learned a lesson I won't soon forget."

Clark wondered what unpleasant job Danforth possibly could have ever had. Caddying at the club on a hot day?

"I enjoyed working with you this time," Danforth continued. Did Clark imagine the special emphasis on the words *this time?* "You did some top-quality research. You'll receive my highest commendation."

Clark bit his tongue. How dare the man? They were peers at the firm, and in Danforth's own words, *partners.* How dare he evaluate Clark's work, as if he were the senior supervisor and Clark but a lowly peon?

He limited his response to: "I did my best."

"Indeed you did. I wonder if it might not be appropriate to involve you in even more of my lawsuits. I know there were some negative feelings on that issue after the TelCon incident, but ..." He let the rest of the sentence drop, as if there was no need to revisit old unpleasantries.

Clark, however, could not leave it be. "The TelCon incident, as you so decorously put it, only became an incident after you butted into my deposition."

Danforth cleared his throat. "That ... was regrettable."

"That was unforgivable!" Clark's hand slapped the arm of the chair. "I had the matter well in hand until you decided to make your cheap grandstand play."

A thin line crossed Danforth's brow. "Surely you noticed that Harvey Kilpatrick was leaving."

"That ... what?"

"Kilpatrick. Our client, remember? He was totally frustrated with your protracted line of questioning. He was on his feet, packing his briefcase. If I hadn't intervened when I did, he would have been out the door." Danforth dipped his nose into his snifter and swirled the liquid in clockwise circles. "Your approach might have worked in the end, but Kilpatrick wouldn't be around to find out. And what's the point of doing a good job if you lose the client in the process?"

Clark's neck stiffened. "I didn't notice anyone rising to their feet."

"I assure you he did. You were probably too involved in your questioning."

Clark seethed. This was unbearable—flinging excuses in his face, trying to justify his behavior. "And I suppose you have an excuse for the way you sabotaged me on the Avonco litigation as well!"

The crease on Danforth's forehead grew deeper. "What are you talking about?"

"Don't act as if you don't remember! It's only been seven years. You hired a staff of temporaries to make me look like a fool! Girls, I think you called them. Probably paid them a bit extra for some additional services, right?"

The light slowly dawned in Danforth's eyes. "Oh, yes. I recall the case now."

"You claimed you thought of the idea on the spur of the moment. But you never fooled me. I knew damn well you couldn't have hired fifteen Kelly Girls in the middle of the night!"

"In fact, I didn't," Danforth said calmly. "Harve Prescott did. He had several shifts of fifteen working around the clock microfilming documents for that huge Kepfield Electronics antitrust case. I simply borrowed his people for eight hours."

"I—I find that very hard to believe—"

"It's true. I wouldn't lie to you. After all, we're partners."

"Partners." Clark spat the word out bitterly. "You may be. I'm not. Not really."

Danforth nodded. "You're referring to your limited partner status. I was against that, you know. I opposed the creation of the class, and I especially opposed its application in your case. But I'm afraid my arguments did not carry the day."

"You opposed it?"

"Perhaps now, though, after your exemplary performance on this case . . ." He looked up abruptly. "Well, I'll speak to the board of directors. Perhaps I can do something for you yet."

This was the most insufferable statement yet. How dare he patronize Clark in this manner? As if William Danforth were of such monumental importance that Clark's entire fate rested on his shoulders. Clark's teeth clenched tightly together, and he felt his fingernails digging into the palms of his hands.

"By the way," Danforth said abruptly, "I hear congratulations are in order. Who's the lucky girl?"

Clark almost didn't tell him. He couldn't bear the thought of this bastard having any part of his darling, even her name. "Sophie Carmichael," he said at last.

Danforth's eyebrows lifted. "Really?"

"You know her?"

"Oh, yes," he replied, nodding. "I know her."

A cold chill shrouded Clark's body. "You haven't dated her, have you? She isn't another of your damned conquests!"

"Oh, no," Danforth said hurriedly. "I haven't dated her. Or anything like that. I assure you." And then, to Clark's horror, he began to laugh.

That was the last straw. Apparently Danforth found humorous the suggestion that he would even consider dating Clark's precious Sophie. This worthless bit of upper-class scum. He could lie to Clark, he could systematically ruin his life. But by God! He would not let the man insult his one true love.

Clark stood suddenly and threw his glass at Danforth's feet. "You son of a bitch!" he cried. "You'll take it back, or I'll tear you apart with my bare hands!"

Danforth's face was the very image of mystification. "What—?" He pushed himself out of the chair, but the spilled drink had formed a puddle at his feet. When he rose, his slippers skidded on the damp carpet. He began to lose his balance.

And in a flash, Clark saw his opportunity.

While Danforth was still off-balance, Clark pressed his hands against the man's chest and shoved him backwards into the fireplace. A look of terror crossed Danforth's face, and an instant later, his head crashed down on the stone hearth. His body stiffened momentarily, then went limp. His head lolled to one side; his eyes closed.

Clark searched for a pulse to confirm what he already knew; Danforth was dead.

He had killed him.

For the first time in years, Clark smiled.

Clark had no trouble dragging the body out undetected; if Danforth had servants, they were apparently not on duty that night. With some effort, he hauled the body to his car and shoved it in his trunk. Later, he would drop the corpse in the river. The police would assume he accidentally fell and hit his head in the darkness; the traces of alcohol in his system would help confirm the verdict of accidental death.

But first Clark had to keep his appointment with Sophie. Even in death, he would not let Danforth keep him from his beloved.

After Clark was shown into the Carmichael mansion, Sophie and her father came downstairs. Sophie kissed Clark on the cheek. "Father has something to tell you," she said. "Try to understand."

Clark looked to Mr. Carmichael with a worried expression. "What is it?"

Carmichael folded his arms awkwardly. He was obviously uncomfortable. "Sophie has told me the two of you hope to be married."

Clark's heart fell. "Surely you don't oppose—"

"No, I don't. On the contrary, I'm all in favor of the match. You're a fine young man, Clark, and I'd be happy to have you in the family. But there's something you need to know first."

Clark unconsciously held his breath. "Yes?"

"Sophie has a brother."

Clark sighed with relief. Was that all? "A brother? Oh, yes. You mentioned him once."

"Did I? That surprises me. He's been something of the black sheep of the family. I'm not going to mince words, even if he is my own flesh and blood. He was arrested fifteen years ago for statutory rape. I took care of the girl and her family, but, well, there wasn't much doubt about his guilt. That's when I gave him my ultimatum. He didn't like it at first. He moved out, even changed his name. I wrote him off. But to my happy surprise, five years later, after a few lessons from the school of hard knocks, he got his life back on track. Asked me to send him to Harvard law school, which I did. When he got out, he got a job with the best firm in the city. Your firm."

Clark felt a sudden clutching in his chest. "M-My—?"

"Oh, yes. I'm sure you know who I'm talking about. I know you've worked with him. I know Sophie encouraged you to do so. She thought your moral influence might help him get himself together. Might make him more like you. Sophie still loves him very much. To be expected, I suppose. After all, they are twins."

Clark gasped. "Twins?"

"Oh, yes. Surely you've noticed the resemblance. Slim tall figures, beautiful blond hair."

"You don't mean—"

"The thing is, I believe the decision to marry is the most important decision a man ever makes, so you're entitled to know exactly what you're getting into. Sophie loves her brother, and I don't think she'd ever marry a man who wasn't on good terms with him. Do you know what I'm saying?"

"Yes ..." Clark's voice was hollow and barren, much like he felt himself.

"I was certain this wouldn't change your feelings, but Sophie's going to have to hear it from you. She's waiting for your answer."

"Sophie ..." Clark murmured, almost mindlessly. "Where is she?"

"Outside." He chuckled. "Said she wanted to take some pictures of you and I together, so she went after her camera."

"Her camera ..." In his mind's eye, Clark saw his entire life coming apart, shattering into shards of broken glass. "Where—"

"Don't worry, she's already gone after it. Said she has her own keys. She left the camera in the trunk of your car."

Clark wanted to cry out, but before he could, the night was split apart by a piercing scream. From outside.

Oil and Water

J. A. Jance

J. A. Jance is an inspired storyteller who has been spinning murder mystery yarns for the past twelve years. Behind the initials is a wife and mother of five who brings a varied background to her writing.

She's been a high school English teacher, spent five years as a librarian on an Arizona Indian reservation and ten years selling life insurance in Arizona and her current home in Washington State.

Her fictional characters include the best-selling, immensely popular J. P. Beaumont series featuring the crusty but lovable Seattle homicide detective. Catch him in *Without Due Process* and *Failure to Appear.* Plus two non-series books: *Desert Heat* and *Hour of the Hunter.*

In her anthology story, J. A. Jance invites you to ride along with two King County Police detectives as they investigate a brutal murder case, one with a history of domestic violence.

But it's one surprise after another when transplanted Chicago cop James Joseph Barry clashes with partner Phyllis Lanier. They are opposites who will never attract or mix just like "Oil and Water" . . .

I was headed into the precinct briefing room when Captain Waldron stopped me. "You're up, Detective Lanier. We've just had a 9-1-1 call reporting a homicide out in May Valley. Detective Barry's gassing up the car. He'll pick you up out front."

Of all the detectives who work for the King County Police Department, Detective James Joseph Barry was my least favorite possible partner. A recent transfer from Chicago P.D., Detective Barry shared his reac-

tionary views with all concerned. Although barely
thirty-five, his unbearably tedious monologues made
Mike Royko's curmudgeonly rumblings sound like
those of a lily-livered liberal.

But newly appointed to the Detective Division, I
didn't dare question the captain when it came to handing out assignments. I shut my mouth, kept my opinions to myself, and headed for the door.

Moments after I stepped outside, the unmarked car
skidded to a stop beside me. As I slipped into the
rider's seat, Detective Barry made a big deal of checking out my legs. He was obvious as hell, but I ignored it.

"So," he said, ramming the car into gear and ca-
reening through the rain slicked parking lot, "how
come a great-looking babe like you isn't married?"

"Homicide dicks aren't much good in the marriage
department," I told him evenly. "A fact of life your
wife must have figured out all on her own."

Touché! The fleeting grimace on his face told me
my remark had hit the intended target. "Shut up and
drive, will you?" I said.

He did, for the time being. Meanwhile, I got on the
horn to ask Records what they knew about where we
were headed and what we'd be up against. From the
radio I gathered that patrol officers were already on
the scene. The victim was dead and the crime scene
secure, so there was no need for either flashing lights
or siren. Detective Barry made liberal use of both.

It was a chilly October night. After a delightful
Indian-summer September, this was winter's first real
rainstorm. The pavement was glassy and dangerously
slick with mixed accumulations of oil and water. Instead of telling him to slow down, I made sure my
seatbelt was securely fastened and thanked God for
airbags.

Over the rhythmic slap of the windshield wipers,
Barry launched off into one of his interminable stories
about the good old days back in Chicago, this one

featuring his late, unlamented, bowling partner—the beady-eyed Beady Dodgson.

"So I says to him, I says, 'Beady, you old billy goat. For chrissakes, when you gonna wash that damn shirt of yours?' And he says back, he says, 'Barry, you stupid mick, after the damn tournament. Whaddaya tink? You want I should wash away my luck?' "

Detective Barry liked nothing better than the sound of his own voice. However, boring tales of reminiscence were far preferable to questions about my current marital status which seemed to surface every time the two of us had any joint dealings. Detective Barry made no secret of the fact that he thought I should be home taking care of a husband and kids. He didn't approve of what he called *girl* detectives. Which is no doubt why Captain Waldron made sure he was stuck with me. Or vice versa.

"Turn here," I said. "Take the first right up the hill."

As we turned off the May Valley Highway and headed up a steep, winding incline, the headlights cut through sheets of slanting raindrops illuminating a yellow "Livestock" warning sign along the road. Detective Barry slowed the car to a bare crawl.

City born and bred, Detective Barry was in his element and totally at home when confronting a group of urbanized, street-toughened teenagers. It was strange to realize that he was petrified of encountering stray cattle or horses on one of King County's numerous rural roads.

At last the radio crackled back to life and the harried Records clerk's voice came over the air to deliver what scanty information was then available. The victim's name was de Gasteneau, Renée Denise de Gasteneau. A computer check of the de Gasteneau address in the 18500 block of Rainier Vista had turned up six priors in the previous six weeks—two domestics, one civil disturbance, and the rest noise complaints. Chances were Renée de Gasteneau was probably none too popular with her neighbors.

"One other thing," the operator from Records added. "Her husband's there on the scene right now. Emile de Gasteneau."

The name was one I had seen in local society columns from time to time but most recently in the police blotter. "Is that as in Dr. de Gasteneau, the plastic surgeon?" I asked.

"That's the one. When officers responded to the first domestic, they let him go. The second time they picked him up. He's out on bail for that one."

"Three's the charm," I muttered.

Domestic disturbances are tough calls for all cops. For me personally they were especially disturbing. "Why do women stay with men like that?" I demanded. "Why the hell don't they get out while there's still time?"

Detective Barry shrugged. "Maybe they stay because they don't have anywhere else to go."

"That's no excuse," I said. And I meant it with every ounce of my being.

I left the very first time Mark hit me—the only time Mark hit me—and I never went back. It was less than six weeks after our wedding—a three-ring circus, storybook, church, and country-club affair with all the necessary trimmings. I came back to the Park and Ride after work late one Friday afternoon and discovered that someone had broken into my little Fiat and stolen both the stereo and the steering wheel.

That Fiat was my baby. It was the first car I had chosen, bought, and paid for all on my own. When I told Mark about it, I expected some sympathy. Instead, he lit into me. He said I should have had better sense than to leave it at the Park and Ride in the first place. The argument got totally out of hand, and before I knew what was happening, he hit me—knocked me out cold.

Once I picked myself up off the kitchen floor, I called the cops. I remember trying to keep the blood from my loosened teeth from dripping into the telephone receiver. The two patrol officers who responded were wonderful. One of them kept Mark out of the room while the other one stuck with me. He followed me around the house while I threw my clothes and makeup into suitcases and plastic trash bags. He helped amass an odd assortment of hastily collected household goods—dishes, silverware, pots, and pans. I made off with Aunt Mindy's wedding present waffle iron, one of the two popcorn poppers, and every single set of matching towels and washcloths I could lay hands on.

The two cops were more than happy to help me drag my collection of stuff downstairs and out the door where they obligingly loaded it into a waiting Yellow cab. Now that I'm a police officer myself, I know why they were so eager to help me. I was the exception, not the rule. Most women don't leave. Ever.

By then our car was rounding a tight curve on the winding foothills road called Rainier Vista, although any view of Mount Rainier was totally shrouded in clouds. Ahead of us the narrow right-of-way and the lowering clouds were brightly lit by the orange glow of flashing lights from numerous emergency vehicles— several patrol cars and what was evidently a now totally unnecessary ambulance.

The figure of a rain-slickered patrol officer emerged out of the darkness. The cop motioned for us to park directly behind one of the medical examiner's somber gray vans.

"How the hell did the meat wagon beat us?" Detective Barry demanded irritably.

"Believe me," I said, "it wasn't because you didn't try."

The uniformed deputy hurried over to our car. Detective Barry lowered his window. "What's up?"

"The husband's waiting out back. I let him know detectives were on the way; told him you'd probably want to talk to him."

Barry nodded. "I'm sure we do."

"That's his Jaguar over there in the driveway," the deputy added.

A Jag, I thought. That figured. Mark loved his Corvette more than life itself. Certainly more than he loved me. He beat the crap out of me, but as far as I know, he never damaged so much as a fender on that precious car of his.

By the time Detective Barry rolled his window back up, I was already out of the car and headed up the sidewalk. He caught me before I made it to the front porch.

"Let me handle the guy, Detective Lanier," Barry said. "I know where he's coming from."

"I don't give a damn where he's coming from," I returned. "Just as long as he goes to jail."

"Jumping to conclusions, aren't we?" Barry taunted.

His patronizing attitude bugged the hell out of me. Yes, he had been a cop a whole lot longer than I had, transferring out to Washington State after years of being a detective in Chicago. But as a transferring officer, he had been cycled through King County's training program all the same, and he had spent his obligatory time in Patrol right along with the new hires. When it was time to make the move from Patrol to Detective Division, the two of us did it at almost the same time. Since scores on training exams are posted, I knew I had outscored him on every written exam we'd been given.

I shoved my clenched fists out of sight in the pockets of my already dripping raincoat. "Cram it, Barry," I told him. "I'll do my best to keep an open mind."

Looking at it from the outside, the house was one of those you expect to find featured on the pages of *House Beautiful* or *Architectural Digest*—vast expanses of clear glass and straight up-and-downs punctuated here and there by unexpectedly sharp angles. The place was lit up like the proverbial Christmas tree with warmly inviting lights glowing through every window. Appearances can be deceiving. Once inside, it was clear the entire house was a shambles.

Even in the well-appointed entryway, every available surface—including the burled maple entryway table—was covered with an accumulation of junk and debris. There were dirty dishes and glasses everywhere, along with a collection of empty beer and soda cans, overflowing ashtrays, and unopened mail. Under the table was a mound of at least a month's worth of yellowed, unread newspapers, still rolled up and encircled by rubber bands.

The human mind is an amazing device. One glance at that hopeless disarray threw me back ten years to the weeks and months just after I left Mark. Once beyond the initial blast of hurt and anger, I closeted myself away in a tiny, two-room apartment and drifted into a miasma of despair and self-loathing. It was a time when I didn't do the dishes, answer the phone, open the mail, pay the bills, or take messages off the machine. Even the simplest tasks became impossibilities, the smallest decisions unthinkable.

If it hadn't been for Aunt Mindy and Uncle Ed, I might be there still. The telephone company had already disconnected my phone for lack of payment when Aunt Mindy and Uncle Ed showed up on my doorstep early one Saturday morning. They knocked and knocked. When I wouldn't open the door, Uncle Ed literally broke it down. They packed me up, cleaned out the place, and took me home with them. One piece at a time, they helped me start gluing my life back together. Six months later I found myself down at the county courthouse, filling out an application to become a police officer.

Thrusting that sudden series of painful memories aside, I took a deep breath and focused my attention on the dead woman lying naked in the middle of the parquet entryway floor. Her pale skin was spotlit by the soft light of a huge crystal chandelier that hung down from the soaring ceiling some three stories above us.

Careful to disturb nothing, I stepped near enough to examine her more closely. Renée Denise de Gasteneau was white, blond, and probably not much more than thirty. She lay sprawled in an awkward, almost running position. One knee was drawn up and thrust forward—as though she had been struck down in mid-stride.

While I bent over the body, Detective James Barry moved farther into the entryway and glanced into the living room.

"I'll tell you one thing," he announced. "This broad was almost as shitty a housekeeper as my ex-wife."

"Believe me," I returned coldly, "housekeeping is the least of this woman's problems."

Tom Hammond, an assistant from the Medical Examiner's office, was standing off to one side, watching us quizzically. "What do you think, Tom?" I asked.

"I've seen worse—housekeeping, that is."

"Forget the damn housekeeping, for godssake! What do you think killed her?"

"Too soon to tell," he replied. "I can see some bruising on the back of the neck, right there where her hair is parted. Could be from a blow to the back of the head. Could be she was strangled. We won't know for sure until we get her downtown."

"How long's she been dead?" Barry asked.

"Hard to say. Ten to twelve hours at least. Maybe longer."

About that time one of the county's crime-scene techs showed up with their photography equipment as well as the Alternate Light Source box that can be used to locate all kinds of trace evidence from latent fingerprints to stray strands of hair or thread or carpet fuzz. What crime techs need more than anything is for people to get the hell out of the way and leave them alone.

"Let's go talk to her husband," I said.

"Suits me," Detective Barry said.

We found Dr. Emile de Gasteneau sitting in an Adirondack chair on a covered deck at the rear of the house. He sat there, sobbing quietly, his face buried in his hands. When he glanced up at our approach, his cheeks were wet with tears. "Are you the detectives?" he croaked.

I nodded and flashed my badge in front of him, but he barely noticed. "I didn't mean for it to end this way," he groaned.

"What way is that, Dr. de Gasteneau?" I asked.

"With her dead like this," he answered hopelessly. "I just wanted to get on with my life. I never meant to hurt her."

My initial reaction was to Mirandize the guy on the spot. It sounded to me as though he was ready to blurt out a full-blown confession, and I didn't want it disqualified in a court of law on some stupid technicality.

Evidently Detective Barry didn't agree. He stepped forward and moved me aside. "How's that, Dr. de Gasteneau? How'd you hurt your wife?"

"I left her," the seemingly distraught man answered. "I just couldn't go on living a lie. I told her I wanted out, but I offered her a good settlement, a fair settlement. I told her she could have the entire equity from the house on the condition she sell it as soon as possible. I thought she'd take the money and run—find someplace less expensive to live and keep the change.

"Instead, she just let the place go to ruin." You can see it's a mess. There's a For Sale sign out front, but as far as I know, no one's even been out here to look at it. I think the real estate agent is ashamed to bring anyone by. I don't blame her. Who would want to buy a $750,000 pigsty—"

"Excuse me, Dr. de Gasteneau," I interrupted. "It sounds to me as though you're more upset by the fact that your wife was a poor housekeeper than you are by the fact she's dead."

The widower stiffened and glared at me. "That was rude."

"So is murder," I countered.

Giving up on any possibility of a voluntary confession, I took my notepad out of my pocket. "Are you the one who called 9-1-1?"

De Gasteneau nodded. "Yes."

"What time?"

He glanced at his watch—an expensive jewel-encrusted timepiece the size of a doorknob, with luminous hands that glowed in the dim light of the porch. "Right after I got here," he answered. "About an hour ago now."

Without a word, Detective Barry stepped off the porch and moved purposefully toward the Jaguar parked a few feet away in the driveway. He put his hand on the hood, checking for residual warmth, and then nodded in my direction.

"Since you and your wife were separated, why did you come here?"

"Mrs. Wilbur called me."

"Who's she?"

"A neighbor from just across the road. She was worried about Renée. She called my office and asked me to come check on her—on Renée."

"Why?"

"I don't know. She was worried about her, I guess. I told her I'd come over right after work."

"Why was she worried? Had she seen strange cars, heard noises, what?"

"I don't know. She didn't say, and I didn't ask. I came out as soon as I could. I had an engagement."

I was about to ask him what kind of engagement when Detective Barry sauntered back up onto the porch. "That's a pretty slick Jagwire you've got out there. Always wanted to get me one of those. What kind of gas mileage does that thing get?"

"It's not that good on gas," de Gasteneau admitted.

Jagwire! The man sounded like he'd just crawled out from under a rock. Renée de Gasteneau was dead, and here was this jerk of a Detective Barry sounding like a hick out kicking the tires at some exotic car dealership. How the hell did Captain Waldron expect me to work with a creep like that?

"How about if we step inside, Dr. de Gasteneau?" I said. "Maybe you can tell us whether or not anything is missing from your wife's house."

What I really wanted to do was to get inside where the light was better. I wanted to check out Emile de Gasteneau's arms and wrists and the backs of his hands to see if there were any scratches, any signs of a life-and-death struggle that might have left telltale marks on the living flesh of Renée de Gasteneau's killer.

Without a word the good doctor de Gasteneau stood up and went inside. "Just wait," Detective Barry whispered over my shoulder as we followed him into the house. "Next thing you know, he's going to try telling us a one-armed man did it. You know—like in *The Fugitive.*"

"Please," I sighed. "I got it. You don't have to explain."

As we trailed Dr. de Gasteneau from one impossibly messy room to another, I stole several discreet glances in the direction of his hands and arms. I was more disappointed than I should have been when there was nothing to see.

Checking throughout the house, it was difficult to tell whether or not anything was missing. Several television sets and VCR's were in their proper places as were two very expensive stereo systems. The jewelry was a tougher call, but as far as de Gasteneau could tell, none of that was missing, either.

"When's the last time you saw your wife?" I asked as we left the upstairs master bedroom and headed back toward the main level of the house.

He paused before he answered. "Two weeks ago," he answered guardedly. "But you probably already know about that."

"You mean the time when you were arrested for hitting her?"

"Yes."

"And you haven't seen her since then?"

"No."

"What time do you get off work?"

"Between four and four-thirty. I'm my own boss. I come and go when I damn well please."

"But you told the neighbor, Mrs. Wilbur, that you'd come here as soon as you could after work. The 9-1-1 call didn't come in until a little after eight. Where were you between four and eight?"

"I already told you. I had an engagement."

"With whom?"

"I don't have to tell you that."

"Phyllis—" Detective Barry interjected, but I silenced him with a single hard-edged stare. I was on track, and I wasn't about to let him pull me away.

"You're right," I said easily. "You don't have to tell us anything at all. But if you don't, I guarantee you we'll find out anyway—one way or the other."

It was nothing more than an empty threat, but de Gasteneau fell for it all the same. "I was seeing my friend," he conceded angrily. "We met for a drink."

Just the way he answered triggered a warning signal in my mind, made me wonder if we were dealing with a lover's triangle. "What kind of friend?" I asked. "Male or female?"

"A male friend," he answered.

So much for the lover theory, I thought. I said, "What's his name?"

De Gasteneau looked at Detective Barry in a blatant appeal for help, but I wasn't about to be derailed. "What's his name?" I insisted.

"Garth," de Gasteneau answered flatly. "His name's Garth Homewood. But please don't call him. Believe me, he's got nothing to do with all this."

"Why would we think he did?" I asked.

We were descending the broad, carpeted stairway when, suddenly, de Gasteneau sank down on the bottom step.

"Garth and I are lovers," he answered unexpectedly. "He's the whole reason I left Renée in the first place. I guess that's one of the reasons she was so upset about it. Maybe if I'd left her for another woman, it wouldn't have bothered her so much."

These are the nineties. Detective Barry and I are both adults and we are both cops. I guess de Gasteneau's admission shouldn't have shocked or surprised either one of us, but it did. My partner looked stunned. I felt like someone who pokes something he thinks is a dead twig only to have it turn out to be a quick brown snake. Once again I was struck by an incredible feeling of kinship toward the dead woman. Poor Renée de Gasteneau. It occurred to me that learning her husband was gay was probably as much a blow to her self-esteem as Mark Lanier's punishing balled fist had been to mine.

"Why?" I said. Not why did you leave her? That much was clear. But why did you marry her in the first place?

The last question as well as the unspoken ones that followed were more reflex than anything else. I didn't really expect Emile de Gasteneau to answer, but he did.

"I tricked her," he admitted, somberly. "I wanted an heir, a child. Someone to leave all this to." His despairing glance encompassed the whole house and everything in it. "Except it didn't work out. I picked the wrong woman. Renée loved me, I guess, but I didn't care about her. Not the same way she did for me. And when it turned out she couldn't get pregnant, it was too much. After a while, I couldn't bring myself to try anymore. It was too dishonest. Now she's dead. Although I didn't kill her, I know it's all my fault."

The tears came again. While Emile de Gasteneau sat sobbing on the bottom stair, Detective Barry tapped me on the shoulder.

"Come on," he said, jerking his head toward the door. "Leave the guy alone. Let's go talk to the woman across the street."

I thought it was uncharacteristically nice of Barry to want to give the poor man some privacy, but outside and safely out of earshot, James Joseph Barry, ex-Chicago cop, let go with an amazing string of oaths.

"The guy's a frigging queer!" he raged. "For all we know, he's probably dying of AIDS. Jesus Christ! Did he breathe on us? You got a breath spray on you?"

Detective Barry's only obvious concession toward society's current mania for political correctness was refraining from use of the N-word in racially mixed company. The word "gay" had neither entered his vocabulary nor penetrated his consciousness. I, too, had been shocked by Emile de Gasteneau's revelation, but not for the same reason my partner was.

We walked across the road together and made our way down a steeply pitched driveway to the house we had been told belonged to a family named Wilbur. This one was somewhat older than Renée de Gasteneau's had been, and slightly less showy, but it was still a very expensive piece of suburban real estate.

Detective Barry continued to mutter under his breath as he rang the doorbell. An attractive woman in her late sixties or early seventies answered the door and switched on the porch light.

"Yes?" she said guardedly. "Can I help you?"

I moved forward and showed her my badge. "We're Detectives Barry and Lanier," I explained. "We're investigating the incident across the street. Are you Mrs. Wilbur?"

She nodded but without opening the door any wider. "Inez," she said, "what do you want?"

"I understand you were the person who called Dr. de Gasteneau. Is that true?"

"Yes."

"Why did you call him? Did you hear something unusual? See something out of the ordinary?"

"Well, yes. I mean no. It's just that Renée was always on the go, rushing off this way or that. When her car didn't move all day long, I was worried."

I looked back over my shoulder. From where I stood on the front step of Inez Wilbur's porch, only the topmost gable of the de Gasteneau roof was visi-

ble over the crest of the hill. Inez Wilbur seemed to
follow both my movements as well as my train of
thought.

"You're right," she put in quickly. "It's not easy to
see from where you are, but I can see her house from
upstairs, from my room . . ."

"Mama," a man's voice said from somewhere behind her. "Who is it?"

"It's nothing, Carl. Go back to your program. I'll
be done here in a minute."

"But it's a boring program, Mama," he replied. "I
don't like it."

The voice had the basso timbre of an adult, but the
words were the whining complaints of a dissatisfied
child.

"Please, Carl," Inez Wilbur said, with a tight frown.
"Change channels then. I'll be done in a minute."

"Who's Carl?" I asked.

"He's my son," she answered. "He's not a child,
but he's like a child, if you know what I mean. All
this would upset him terribly."

"All what would upset him terribly?" I asked.

A look of anguished confusion washed over Inez
Wilbur's delicately made-up face. "About Mrs. de
Gasteneau."

"What about her?"

"She's dead, isn't she?"

"Mama," Carl said behind her, "who is it? Is it
company? Are we going to have dessert now?"

Inez let go of the doorknob and covered her face
with her hands. Slowly, as though being pushed by the
wind, the heavy wooden door swung open.

A large, open-faced man with a wild headful of
slightly graying hair stood illuminated in the vestibule
behind her. He was wearing a short-sleeved shirt and
expertly playing with a yo-yo. His muscular forearms
were raked with long deep parallel scratches—a last
desperate message from a dying woman.

"Hello, Carl," I said quietly. "My name's Detective

Lanier and this is Detective Barry. We'd like to talk to you for a few minutes if you don't mind."

Inez stepped aside and let us into the house while Carl Wilbur's mouth broke into a broad, gap-toothed grin. "Detectives? Really? Do you hear that, Mama? They're cops, and they want to talk to me!"

Inez Wilbur's face collapsed like a shattered teacup, and she began to cry.

Detective Barry pulled his Miranda card out of his wallet. "I'll bet you've seen this on TV, Carl. It's called reading you your rights. You have the right to remain silent . . ."

It was six o'clock the next morning before we finally finished our paper. Inez Wilbur had tried to explain to Renée de Gasteneau that Carl was watching her, that she should always pull her curtains and be more careful about walking around the house without any clothes on. But Renée had ignored the warnings just as she had ignored Carl himself.

In the aftermath of Emile's defection, Renée de Gasteneau had searched for validation of her womanhood by taking on all comers. Carl Wilbur, her curious neighbor, had watched all the proceedings with rapt fascination, learning as he did so that there was more to life than he had previously suspected, that there were some interesting things that he wanted to try for himself. And when those things were denied him, he had responded with unthinking but lethal rage. He had thrown a lifeless Renée de Gasteneau to the floor, like a discarded and broken doll.

I was dragging myself out to the parking lot when Captain Waldron caught me by the front door. He hurried up to me, his kind face etched with concern.

"Are you all right?" he asked.

"Just tired. Worn out."

Detective Barry drove by out in the parking lot. He tapped on his horn and waved. I waved back.

"Tough case," Captain Waldron said, "but you han-

dled it like a pair of champs. How do you like working
with Detective Barry?"

"He's okay," I said.

Waldron nodded. "Good. I was worried about
whether or not you two could get along."

I laughed. "Why? Because Barry's an asshole?"

"No, because of his divorce."

"What about his divorce?"

"You mean you don't know about that? It's common knowledge. I thought everyone knew. His wife
left him because he beat her up and she turned him
in. That's why he transferred out here from Chicago.
Her father's a captain on the Berwyn P.D. somewhere
outside of Chicago. I guess things got pretty sticky for
a while, but with his track record for cracking serial-
killer cases, the sheriff was willing to take him on."

"No questions asked?" I demanded.

Waldron shrugged. "I think he had to complete one
of those anger-management courses."

"Did he?"

"As far as I know. I just wanted to let you know
how glad I was that the two of you were able to get
along."

"We got along, all right," I said. "Just like oil and
water."

See What the Boys in the Locked Room Will Have

Bill Crider

Bill Crider's first Sheriff Dan Rhodes novel won the Anthony Award. You can enjoy his newest adventure, *Murder Most Fowl*.

Then came the Truman Smith series and *Dead on the Island* was promptly nominated for a Shamus Award. Now Bill adds English professor and reluctant amateur sleuth Carl Burns in the upcoming novel . . . *A Dangerous Thing*. Plus two non-series books *Blood Marks* and *The Texas Capitol Murders*. If you ever get the chance to hear him speak, Bill is a delightful raconteur.

And that accomplishment shows in the following pages— Welcome to the 1950s where Janice Langtry and Bo Wagner are hard at work on another best-selling mystery novel. Together they create and solve the most puzzling crimes, at least on the printed page. But now there's a real crime to solve. Janice and Bo accept the challenge. Will you? Turn the page and "See What the Boys in the Locked Room Will Have" . . .

I

Outside, the rain fell softly from a heavy gray sky, but the only sound in the room was the clacking of the keys on the old Royal typewriter as Bo Wagner's stubby fingers danced over the keyboard.

Bo was working on the final chapter of another in one of the most promising series of detective novels the 1950s had yet seen, all of them featuring Sam Fernando, the Gentleman Sleuth. The scene was one that Bo regarded as obligatory in all the books, the one in which the suspects are gathered in one spot, waiting for Sam Fernando to explain to them the mechanics of the seemingly impossible murder that formed the basis for the book's plot and, not incidentally, to reveal to all of them and to the no doubt completely bumfuzzled reader just exactly who had committed the heinous crime.

Bo was really smoking along, never glancing at the keyboard but instead keeping his eyes glued to the handwritten pages on the wooden typing stand beside the Royal. He typed so fast that it seemed a miracle that the keys didn't collide and jam. He was so intent that he didn't even notice the statuesque blonde who was standing not six inches behind his chair, reading every word as it appeared on the clean white typing paper:

> Sam Fernando leaned against the oak door frame and looked over the suspects who were crowded into the study of the deceased Dr. Dorman. Mrs. Hutchings sat in the overstuffed leather chair near the desk, her black eyes darting left and right, her double chins quivering. Harley Montfort was on the couch opposite the desk, his long legs sticking straight out in front of him, his ankles crossed, while next to him Missy Tongate, her bright red hair a mass of timpting tangles, squirmed . . .

"Just a cotton-pickin' minute, there, Bo," Janice Langtry said in her soft Texas drawl. "What're you writin' here, a sequel to *Forever Amber?* Let's have us a look at this draft copy."

She reached out a hand big enough to fill a catcher's mitt and picked up the handwritten sheets. She shook them under Bo's nose. "Can you tell me where it says anything about any 'mass of timptin' tangles'?"

Bo admitted reluctantly that he couldn't find such a phrase. "But—"

"Don't *but* me!" Janice said. "I know it's not there, and you know it's not there. You spelled *temptin'* wrong, too."

Bo almost told her that she was right. That he put a *g* on the end of it. But he restrained himself.

Janice Langtry was nearly six feet tall, and she was wearing a man's crisply starched white shirt with the sleeves rolled up halfway to her elbows, faded Levi's with the bottoms turned up into cuffs and black suede loafers with white socks. Her long blond hair was pulled back into a ponytail and tied with a red scarf.

She was also wearing just the slightest touch of White Shoulders perfume, the scent of which always made Bo a little horny—not that he ever dared mention *that* fact to Janice Langtry.

"And what about that *squirmed?*" she asked. "I bet you a dollar the next word you were goin' to type was *deliciously*."

"Maybe, but—"

"I told you not to *but* me. You couldn't spell *deliciously* if you tried, anyhow. Our agreement is that you type it up on the page just like I wrote it out by hand and not change a thing. Have you been readin' those Mickey Spillane books again?"

"Maybe, but—"

Janice put the handwritten sheets back on the wooden stand. Then she put her hands on her considerable hips and looked Bo right in the eye. A lesser man might have quailed, but Bo managed to meet her gaze squarely.

It wasn't easy. After all, he was sitting down. Even standing, he was nearly three inches shorter than she, and where she was neat, he was pretty much of a slob. His green shirt was wrinkled and there was a dark stain near the second button. Bo didn't know what the stain was. His jeans had a small rip in one knee, and his shoes looked worse than the ones the photographers had caught Adlai Stevenson in.

"I write the words," Janice said. "You just type 'em. That's the agreement, right?"

"Right." Bo nodded. He reached into his shirt pocket and brought out a crumpled pack of Camels and a folder of matches. He stuck a Camel in his mouth and lit it.

"Those things are goin' to kill you," Janice said, waving a hand in front of her face to shoo away the smoke.

"Hey, Mickey Mantle smokes these," Bo protested. "They soothe his T-Zone."

"That's Lucky Strike."

Bo let a trickle of smoke out his nose. "Nope. Lucky Strike's slogan is LS/MFT. 'Lucky Strike means—' "

"I really don't give a big rat's rump *what* it means. You're just changin' the subject. You're the plotter, I'm the writer. That's the agreement. You don't change my words, I don't change your plots."

"I'm also the typist," Bo pointed out, trying not to sound defensive.

It bothered him more than a little that while his head teemed with plot ideas, he could hardly write a complete sentence without help. He had convincingly murdered people onstage during a performance of *Twelfth Night,* with the audience watching; in airplane cabins in full view of all the passengers; in classrooms full of students; in automobiles with all the windows rolled up and the doors locked; and in any number of other "impossible" places, including not a few very much like the study of the unfortunately deceased Dr. Dorman.

But the truth of the matter was that while he could plot like a demon, he couldn't write for spit. His spelling was loathsome, his grammar was atrocious, and his sentence structure was indescribable.

He knew all that, but he didn't like it, which was why he constantly studied the masters of detective fiction prose, like Mickey Spillane, a writer he greatly admired, hoping some of their stylistic magic would rub off on him. So far, none of it had.

Spillane's style was different from Janice's, of course, and probably not suited to the adventures of the Gentleman Sleuth, but it was exceptionally effective nevertheless, or so Bo believed. And besides, Spillane's books outsold the adventures of the Gentleman Sleuth by about ten to one. It never hurt to add a little spice to things, and that's all Bo had been trying to do.

"You're only the typist because you said you wanted to do it," Janice reminded him. "I can type just as fast as you. Probably faster."

She was right. Bo stubbed out his Camel in the ashtray by the typewriter and rolled the paper from the machine. He crumpled it and threw it in the trash can by the desk.

While he was rolling in a new sheet, Janice tapped the typewriter. "By the numbers this time."

"You're the boss."

Janice nodded, the ponytail bobbing. "You said it."

Bo began typing again. This time he didn't add any squirming or "timpting tangles." He tried to tell himself that he didn't really care about all that descriptive stuff anyway, but it would have been nice once in a while to have something of his own in the writing. What really interested him, however, was the mechanics of the plot, and that's what he was getting to. His fingers jumped over the keys:

... Missy Tongate brushed her red hair off her forehead. Ferdy Forman was behind the doctor's old desk, trying to look at home but failing miserably. Detective Lomax stared at each one of them in turn, then looked at the Gentleman Sleuth.

"I don't know what you're thinking of, Fernando," Lomax sneered. "You know as well as I do that everyone here was outside the room when they heard the shot that killed Dorman. And the door was bolted from the inside. The gun was on the floor beneath Dorman's body. It's a clear case of suicide."

Sam Fernando smiled. It was a smile that seemed to infuriate Detective Lomax, who had seen it all too often. "That's where you are mistaken," Fernando said.

"That's great, that's really great," Janice said. "The readers love it when Lomax does that slow burn. They know that Sam is going to drop the bomb on him one more time."

Bo turned around. He tried to avoid looking at Janice's breasts, which were quite close to him. He'd looked at them a tad too admiringly a month or so ago, and she'd belted him one right in the kisser.

"You really like that part?" he asked.

"I said I did, didn't I? Why would I lie?"

"No reason." Bo turned back to the typewriter.

The slow burn was Janice's idea, and Bo thought it was corny. He often wondered why the readers never seemed to get bored with it. If he were Detective Lomax, he'd retire or move to another city where he'd never have to see Sam Fernando's smugly smiling face again.

What Bo wanted to do was write a scene where his hero's nerves jangled with the kill-crazy desire to smash some greasy-haired hood's teeth down his stinking throat and rub his nose off on the filthy bricks of the nearest building. But of course he *couldn't* write it, and Janice *wouldn't* write it, so there they were.

"You see," Fernando explained, still wearing the smile that seemed to enrage Lomax and cause the policeman's face to grow almost purple and pointing to the window frame, "if the thumbtack had fallen to the *outside*, then we would never have known the truth. But the killer obviously miscalculated. Therefore—"

The telephone rang in the next room, and Bo stopped typing while Janice went to answer it. He leaned back in the chair and tried to overhear what his writing partner was saying. Her voice was muffled, and he could make out only part of it.

"Yes, we're busy," she said. "We're working on our next book ... *What?* ... And in a locked room? ...

You're sure about that? ... Yes ... Of course ... We'll be right there."

Bo heard the heavy click as she hung up the handset. She came back into the study with a stricken look on her face.

"What's happened?" Bo asked. "What's the matter?"

"That was Lieutenant Franklin."

Bo knew Franklin, of course. Every writer of mystery stories needed to know at least one good source of matters relating to police routine and procedure, and Franklin was theirs. He read each of their books to insure an air of something approaching authenticity, though Bo insisted that authenticity didn't really matter. His theory was that he and Janice were selling fantasy.

"From the way you look, I'd say he didn't call to talk about some new plot device he's dreamed up for us."

Janice shook her head. The ponytail danced. "No. It wasn't that."

"Well, what was it, then?"

"He called to tell us that somebody's murdered Ray Thompson. In a locked house. In front of three or four witnesses. And there's no murder weapon to be found."

II

Bo Wagner was thirty-five-years old, but, as Janice often reminded him, he had never grown up. Which was why they were zipping through the streets in a black chopped and channeled "49 Merc" and why Bo was wearing a red jacket just like the one James Dean had worn in *Rebel Without a Cause*. The radio was blaring "C'mon Everybody" by Eddie Cochran. The wipers swished rain from the windshield.

"Are they sure Ray's dead?" Bo asked, taking a corner on two wheels. He worked the clutch and shifted smoothly down into third gear as the car straightened out from the turn. "Sometimes they can do wonders in the hospitals these days."

"Ray's dead all right," Janice told him. "That's what Lieutenant Franklin said. He was shot twice."

"Where?"

"Somewhere in the house. That's all I found out. I just said we'd get there as fast as we could."

They were on a long, straight street, and Bo mashed the accelerator to the floor.

"Not this fast!" Janice yelped. "Not on this wet street!"

Bo slowed down, but not much. He couldn't believe Ray was dead. There had to be some mistake, but it was pretty unlikely that Lieutenant Franklin would be wrong about something that important. If he said Ray was dead, then Ray was no longer among the living.

"C'mon Everybody" ended and was followed by a string of commercials. Then "It's Only Make Believe" came on.

"That guy sounds a lot like Elvis."

"He wishes," Janice said, but her heart wasn't in it. Bo could tell she was thinking about Ray.

Ray Thompson had been among their earliest admirers. After the publication of *The Red and Blue Clue,* the first Sam Fernando book, Ray had called Bo.

"I just wanted you to know how much I enjoyed your work," he said. "Both yours and Miss Langtry's. I assume you share the work equally?"

Bo told him that was right.

"Well, you do it very well indeed. I haven't enjoyed anything quite so much since the first Ellery Queen novel I ever read. *The Roman Hat Mystery,* I believe. And to think that both you and Miss Langtry live right here in the city! I wonder if you would do me the honor of having dinner with me some evening?"

Ray had gotten their names from an article that appeared in the local newspaper after the publication of *The Red and Blue Clue.* No other newspapers had been interested, which was fine with Bo. He thought

writers should write and not have to worry about pub-
licizing their work.

The young reporter who came to do the interview
had been struck by the fact that the book was a collab-
oration between a man and a woman, and he'd written
a long story about how the two had met (at the library), discovered their mutual interest in mysteries
(they were in the mystery section, and both of them
reached at the same time for the latest John Dickson
Carr novel), and decided to write together (both had
friends who said things like "You read so many of
those things, why don't you write one?" but neither
felt competent to try it alone).

Ray Thompson loved reading, especially mysteries,
and he had time to indulge himself thanks to his envi-
able financial situation. His father had bought a few
acres of land to raise cows on and had forgotten all
about the cows when a drilling company discovered
oil there. He retired from raising cattle and doing
much of anything except counting his money, and Ray
had followed in the old man's footsteps, except that
now most of the oil was gone and the money came in
from investments.

Janice and Bo had gone to dinner at Ray's house a
few days after the phone call. Neither had ever been
in a place quite like it. When they entered the front
door, they were only a few steps from the largest private library in the city. Wooden bookshelves were
filled from floor to ceiling with nothing but mystery
novels, first editions by Agatha Christie, Ngaio Marsh,
Ellery Queen, Dorothy L. Sayers, Cornell Woolrich
(and his alter ego William Irish), John Dickson Carr
(and *his* alter ego, Carter Dickson), and even (to Bo's
secret delight) Mickey Spillane.

Ray was as fascinated with the two writers as they
were with his book collection. For all his love of reading, he had never met an actual writer before, and
now he was talking to two of them. After that evening
they were fast friends, and Janice and Bo were fre-
quent guests in Ray's home. But now he was dead.

"I just can't believe it," Janice said as Bo pulled to the curb in front of Ray's house.

There were several cars already there: two police cars, Lieutenant Franklin's unmarked Ford, and a black Lincoln Continental.

The two-story house was huge and impressive, if not exactly tasteful, with a wide front and two wings that extended backward. The outside was mostly red brick, and there were flower beds along the front and down the sidewalk.

"I'm not sure I want to go in there," she hedged.

Bo wasn't so sure either. He was used to murder on the clean white pages he typed, but he had never been on the scene of an actual killing.

"We have to go in—for Ray."

He got out of the car and went around to open the passenger door for Janice. It was still raining lightly, and the December wind moaned out of the gray sky and whipped down the street, cutting right through Bo's red jacket. Janice was wearing a long all-weather coat with a raccoon collar. The bottom of it flapped against her legs as she stepped out on the curb.

There were two tall oak trees in the front yard of the house. The wind scattered dead, wet leaves across the yard and down the sidewalk, and they brushed across Bo's shoes as he approached the door.

The door was made of heavy carved wood, and there were long windows on either side of it. On the wall beside the windows there were drainpipes coming down from the roof gutters. The water from the drains flowed into the flower beds. There was a steady stream from one pipe, but only a trickle from the other.

In the center of the door there was a heavy brass knocker in the shape of a cowboy boot. Bo reached out for the knocker, but he didn't have to use it. The door was pulled open by Lieutenant Franklin, who was standing in the short hallway. Franklin had a broad face with a downturned mouth, a nose like a potato, and the suspicious eyes of the career cop.

"C'mon in." His voice was deep and husky, as if he

had a terrible cold, which he didn't. He sounded like that all the time.

Bo and Janice walked past him, and he shut the door behind them. Bo helped Janice off with her coat, getting another tiny whiff of White Shoulders, and hung it in the hall closet. There was already a topcoat inside. The shoulders were slightly damp with rain. The coat looked expensive to Bo, but he wasn't really much of a judge.

It was only a couple of steps from the hall to the library, which looked pretty much as it always had except for the two cops who were going over it looking for clues. The major crime-scene investigation had already been done, and there was fingerprint powder on every smooth surface that Bo could see. One of the cops was poking through the drawers of the desk. The other was taking books off the shelves and thumbing through the pages.

The library was a large room, about fifteen feet wide by twenty feet long, with most of the available wall space being taken up by the bookshelves. There was, however, a large stone fireplace on the wall at the right end of the room. Opposite the room's entrance there was a big oak desk, and behind the desk were French doors leading onto a stone patio and into the yard beyond. Bo noticed that one of the doors had a broken pane.

"That's where it happened." Franklin waved a hand toward the library. "The body was right there by the desk."

"You said he was shot, didn't you?" Janice asked.

Franklin nodded.

"What about the gun, then?"

"She means the murder weapon," Bo said, trying to show Franklin that they knew the jargon.

Franklin wasn't interested in jargon, however. He obviously had something else on his mind.

"The gun's one of our problems."

"You said you couldn't find it," Janice prompted.

"That's right. Listen, why don't you two come in the library with me for a minute?"

Franklin moved away without waiting for an answer. Bo looked at Janice, who shrugged, and the two of them followed the police lieutenant.

Franklin stopped just inside the library, "Let's not get in anybody's way."

The two cops went about their business. The one looking through the books put the one he had been examining back on the shelf and took another one down. The other cop was finished with the desk drawers, and he moved to another part of the room and began examining books just as his partner was doing.

Bo noticed the floor beside the desk. There was a large dark stain in the carpet.

"Why did you want us to come in here?" Bo asked, trying not to look at the stain.

"Because there are some other people being interviewed in the den," Franklin explained. "I've already talked to them, but Simmons is going over things with them again."

Simmons was a homicide detective. Bo and Janice had talked to him a few times when he dropped by Franklin's office while they were visiting.

"We couldn't talk in here," Franklin went on, with a glance at the stain that Bo was trying to ignore. "The den was the best place."

The den was in the wing of the house to the left of the library. The downstairs area of that wing also held the game room and a large storage room. The other wing was for the kitchen, the dining room, and the office where Ray took care of his business interests. Bedrooms were upstairs in both wings.

"Why did you want us to come over here, anyway?" Janice asked. "Ray was our friend, but that's not why you called. Is it?"

Franklin looked uncomfortable. "No," he admitted. "That's not why I called."

Janice wasn't satisfied with that. "So why did you call, then?"

"You know how these things are. Real murder's not like it is in those books you write, or it's not supposed to be."

Bo was getting interested. "What do you mean?"

"I mean, murder's usually something that's pretty straightforward. You have witnesses. You have clues. You have people who know things."

"But not this time?"

"Not this time. This time it *is* like one of your books."

"Tell us about it," Janice said.

III

Franklin told them what he knew. The missing gun was the least of his problems. What he had was a locked-room crime.

"Hank Rollins heard the shots," the lieutenant said. "He's a handyman who Thompson used for all kinds of work around the place. In the summer he mows the yard, and he makes general repairs when they're needed. This morning he was out in the back, cutting some dead limbs out of the pecan trees when he heard what he thought were two pistol shots. They were muffled, as if they'd come from the house, so Rollins ran to the patio and looked in through the French doors.

"Thompson was lying on the floor," Franklin continued. "There was no one else in the room. Rollins couldn't get in because the French doors were locked. He broke out one of the door panes and came inside. When he got in, he could hear someone banging on the front-door knocker. He looked down at Thompson, figured he needed help, and went to the door. There was a guy named Walton standing there."

"Jeffery Walton?" Janice asked.

Franklin nodded. "That's right. You know him?"

Bo had heard the name. "Ray's business manager. Ray's talked about him to us. We've never met him."

"Well, he was the guy at the door. He and Rollins

went back to the library, and the daughter was there by that time, standing by the body and screaming. Walton took her out of the room, and Rollins called us."

"They didn't see the gun?" Janice asked.

"They didn't see anything," Franklin replied. "So they say. But there were some other people here."

"Who?" Bo wanted to know.

"Thompson's kids."

"Dolly and Jimmy," Janice said. "Them, we've met."

"They're the ones. The girl was upstairs in what she calls her 'sewing room.'"

"Sewing's her hobby," Janice explained. "She's very good."

Franklin didn't look as if he cared a thing about Dolly's sewing skills. "Yeah. Anyway, the room's right by her bedroom, and she was making a dress or something, running a little Singer machine. She says she heard the shots, but they were muffled, like someone hitting a nail with a hammer. She didn't know what they were. She left the sewing room to check, and then she heard the glass break. She got downstairs just about the time Rollins was letting Walton in the front door."

"Did anyone hear the door knocker before the shots?" Janice asked.

"That's an interesting question," Franklin said. "And the answer is no, and as far as anyone knows, there was no one downstairs except Thompson."

"What about Jimmy?" Bo asked.

"He didn't hear the door knocker or the shots. Says he was in the garage, working on his car."

The garage was separate from the house, just in back. There was a door that led from the kitchen to a short covered walk that went to the garage.

"He likes that car, all right," Bo agreed. "It's a '55 Chevy Bel-Air with a V-8 engine and—"

"I don't care about the damn car," Franklin growled. "Don't you see what we've got here!"

"I do," Janice said. "It's like something from one of our books. A man was murdered in this room, by someone that no one knows was in the house. The victim had a door behind him and a door in front of him, but it seems that the killer didn't go out either of them. He didn't go out the back door, or Jimmy would've seen him from the garage. And he didn't go upstairs to the bedrooms on Dolly's side, because she didn't see him there."

"What about the den?" Bo asked. "Aren't there French doors in there, too?"

"Bolted," Franklin said. "On the inside."

"Then the killer's still somewhere in the house."

"He's not in the house," Franklin told Bo. "You can bet on that. We've searched."

Bo looked over at the fireplace. There hadn't been a fire in it in a long time; Ray thought the smoke wasn't good for his books. There seemed to Bo to be an excess of soot on the hearth, as if someone had disturbed the interior of the chimney. Bo had no idea how big the chimney was, but it was certainly possible that someone could have climbed up it. Chimney sweeps did it in London well into the nineteenth century, though of course they were mostly small children.

Of course Dr. Gideon Fell, one of John Dickson Carr's famous fictional detectives, didn't approve of chimneys as a means of escape in locked-room murders, but maybe Thompson's killer didn't know that.

"If the killer's not in the house, and if no one saw him making his escape, where does that leave you?" Janice asked Franklin.

"I don't know," he said. "That's why I called you two. Most murders are really pretty simple. There's not any puzzle to figure out. You just look for motive, means, and opportunity, and when you've got all that sorted out, you can find your killer."

"Speaking of motives, you have a couple of people here who have one." Bo ignored Janice's glare and went on. "Let's face it. We like Ray, but Dolly and Jimmy didn't get along with their father."

"Those kids"—Franklin nodded—"we know about them, too."

It was an old and familiar story. The mother dies when the children are young, and the father tries to compensate by being overly strict, possibly a bit dictatorial.

Ray Thompson had wanted Jimmy, the eldest, to make his own way in the world, while Jimmy had become more than a little resentful when he did not receive the help he expected. Jimmy had managed well enough, however. He worked his way through college and law school, and he was now living at home while studying for the bar exam. His one luxury was the '55 Chevy that Ray had recently bought him. Ray had told Bo and Janice that he was getting older and that it was time he started loosening the purse strings.

Dolly was twenty, five years younger than her brother, and not nearly so resentful, though it was no real secret that she felt a bit ridiculous wearing homemade clothes while most of the girls from other families she knew were wearing designer originals.

"The daughter's been known to comment that she wouldn't mind getting her hands on her inheritance," Franklin stated. He smiled as much as it was possible for him to do so. "Don't you think I move in the right social circles?"

"What do you know about Hank Rollins?"

"Glad you asked," Franklin said. "There's no police file on him, not even a parking ticket. He's worked for Thompson for years, mowing the yard, painting, things like that. And he's done odd jobs for a lot of people in the neighborhood. There's never been a complaint."

"Sometimes it's the one you least suspect," Bo muttered.

"Could be," Franklin said. "Maybe he thought there was some money in the desk. But then why would he answer the front door?"

"What about Walton?" Bo asked.

"Well, now, he doesn't have a record, either. But he and Thompson haven't exactly been getting along lately, and Walton came here with some bad news."

"What bad news?" Janice asked.

"It seems that nearly all Thompson's investments have gone south on him. Walton was going to tell him that he was practically broke."

"That might give *Ray* a motive for murder, if he blamed Walton. But it wouldn't give Walton a reason for killing Ray."

"I'm just telling you what I know, Janice. Maybe none of them did it. Maybe Thompson was killed by the Invisible Man, who just walked out the front door without being seen."

"I didn't notice Claude Rains walking the streets on the way over here," Bo said.

"And I didn't ask you here to make jokes!" Franklin retorted. "I thought maybe you'd have some ideas."

"And we do, we do." Janice's comment surprised Bo, who had no ideas at all. "Can we talk to everyone?"

"Together?" Franklin asked.

"No. One at a time."

"Sure. I'll arrange it. In the den be okay?"

"I'd rather use the kitchen. I want to talk to Bo in there first. Alone."

"You two go ahead and I'll get things set up."

Janice thanked him and started for the kitchen. Bo watched her go. She turned back. "Are you coming?"

"I guess so," Bo said, still wondering what she knew that he didn't.

IV

As soon as they got into the kitchen, Bo lit up a Camel. He looked around for an ashtray, but there wasn't one. He tossed the match in the sink.

"That's a disgusting thing to do," Janice said. "I suppose you're going to put your ashes there, too?"

"That's right. It may be disgusting, but it's safer than flicking them in the trash can. Don't worry. I'll wash out the sink when I'm done."

Janice started out of the kitchen. "I'm sure you will."

"Hey, where're you going?"

"To look at something. You just smoke your cigarette. I'll be right back."

Bo inhaled deeply and let the smoke trickle out through his nose. *Fills your lungs with tiny little vitamins,* he thought. He looked around the kitchen. Ray had a housekeeper, but maybe today was her day off. She kept the place excessively clean, in Bo's opinion. The countertops sparkled, and the porcelain sink was so white that it hurt his eyes to look at it. All of which led him to wonder again about the chimney and all that soot.

He was thinking about that when Janice came back into the room.

She looked pointedly at the cigarette. "Aren't you finished yet?"

Bo was only about halfway down the Camel, but he stuck it under the tap and turned on the water. The cigarette fizzed and went out. He dropped it in the sink.

"I'll get it. I promise."

"You'd better. Now, what do you think about all this?"

"It's obvious," Bo said. "The chimney. Did you notice all the soot on the hearth? I think someone killed Ray and escaped up the chimney. That's the only way it could've been done."

"Assuming someone could actually climb up the chimney," Janice said, "which I doubt, where did he go after that?"

"The roof."

"And then?"

"Down a drainpipe maybe. There're two of them right by the front door."

"Wouldn't he have been seen?"

"Maybe there's a drainpipe in the back." Bo rubbed his hands together, getting into the spirit of it. "Here's how I'd plot it. The killer comes in, argues with Ray for some reason or another. Then something gets Ray really upset and he goes for that pistol he keeps in his desk—"

He broke off and looked at Janice. "The pistol! Ray showed it to us one night. It's in the middle drawer of the desk! I've got to tell Franklin."

He started for the doorway, but Janice stopped him. "The pistol's not there. I looked."

"So that's where you went. Did you tell anyone?"

Janice shook her head. The ponytail jiggled. "I mentioned it to Lieutenant Franklin."

"Good. What did he say?"

"He said they'd look for it."

"All right. Anyway, it all fits. Ray goes for the pistol. They struggle, and the killer takes the gun away from him. Ray charges. The killer fires. Ray drops, and the killer is horrified by what he's done. How can he escape? His eyes dart around the room. Suddenly, he hears the knocking on the front door! He sees Rollins coming toward the patio from the backyard! Maybe he even heard Dolly coming down the stairs!"

Bo was half-crouched in the middle of the kitchen now, his palms held outward at shoulder level. He was taking the part of the killer, and his head swiveled from right to left as he searched desperately for an exit.

"Where can he go? There's no way out! But then he sees the chimney! Can he get inside?"

Bo glided across the kitchen toward the Chambers range. He opened the oven door and looked inside.

"It looks awfully small, but he has to try! It's his only chance!"

"You're not really going to try to get in there, are you?" She asked, as Bo stuck his head inside the oven.

Pulling his head back, he grinned sheepishly. "Sorry, I guess I got a little carried away. But you see how it would work, don't you?"

"Maybe." She didn't look or sound convinced.

"Just think about it. Close your eyes and imagine it. He scrabbles up the chimney and comes out on the roof, covered in black soot. The wind is howling around him—"

"The wind is a little gusty, but it isn't howlin'."

"Hey, we're working on a story here. Give me a little poetic license."

"All right, all right. Go on. 'The wind was howlin' around him—' "

"Right. It's dark, and the moon is hiding behind the thick clouds—"

"Dark? It's overcast, but it's not dark."

"It is in the story, all right?"

"Fine. It's *your* story."

"Damn right. Do you want to hear the rest of it?"

"Of course. But why don't we talk to people first? They might give you some ideas."

Bo could see the sense in that, though he hated to stop when he was on a roll. Nevertheless, he said, "You're right. Are you ready?"

"I think so. Would you like to talk to Dolly first?"

"Why not? You want me to have Franklin send her in?"

"Not until you clean up that mess in the sink!"

V

Dolly was tall and slender, with black hair, black eyes, and pale skin. Her eyes were red now, as if she had been crying. She was sitting at the sturdy oak kitchen table across from Janice. Bo was sitting at the end, in the only chair with arms.

Dolly explained that after hearing the shots, though she didn't know at the time what they were, she thought she had better see if something had happened in the lower part of the house.

"It was such an *unusual* noise," she said. "And when I got downstairs, there was Father, lying on the rug."

Her voice broke, and she looked down at the table-top. Janice reached across the table to take her hand. "Let's not talk about that part. Tell me about what you heard before the shots."

Dolly looked up. "Before the shots?"

"Yes." Janice prodded. "Did you hear anything? The door knocker? Anything at all?"

"Mr. Franklin asked me that, too." Dolly frowned thoughtfully. "I told him no. I didn't hear a thing."

"Think hard," Janice coaxed, and Bo wondered what she was getting at. "Close your eyes and try to imagine that you're back in your room. You're sewing, and the house is quiet. Can you hear anything at all?"

For a full minute Dolly was quiet. Then she said, "Maybe ... I hear voices. But not loud. It's hard to hear things up there on the second floor."

"What kind of voices?" Janice asked.

"Angry maybe. I'm just not sure."

Bo was sure. And he was elated. It was just exactly as he'd thought. An argument. Could he plot, or could he plot?

Dolly left the kitchen and Jimmy came in. Though he had just completed his law degree, he looked more like a mechanic than an attorney. He was wearing overalls with black grease stains on them and a blue work shirt that looked even worse than the overalls. There was even a smear of grease on his face.

Jimmy told them even less than Dolly had. From the garage he could hear nothing at all.

"Were the garage doors open?" Janice asked.

Jimmy told her that they weren't. "Too windy," he explained.

Bo didn't know the point of that exchange, either. What difference did it make whether the garage doors were open? But he didn't worry about it. He had everything figured now. He pictured the killer climb-ing carefully down the drainpipe, then slipping quietly away through the dripping pecan trees in back of the house.

Jimmy couldn't tell them anything else. "I wish I had heard someone," he said. "Maybe I could have done something."

Bo didn't think he really seemed all that concerned.

"Or maybe you would have been shot, too," Janice told him.

"Maybe." Jimmy nodded, and then left the room.

Jeffrey Walton was next. He came in with his hand out and a smile like a used car salesman. He was wearing a light gray wool suit that Bo figured had set him back about three Sam Fernando royalty statements. There was a dark stain on one knee of what should have been immaculate trousers.

"I'm Ray's business manager," Walton said. "He often told me about you two. I'm sorry we have to meet under these circumstances."

Bo shook Walton's hand. "It's not your fault."

"How long have you been associated with Ray?" Janice asked.

Walton thought for a moment. "Fifteen years, give or take a few months. We did a lot of business together."

"But things haven't gone so well lately, have they?" Janice asked.

Walton lost his smile. "That's correct. The market hasn't behaved as a lot of us thought it would."

Bo didn't know a thing about that, and he didn't think Janice did, either. Neither of them had any money in the market, though the Gentleman Sleuth books were beginning to pay off. Bo had a fairly sizable savings account, and it was time he started thinking of other kinds of investments.

"I don't suppose Ray was happy about that."

"Neither was I," Walton told Janice.

"Is that your camel's hair coat in the hall closet? It's very nice."

"Yes, it's mine. I'm glad you like it."

"Can you think of anyone who might have wanted

Ray dead?" Bo was getting tired of all the irrelevant questions Janice was asking.

"Several people." Walton looked over his shoulder toward the other part of the house. "I don't want to talk about anyone, but—"

"Never mind," Janice interrupted. "We know that Ray wasn't on the best of terms with his children."

"I meant anyone outside the family," Bo continued.

"I really can't think of anyone," Walton admitted. "Ray was on pretty good terms with everyone."

He gave it some more thought at Bo's urging, but he still couldn't come up with any names, so Janice asked if there were any cars in the street when he drove up.

"I didn't see any."

Bo didn't see the point of that one. He started to say so, but Janice was already asking Walton to send in Hank Rollins.

Rollins was tall and slender, with a weathered face and hands. He was wearing a flannel shirt, a denim jacket, and faded jeans. Janice asked him to tell what had happened earlier.

"I heard the shots." Rollins's voice quavered slightly. "Two of 'em. I got to the house quick as I could, but I was cuttin' some dead limbs out of those pecan trees in back, and it took me a second or two to get movin'. I looked in through those funny doors, and I could see Mr. Ray was lyin' right there on the floor."

"And there was no one else in the room?"

"Not a single, solitary soul, ma'am. I broke out one of them little glass panes and opened the doors. I seen right off there wasn't a thing I could do."

"And then someone was knocking at the front door?" she asked.

"Yep. It was that Mr. Walton. I let him in, and by that time Miss Dolly was in the library. She seen her daddy lyin' there and busted out screamin'. Mr. Walton took her in the den to try calmin' her down, and I called the cops."

"Did you see any cars on the street when you opened the door?"

"No, ma'am. Just that big Lincoln that Mr. Walton drives."

Bo finally figured out why Janice had asked Jimmy about the garage doors. She wanted to know if he could see the street. But he still didn't see why she wanted to know. By the time he'd thought about it for a few seconds, Janice was asking Rollins what exactly Walton did when he went into the library.

"Well, that's hard to say. Miss Dolly was standin' there, and Walton got down on his knees to see if Mr. Ray was dead."

So, the dark stain on the knee of his slacks was blood, Bo mused.

"I hope he didn't get any blood on his expensive topcoat."

Rollins frowned and shook his head. "Oh, he wasn't wearin' any coat."

Bo wondered about the man who'd gone up the chimney. He ought to be easy to spot. His coat and pants would have soot all over them. He hoped the police were doing a search of the neighborhood.

When Janice was through with Rollins, he left the room, his shoulders slumped as if he were carrying something heavy. He looked as if he were the only one who was really sad about Ray Thompson's death.

"Are you finished talking to them?" Bo asked.

"I think so. Are you ready to play Sam Fernando?"

"Huh? What are you talking about?"

"I'm talking about calling all the suspects together in the den and pulling the killer out of a hat."

"That's a mixed metaphor. At least I think it is. I figured you for a better writer than that."

"You know what I mean. Are you ready?"

"You mean you're *not* kidding? Do you have any idea what you're talking about?"

Janice smiled. "Of course I do. Don't you?"

"The chimney! It has to be the chimney."

"Don't be silly. All that soot? The police must've

caused that when they searched it. You don't think they'd miss somethin' that obvious, do you?"

"Rats," Bo sighed. "Probably not."

"And if the killer kicked out the soot, wouldn't Mr. Rollins or Mr. Walton or Dolly have noticed it fallin' out of the chimney? Wouldn't they have heard him scrabblin' around in there?"

"I guess so." Bo was quite disappointed. It had all seemed so logical.

"You get it now, though, don't you?"

Bo didn't. Not quite, anyway, so Janice told him.

VI

Jimmy Thompson sat uncomfortably in an over-stuffed leather-covered chair that looked as if it belonged in a lawyer's office instead of a den. Jeffery Walton and Dolly sat on the long floral-covered couch. Hank Rollins sat in a wingback chair. Franklin, Bo, and Janice stood near the center of the room. Detective Simmons was standing at one end of the couch. It was time for the big moment.

Franklin had everyone's attention as he began speaking. "As you all know, Miss Langtry and Mr. Wagner are more or less experts in unusual murder cases like this, and they were also friends of the victim. I asked them to come over and give us the benefit of their expertise, and they tell me they know who killed Mr. Thompson."

Everyone looked a little shocked at that bit of news, and Jimmy Thompson leaned forward. "Are you joking? They're just writers, not trained investigators. They don't know anything about real life."

Bo had never particularly disliked Jimmy before, but now he saw that, given the opportunity, he could develop quite an antipathy to the young man.

"They may be writers, but they do know something about locked rooms. Mr. Wagner?"

Bo straightened and tried to look dignified in the Sam Fernando manner. But it wasn't easy while wearing a green shirt and a red jacket with jeans that had a hole in one knee. Sam Fernando wouldn't have been caught dead in any such getup. Bo thought Janice would have been much more impressive in the role, but she wanted him to do it.

"When you have a murder like this," Bo began solemnly, "you have to consider the usual things: motive, means, and opportunity. The problem with this particular case is that there doesn't seem to have *been* an opportunity." He paused dramatically, just as Sam Fernando often did. "But there was."

"Baloney!" Jimmy blurted. "There was no one in the room when Rollins came in, and my father was already dead."

"But there was someone in the room," Bo returned. "Or there had been."

Jimmy was still belligerent. "So how did he get in? Dolly didn't ever hear the knocker. Neither did I."

"You tell 'em, Janice." Bo wanted her to get some of the glory. After all, it was *her* idea. That way, she could also take some of the blame if it all turned out to be wrong.

"No one heard the knocker because no one used it," Janice continued. "We didn't use it when we came. Lieutenant Franklin was waiting at the door for us, and he saw us coming through the glass panes on either side. Ray was waiting for someone he badly wanted to see. When that person arrived, Ray was at the door and opened it for him."

"And who was this imaginary person?" Walton asked.

"You should know," Bo said. "It was you."

Walton half rose from the couch. "That's ridiculous."

"No, it isn't. Ray let you in. I think he suspected that you'd been jiggling his accounts, maybe stealing from him. He told me and Janice that he was thinking about letting Jimmy and Dolly have a little more money, and I figure that when he discussed that with you, you told him that the money wasn't available. He wanted to know why. Maybe you stalled him for a while, but you couldn't put him off forever. He demanded a face-to-face meeting and an accounting. There was an argument. Maybe you threatened him. He went for the pistol he kept in his desk. You took it away from him, and then you shot him."

Walton was breathing hard. "Utterly ridiculous. You can't prove a word of it."

"There were no other cars on the street," Bo went on. "Therefore the killer either walked here, which is pretty unlikely in this weather, or he drove. Only one person drove."

"He could have been here already," Walton pointed out. He was getting his breathing back under control. "What about Dolly and Jimmy? What about Rollins?"

"I guess it could be one of them. But it wasn't. Tell him what gave him away, Janice."

"That topcoat you said was yours," she told Walton. "It's hanging in the closet. You took it off when you came in the first time, and you didn't have time to put it back on. Maybe you didn't even think about it, but you were mighty calm if you ask me. Calm enough to know that if you hurried, you could get back outside before anybody got here to investigate the shots. Then you could bang on the door and pretend you were just arrivin'. But Mr. Rollins will swear that you didn't have the coat on when he let you in. Won't you, Mr. Rollins?"

"I sure as to God will!" Rollins looked as if he would like to come out of the wingback chair and throttle Walton right there in the library.

"You still can't prove I killed him," Walton said. "There's no weapon."

"Not right now," Bo said. "But it couldn't be far. In fact, I'd bet it's jammed up the drain spout right out there by the front door. The one that looks to be stopped up."

That was when Walton jumped for him.

Bo squared off and raised his fists, much as he imagined Mike Hammer would have done in a similar situation had his .45 not been handy, but Bo didn't get to test his talent for violence. Detective Simmons put a big hand on Walton's collar and jerked him back down on the couch.

"There, there," Simmons cautioned. "None of that."

Walton snorted and tried to twist out of Simmons's grip, but he couldn't. He sat and stared balefully at Bo and Janice.

Dolly was looking at Walton strangely. "I don't understand," she said. "Why didn't he just get in his car and leave?"

"He was probably afraid someone would see him," Bo said, though he wasn't sure about that part. Janice hadn't told him what she thought.

Now, however, she did. "It was probably because he was afraid someone here would know that he had an appointment with Ray today. I don't think anyone did, but what if Ray had written it on his calendar? Walton could have justified being late, but he might not have been able to explain things if he didn't show up at all."

"It's on his calendar, all right," Franklin said. Then he called the two policemen who had been in the library earlier and told one of them to check the drainpipe. The man was back in less than a minute.

"It's in there, all right. I didn't want to touch it."

"We'll get it later," Franklin said. "It's not going anywhere, and those fingerprints won't wash off easily. Take Mr. Walton to the station, boys."

"With pleasure," Simmons said, jerking Walton up off the couch.

Walton tried to say something, but his voice was too choked by Simmons's grip on his collar to be intelligible. Bo figured that was just as well.

VII

While they were driving back to the house to finish work on their book, Bo sulked behind the wheel.

After they had gone a few blocks, Janice said, "You don't seem too happy that we cracked the case."

Bo stared out moodily through the windshield. It was no longer raining, but the sky was still heavy with clouds. The radio was playing "Walking Along" by the Diamonds, a number that would normally have cheered him up. But not this time.

"I didn't crack anything. You did."

"What difference does that make? We made sure that Ray's killer didn't get away with it."

Bo turned his head to look at her. "I didn't make sure. I thought all the time that it was the chimney." He faced front again.

"That doesn't matter. You were looking at it like a story. I was looking at it like real life. Besides, we're a team. Partners. I learned everything I know about figuring out plots from reading your outlines. Even if the spelling is atrocious."

"Really? You mean that?"

"Sure I do. I couldn't have figured it out without knowing the way you think about things."

"Maybe you don't need me anymore, then."

"Now you know better than that. Didn't I say we were a team? Just like Crosby and Hope."

"Right! Ruth and Gehrig."

"Martin and Lewis."

"They broke up."

"Well, we won't. Just like Burns and Allen."

Bo laughed. "Abbott and Costello."

"Frick and Frack," Janice said, joining in his laughter.

"Damon and Pythias."

"Aeneas and Achates."

"Sodom and Gomorrah," Bo added, hopefully.

"Forget it, bub!"

But Bo thought about *it* all the way home. Especially since the scent of her perfume seemed so much stronger inside the confines of the car. And then there was the "timpting" blond curve of her ponytail. And the way she began squirming deliciously the more he looked.

No Simple Solution
Jan Grape

Jan Grape is an accomplished mystery short-story writer. Her "Whatever Has to Be Done" was chosen for the honor roll in *The Year's Best Mystery and Suspense Stories 1993.* You can also add to your reading enjoyment her stories in: *Santa Clues, Mysteries for Mother, Deadly Allies II,* and *Mickey Spillane Presents: Vengeance Is Hers.*

Jan, with her husband Elmer, co-chaired the Southwest Mystery/Suspense Convention and own Mysteries & More, Inc., a bookstore in Austin, Texas. Jan is currently working on her first novel.

Austin is where you'll find PI's Jenny Gordon and C. J. Gunn. These two accomplished partners take on a case that proves, with murder, there is "No Simple Solution" . . .

I

"It sounded like an open-and-shut case to me when I first heard about it. And besides, who can blame the guy?" I said. "If my five-year-old child had been killed in a drive-by shooting, I might have done the same thing Eloy Stewart did." The drive-by shooter had been tried and acquitted and that's when Mr. Stewart took matters into his own hands, allegedly killing Benito Alvarez, age twenty, three days ago. Also killed was a sixteen-year-old girl who'd been with Alvarez.

C. J. snorted. "No *might have* in my mind, Jenny. I'd have gone after the little turd with my bare hands," she said. Her full name is Cinnamon Jemima Gunn, but only close friends know her secret. When she gets that haughty look she reminds me of photos I've seen of Nefertiti.

C. J. and I have owned and operated a detective agency since my ex-cop-turned-private eye husband,

Tommy Gordon, was killed three years ago. We had teamed up back then to catch the killer.

C. J.'s mind held no gray areas when it came to murdered children—the innocents—everything was in stark black and white. She'd learned this philosophy the hard way. Harsh maybe, but her own little girl had been killed a few years ago, along with her policeman husband, and anytime she heard of a child being killed she was immediately ready to hang the guilty herself. I'll admit I felt almost as strongly as my partner did. And we don't always see eye-to-eye about a lot of things.

The Austin and national news had told and retold the story of how Eloy Stewart, his wife, and little girl had gone to a downtown restaurant—a totally innocent evening out—and after eating had walked to the side parking lot on the way to their car.

Two rival gangs were chasing each other down the street, both groups in automobiles. The lead gang-banger's car stopped directly in front of the Mexican food restaurant and started firing at the approaching rival's car. A stray bullet hit the Stewart's little girl, killing her instantly. No one else had been injured.

Both gangs claimed the other side fired the fatal bullet. And too many questions about the bullet's trajectory mystified the jurors, so Benito Alvarez had won an acquittal.

The same day we'd been discussing the Alvarez case, Stewart's father came to see us at G & G Investigations, and asked for our assistance. We both agreed to talk to him.

Albert Stewart arrived shortly after lunch. "I ain't saying he wouldn't of killed that boy," he said. "Eloy admits he went over there with that in mind, but I'll never believe he'd of killed Alvarez's girlfriend."

"The police found him standing over the bodies with a gun in his hand," C. J. reminded him.

The older man was a smaller, diminished version of the son I'd watched during the local news coverage. His shoulders were stooped as if just carrying his head around was too much to bear, but there was still a fire in his brown eyes and a strength in his seventy-ish voice. And you could also see where the son got his good looks. Something in their manner reminded me of farming folks, raw-boned, sturdy people much like the pioneering Europeans—Germans, Slavs, Poles, or perhaps the Scandinavians—who had settled central Texas in the early 1830s.

They weren't farmers, however, Albert Stewart was retired from managing an automotive parts store and Eloy had taught junior high school, at least until his daughter was killed.

"It weren't his gun." Mr. Stewart's speech was pure country.

"I spoke with Lieutenant Hays of Homicide," I said. I'd called the lieutenant for details just before escorting Albert Stewart into the inner office.

Larry Hays and my late husband graduated from the Austin Police Academy in the same class, part-nered for ten years on the force, and remained friends when Tommy left APD to become a private eye. Larry treated me like he was my big brother and I often asked his advice in police matters, although I didn't always take it.

I continued, "He says a second gun was taken from Eloy which hadn't been fired. But the one found in Eloy's hand was definitely the one used to kill Benito and Emily."

"I know how it looks. Bad as it can get, I guess. Eloy says Benito and Emily were already dead when he got there. But he also says just when he got out of his car, he saw a blond-haired girl dartin' out from behind a house two doors down from Alvarez's. When she got on the sidewalk and saw Eloy, she ran. He figures she saw who done the killing or maybe she was there and got skeered and ran. If you could find this girl, maybe she'd testify. Maybe she could verify that after seeing him, he didn't have time to do the killing before the police showed up."

"And what do the police say about the girl?" I

asked and wondered why it didn't occur to the Stewarts that the running girl had done the killing.

"They didn't care to listen. Far as they're concerned they have their killer and the case's closed," Mr. Stewart said. "One officer did say if we knew something to clear Eloy, we oughta tell his lawyer."

"Who is your son's lawyer?" C. J. wanted to know.

"The court appointed this young gal. Eloy's flat broke since he ain't worked in over a year. My daughter-in-law went back up to St. Louis to stay with her family several months ago. She was here for Alvarez's trial but soon as that was over, she took off again. What little savings they had is gone. I'm trying to raise money for his bail myself, but my wife's in a nursing home. Her expenses are huge and Medicare doesn't pay for custodial care, so there's not much I can do."

The lines around the older man's mouth and eyes showed his grief. "This lady lawyer's a nice person," he said, "but she's overworked and don't have time to be bothered. She told Eloy to plead guilty to jus-ti-fi-able homicide and the judge'd probably go easy. Even that prosecutor said he'd recommend leniency if Eloy pled guilty. Said Eloy'd probably only serve two, three years at the most."

"But he won't plead?" I looked at the old man and wondered how to get him to understand we probably couldn't help. What he was telling us was too vague, too iffy.

"No way. Eloy says he didn't do it, Miz Gordon, Miz Gunn," he said, looking at each of us in turn. "I'm just a countrified-foolish-old man, but I believe my son. I knowed if Eloy'd killed them two—he'd say so. He'd go to prison or take whatever punishment was handed out to him."

"I think you're trying to be a good father," I said, "and help your son." But I couldn't see a killer leaving the girl alive as a witness. "A man seeking revenge . . ."

He was nodding his gray head. "If Eloy'd walked in there and found Benito alone, he might not've hesitated pulling that trigger. But with that girl there—an innocent bystander—another child would die for no reason. He wouldn't do that to another mother. To another family. He's just not capable."

Maybe, maybe not, but we said we'd look into the matter for him. After a small argument—with us trying to give him a discount and him protesting weakly—he paid a reduced two-day retainer and left.

"Guess I was wrong about this being an open-and-shut case."

"You got that right, girlfriend," said my partner. She was thoughtful for a few moments. "Something about that old man bothers me. He's too, too . . ."

"Too what? I'll swear, C. J., you'd be suspicious of your own grandmother."

"My grandmother was a bootlegger and a hooker. I wouldn't trust her as far as I could throw her."

"I don't believe that. Too bad she isn't alive to defend herself." C. J. and I have worked together three years and we're close, but she doesn't dwell in the past or talk about it much.

"Look it up in the newspapers if you don't believe me. Or better yet, ask my mother. She'll tell you."

"One of these days I just might," I told her, knowing full well I wouldn't. It was more fun to think her granny had been a character and added to C. J.'s mystique.

Since many police officers have a negative opinion of private investigators, it wasn't easy for us to get permission to visit Eloy Stewart in jail. Lieutenant Hays helped to arrange things from the police department's standpoint and then we tackled Stewart's attorney, Jacqui Johnston. I don't know if it was because of her heavy work schedule or what, but for a moment she acted as if she didn't remember him. Hard to believe with all the media attention, but I gave her the benefit of a doubt when she got us on the visitor's list.

Travis County Jail is next door to the county courthouse. Some pretrial inmates are kept there, some are sent to the Del Valle jail out near Bergstrom Air

Force Base, and some stay downtown at the city jail. The inmates placement has to do with certain aggressive cases going here and nonaggressives going there and attempting to keep a racial balance, but I'll never understand how it's determined who goes where.

Eloy Stewart was brought into a small interview room with a table and three folding chairs where we waited. He was wearing the dark-green clothing, made like a scrub suit with TCJ for Travis County Jail stenciled on the breast pocket, which is worn by inmates at this location.

Stewart was forty-one, around five-foot-ten, and weighed close to 180 pounds—most of it solid muscle. The dark-green scrub suit made his hazel eyes look greener. They were set too close together to be attractive, but his dark eyelashes were long and to die for. He smiled, but only with his mouth. I'd guess he didn't have much to smile about.

"It's like my father told you," he said in a monotone. "I went over there ready to punish Benito. I found him and the girl dead. I remember feeling angry because Benito had died and I didn't get to see his face when it happened."

Eloy had a three-day stubble and bloodshot eyes. "Someone beat me to it but only by a few minutes because the girl made a gurgling sound just as I entered the room. I felt her pulse and there wasn't any. That bothered me . . . a lot."

"Did you call 9-1-1?" I asked.

"No. She was dead and I, uh, I wasn't thinking too clearly."

"Why did you pick up that gun—the murder weapon?" C. J. asked.

"I don't remember doing it. The next thing I knew, the police charged in the front and back doors and told me to drop the gun and get down on the floor. I didn't even hear them drive up or knock or anything."

"Tell us about that girl," I said, taking out a notebook. "The one your father thinks might help clear you."

"She was just a girl. Blond hair put up in uh, a double ponytail thing—you know one bunch tied off near the top of her head and the long part tied off separately. She wore shorts and a pair of red cowboy boots. I couldn't see her face too well, but she looked young and pretty. At least that was my impression."

"How young?" I asked, making notes.

"About the same age as Emily Jimenez, sixteen, seventeen," he said, closing his eyes. They popped open quickly as if the memory was too vivid and he shivered. "It was horrible seeing them like that."

"Did you see this blond girl go into a house or getting into a car?" asked C. J.

"No, I didn't."

C. J. and I looked at each other and I knew we thought the same. We weren't getting much enlightenment here.

I asked about gunpowder residue and he said the tests were inconclusive.

"Uh, I guess I should tell you . . ." He hesitated.

"Anything you think that might help," I urged. "To be honest we don't have much that can—"

Eloy interrupted. "You should know how much I wanted Benito dead. I doubt you can understand that, but losing a child is something that'll make you totally crazy."

C. J. nodded—she understood. Her daughter had been killed ten years ago, back when she was working for the Pittsburgh police department. She had caused some heavy grief for an organized drug syndicate. They had retaliated by planting a bomb in her car one Sunday morning. Her husband decided to use her car when he went to buy doughnuts and took their little girl with him. There wasn't much of either one left to bury.

Since my husband had been murdered, I could sympathize, but I couldn't imagine the grief of losing a child.

"I couldn't eat or sleep. I couldn't give comfort to my wife, I couldn't take comfort from her or anyone.

My life felt like it was over. I still don't have much of a life but I do feel some responsibility for my parents. If anything happens to me ..." He let his voice trail off and began tracing his right index finger on the tabletop, making circles around and around in the same spot.

"We'd wanted a kid so much, we'd tried unsuccessfully for thirteen years and when my wife got pregnant, when Rachel Ann was finally born it was like a miracle." He kept tracing that circle and I wondered if he would wear a groove in the table.

"Rachel Ann was ... precious," he said. "Smart and funny and the cutest little thing you ever saw."

His voice broke and his eyes filled. He shook his head and rubbed them with his left hand. I thought he was probably a man who couldn't handle anyone seeing him cry and, I was right. He got up and walked over to stand facing the wall.

When he was back in control and resumed speaking, his voice cracked but he stayed where he was—staring at the wall. "I have trouble even now believing she's dead and it's been thirteen months."

Neither C. J. nor I spoke. There was nothing for us to say, his wound was still too raw, too painful.

In a few seconds Eloy began a slow pace around the room, making a complete circuit and another and another. "I keep telling myself I probably wouldn't have killed Benito if he'd been alive when I got there. But I just don't know because he was already dead. I didn't have to stand there and decide whether or not to pull the trigger. I know I wanted him dead. I thought it would ease my pain if he died but I was wrong. It didn't stop it and I guess it never will."

"But what about Emily, the girl with him?" I asked.

"No one wants to talk about that. The police think that I killed her to keep from leaving a witness. Even if she'd testified—it wouldn't have mattered—I still wouldn't have shot her. My plan all along was to confess and turn myself in."

He stopped pacing and looked at me without batting an eye and I believed him. "If I'd killed either of them," he stated, "I'd take my punishment because I don't much care what happens to me. But being accused when I'm innocent is a different story."

He laughed then, a hollow laugh, "Guess that sounds like I do care about something. A kind of survival instinct probably. And maybe eventually I really will care again."

I'd never have predicted what happened next in a million years. C. J. walked over to Eloy Stewart and talked quietly to him for some minutes, then said in a voice loud enough for me to hear, "Don't worry, Mr. Stewart, we'll find that girl and clear you."

She's the one usually accusing me of letting emotions get in the way of my good judgment, but I knew she'd been touched by his little girl's death. And yes, my emotions were involved too, what can I say? I'm a sentimental slob.

We were about to leave; Stewart was being escorted down a hallway by one of the deputies from the Sheriff's Department (they run the jails in Austin) and C. J. and I were partway through the security door when Eloy stopped and asked the guard if he could say one more thing to us. "Make it quick," the deputy replied.

"I just remembered. Something was weird about that girl."

"Weird? How?" I asked.

"I can't put my finger on it ... maybe." He shook his head. "No, I just don't know ..."

The deputy said, "Come along. You can talk again tomorrow."

"See if you can get permission to phone our office. Just give us anything else you might think of," C. J. called to Eloy.

"I'll call tomorrow," he said.

But something in his voice made me wonder if he would.

II

After a brief discussion we decided to canvass the neighborhood around the Alvarez house and see if we could turn up a witness who had seen the girl. The girl seemed to be Stewart's only chance. Maybe folks had remembered something they hadn't told the police last week or we might find someone who'd not wanted to get involved before. It happens more times than the police will ever admit.

C. J. likes to drive when we travel together but her new pickup was in the shop having its five-thousand-mile checkup. I'm a good driver, Tommy had raced cars in his youth and he'd taught me defensive driving, but she complained when I drove. I think it's a control thing with her. She grumbled while I unlocked my silver Omni, but she got in and we headed south on Loop 1, known to the locals as Mo-Pac (so named for its proximity to the Missouri-Pacific Railway).

The late afternoon sky was still so bright it hurt to look at it. The heat was never-ending this summer and although the Midwest was washing away in floods, we hadn't had a decent rain in months. Luckily, the Omni had a good air conditioner and I kept the blower on high while we listened to a Garth Brooks tape.

The neighborhood the Alvarez family lived in consisted of small frame houses on Austin's south side, not far from South Congress Avenue. It was a mixture of decent-looking little homes with others sliding into total neglect.

The corner house, the one young Alvarez had died in, fit the latter category. It was painted a pale green that reminded me of that sickly color that used to always be used for hospital walls. A water-cooled air-conditioning unit sat in the front window, dripping and leaving a limestone calcification on the wall.

An old car with no wheels, its headlights rusted and falling out, was on blocks at the side of the house next to the street. The grass was dead, but with the heat we'd had this summer, that wasn't unusual in any part of town.

C. J. and I parked and walked to the door on the south side of the Alvarez house. Logically, the girl must have gone through this backyard to come out two doors down. An attempt had been made to keep this house among the decent-looking. The white paint was probably no more than two years old. New porch steps made of treated lumber had been installed, but were as yet unpainted. Two ferns hung in baskets along the porch's outer edge and three pots of peppers were on the floor near the front door.

C. J. knocked. A lady with a face as wrinkled as an unironed cotton blouse pushed aside the lacy curtain at the front window and peered out. She must have been satisfied with what she saw because a moment later she opened the door. Her hair was iron gray, but her dark eyes sparkled with vitality. "Are y'all from the newspapers?" She had an artificial-looking smile pasted on her face.

"No, ma'am," said C. J. "We're private investigators. I'm C. J. Gunn and this is Jenny Gordon. Would you have a moment to talk?"

The woman frowned briefly before she said, "Oh my, y'all better come inside before some of those gang boys see you out here, although I guess with Benito dead they won't be paying so much attention."

She said her name was Juanita Hidalgo and she led us into a front parlor with dark-wood paneling and velvet upholstered furniture. Crochet doilies were pinned to the backs and armrests of the chairs and sofa, and an afghan made of bright-colored yarn covered the back of a platform rocker. A small religious shrine stood in the far corner. C. J. and I sat on the sofa and Mrs. Hidalgo insisted we have some fresh lemonade she'd just made.

"I feel sorry for Mrs. Alvarez," she said. It had taken her only a moment to bring the refreshments as if the tray had already been prepared. "She's had a rough time. Her husband ran off and left her with six little ones. She does the best she can, works all the time, but that means her kids never have much supervision. The older ones are grown now and they're all good kids except for that one—Benito. He always was mean. Running with a bad crowd, getting in trouble with the police. I knew he'd cause his mother grief one day.''

She handed over our glasses and offered homemade sugar cookies which looked too good to refuse. She placed the tray on the coffee table and sat in the rocker opposite us, rocking slowly. "It's been so exciting around here, neighbors, reporters, and policemen and, now, you young ladies. I haven't had so much company in years." The pasted-on smile was back in place. "What was it you wanted to ask?"

I glanced at C. J., and saw my partner's tiny shrug. "We're trying to help clear the man accused of killing Benito and his friend, Emily," I said. "Mr. Stewart says the boy and girl were already dead when he got there." Mrs. Hidalgo had been nodding as I spoke but didn't interrupt. It suddenly dawned on me that her weird smile had to do with the fact she wore dentures.

I continued, "Mr. Stewart saw a girl. He thinks she came from the Alvarez's house, crossed your backyard, and came out in front of the house on the other side of you. He's hoping the girl could say what time she saw him and help prove his story. Do you know a blond-haired girl who lives down that way?"

She shook her head. "No. But boys and girls always went in and out all the time visiting Benito."

"Were you at home the day the shooting took place?" C. J. asked. "Last Saturday?"

"Oh my, no. Saturday's my shopping day. My youngest son picked me up early and after shopping, took me back to his place for dinner. I never get home until late on Saturday." She glanced at the array of family photographs lined up on the credenza next to the sofa. "My children," she said, proudly. "They all live in Del Rio except for Tony, my youngest."

"Nice family," I said sipping the lemonade. I real-

ized I'd been counting on her, she was the type to
see everything in the neighborhood. I swallowed my
disappointment and it tasted like the drink, a little
tart.

"I'd like to help clear that young man," she said.
"I feel sorry for him losing his little girl like that and
then being arrested for Benito's murder. Oh my, it
just doesn't seem fair."

She stopped the rocker and looked at me. "I'll just
bet he didn't do it—I'll bet it was one of those awful-
looking boys that come around all the time that shot
Benito. They have guns and knives and no telling what
all. I'm sure they're all gangsters."

"Do they bother you?" C. J. asked. "Or do damage
to your house?"

The old woman laughed out loud. "Oh, my goodness, no. You should see my Tony. He's big and strong
and he warned Benito a long time ago. Told that boy
he'd pull his head off and beat him with it if I ever
got mistreated. They throw their beer cans and trash
in my yard, but they know better than to cause me
trouble."

Mrs. Hidalgo continued talking, telling about the
gunshots that filled her neighborhood at night, especially on the weekends. "I'm sorry I haven't been
much help." She stopped the rocker again and this
time she wasn't smiling.

"Well," I said, "we need to visit some other neighbors and we probably shouldn't take any more of
your time."

"Time is all I have most days and it gets lonesome
when you're alone. I know Tony has his own life to
live so I make sure I have other things to do: sewing,
knitting, crocheting, reading, yard work, my baking,
and housecleaning. I don't want to be a burden on
anyone."

"I'm sure you'd never be a burden," I said.

"Your cookies were delicious," C. J. said as we
stood.

"Would you like the recipe?" Mrs. Hidalgo asked.

"If it's not too much trouble," said C. J.

Mrs. Hidalgo went to the credenza and opened a drawer, taking out an index card. The recipe was already written under the heading of Juanita's Sugar Cookies. She handed the card to C. J. and walked with us to the front door.

"I wonder," she said. "Maybe the girl Mr. Stewart saw was that little blond-haired girl Benito dated for a while. I don't know why she doesn't come around anymore."

"Was Emily Jimenez his current girlfriend?" I asked.

"She might have been special, but Benito had many girlfriends. They were always chasing after him. But that blonde hung around here the longest, up until a few months ago."

"Do you know the girl's name?"

She furrowed her brow. "Seems like I heard them call her Stacy. But I don't know her last name. You could ask Mrs. Alvarez, she might know."

"Did Stacy ever wear cowboy boots?" I asked.

"She sure did, red ones. Wore them all the time. Looked funny too with her shorts, but young folks dress wild and crazy these days."

"Well, thanks for your help and for the refreshments."

"And for the recipe," said C. J. "I can hardly wait to try it."

"They'll be good every time you make them," Mrs. Hidalgo promised. "Everybody raves about them."

"Thanks again," we said, and I felt sorry knowing she was going to be lonesome for the rest of the day.

"What a character," I said. "But the poor soul is starved for company."

"Might be you or I someday, girlfriend," commented C. J. and it was a sobering thought.

We walked across the lawn and knocked on the door at the Alvarez house, but no one answered. As we stepped off the porch, a dark-haired boy about nine or ten years old came riding up the driveway on a beat-up old bicycle. "Hi! Are you looking for my mother? Need some ironing or housework done?"

"Is Mrs. Alvarez your mom?" C. J. asked.

"Yeah. But she ain't home now." He had put one foot down on the concrete, stopping the bike and stood straddling it.

"When will she be back?" I inquired.

"Tomorrow. She's staying with my sister who's getting a new baby."

We laughed and C. J. said, "We'll try to come back tomorrow."

We had already started toward the car when I stopped and walked back to where the boy was trying to turn the bicycle around. "Maybe you could help. I'm looking for Stacy. She was a friend of your, uh, Benito." C. J. continued to walk to my car and leaned against the fender while she waited.

"Yeah. I know Stacy. She worked at the Dairy Queen, but I don't think she does anymore."

"The Dairy Queen down on Ben White Boulevard?"

"Yeah, that's the one."

"Thanks," I said. "And your name is . . . ?"

"George Alvarez."

"Thanks, George. By the way, you're not staying here all by yourself with your mother gone, are you?"

"No. I'm staying down there with her." He pointed to a house three doors down and across the street.

I guess I looked funny because he grinned. "My sister lives there."

He hopped back up on the bike and peddled out into the street. "See you." He waved.

"Yeah, see you, George."

I told C. J. what George had said and we drove to the Dairy Queen, parked, and got out. "A hot-fudge sundae sounds good."

"You don't need one," C. J. said. "You just ate three large sugar cookies."

"I know I don't need one, but—"

"You don't have to explain it to me but remember

if you do eat ice cream you'll have to do an extra workout tomorrow."

It wasn't fair. She stands six feet tall in her stocking feet and is blessed with a body that never puts an extra ounce on it even if she eats like a football player. I'm only five feet six and every time I smell food I add another half-pound to my 125-pound weight.

When we got to the counter, I resisted temptation and asked to speak to the manager. He was a plump young man wearing glasses and had a bad case of acne. He told us Stacy's last name was Carson and gave us the girl's address in Westlake Hills. We left right after that so I wouldn't have to suffer hot-fudge deprivation.

C. J. took an Austin city map from the glove compartment to look up Stacy Carson's address as I drove west to pick up Loop 1 and headed north again.

Westlake Hills is what its name implies: it's west Austin, has a lake and hills. It also has canyons, twisting roads, and prime real estate with huge price tags.

"Pretty ritzy neighborhood," said C. J. "Wonder how Stacy got hooked up with the likes of Benito Alvarez? And why was she working at a Dairy Queen over in that part of town? We're miles from her stomping grounds."

"Maybe when we talk to her we'll find out."

Stacy Carson's house was as we expected. It *was* ritzy—a two-story white brick with Colonial pillars holding up the front porch. A spot of rust wouldn't dare appear on the red Mustang convertible which sat in the circular drive. Magnolia, elm, oak, and mimosa trees shaded the house. Late summer roses bloomed in a diamond-shaped landscaped area on one side in front of a gazebo. A gardener was pruning shrubbery and a sprinkler twirled lazily on the lush green lawn. Only people with big bucks can afford the upkeep on such a yard with the drought we'd been having.

A girl who looked about sixteen with her blond hair gathered up in a double ponytail answered the door-bell. She was wearing shorts and red cowboy boots.

Her face was pale as if she hadn't been outside all summer or maybe she'd been sick.

"Stacy?" I asked. When she nodded, I introduced us and said we were private investigators and would she be willing to answer a couple of questions.

"Private eyes like V. I. Warshawski, huh?" she asked. "I saw the movie."

"Well, not exactly," I said. "I'm not too crazy about baseball."

Stacy laughed and invited us inside.

"Who is it?" asked a soft voice coming from behind the girl. A young Mexican-American woman of about twenty-five came bustling up, her dark hair braided and hanging down her back. She wore a worried frown. "You shouldn't be up answering the door, Miss Stacy. That's my job and besides you shouldn't be out of bed yet." She turned to us. "We're not interested in buying anything today."

The woman reminded me of someone I'd seen recently and suddenly I realized she looked like an older version of George Alvarez, Benito's little brother. I glanced at C. J. and couldn't tell from her expression if she'd noticed or not.

"It's okay, Consuela," said Stacy. "They're private investigators not salespeople."

"Investigators?" The woman's concern was obvious. She placed a protective arm around the girl. "I don't know. I don't think your father ..."

"Screw my father," said Stacy and shrugged off the arm. "Come along, Ms. Gordon, Ms. Gunn." We followed her across the huge entry hall and she said to the woman in passing, "We don't want to be disturbed, Consuela. Except you could bring something cold to drink."

"Nothing for me," I said and C. J. echoed my statement.

"Fine. We'll go to the sunroom." Stacy led the way. I tried not to stare at the exquisite furniture, paintings, and expensive antique art objects decorating the huge living and dining rooms we passed.

The sunroom with glass all around, including the roof, was carpeted in a pale shade of blue and was large enough to hold the living/kitchen area in my apartment. One end of the room was devoted to plants, some in hanging baskets. The other end held an arrangement of chairs and love seats, each decorated in various shades of blue and white.

Stacy Carson invited us to sit while she sat opposite and asked, "How did you find me? I'll bet that old busybody next door told you about me, didn't she? She's always snooping where she shouldn't."

"Stacy," I said, "we're trying to locate a witness who was seen leaving the scene where a murder was committed."

Her face flushed, and she wouldn't look at me. In a minute, she composed herself and said breathlessly, "Wow. You investigate murderers? How exciting."

"Murder isn't glamorous or exciting," stated C. J. "It's quite an ugly, serious business."

"Of course, how thoughtless of me." She sounded contrite, hooked one finger in a wisp of hair that hung in front of her ear, and began twisting it. "You do know that some people just deserve to die."

"I understand you spent a great deal of time at the home of Benito Alvarez," I said. "Did he deserve to die?"

She flinched when she heard his name but she kept her cool.

"Yes, I was there once or twice. Consuela is, was, Benito's older sister. But I know nothing about his death. I feel sorry for his family. I even feel sorry for the poor man who killed Benito." She stopped twisting her hair, and shrugged. "But this doesn't have anything to do with me."

"Were you at the Alvarez's house the day Benito was killed?" C. J. asked.

She fidgeted a moment, gave a small shudder, and I saw goose bumps pop out on her arms.

"No. I don't believe so." She stood. "Is that all the questions you have?"

"How well did you know Benito?" I asked, but she ignored me.

"I must ask you to leave now," she said. "My father is returning home from Russia the day after tomorrow. We're having a welcome-home party."

"Your father's in Russia?" I stood. "Where is your mother?"

Her mouth grimaced slightly and one large tear rolled down her cheek. But I couldn't tell if her feelings were fake or genuine.

"My mother died last year."

"I'm sorry," I said, and meant it. My own mother had died when I was twelve and I still miss her, almost every day. It's not easy being a young girl with only a father to take care of you, and it would be even more difficult if your father had to be away. "Does your father travel often?"

Stacy nodded. "This time he's been gone for six months and I've missed, well, never mind."

"You don't stay here alone, do you?" C. J. asked as Stacy led us toward the front of the house.

"No, Consuela's my companion. She keeps me from being lonely."

"Thanks for your time." I was frustrated but knew we couldn't force her if she refused to answer our questions.

"Sure, and I hope you find your witness."

"Oh, we will," C. J. said. "In fact, I think we've already found her."

Stacy gave us an odd look as we turned and walked to my Omni.

"What was that?" I asked C. J. "Is she for real?"

"She was there that day. And she knows something."

"You'll get no argument from me, but we need to get a photo and see if Eloy can identify her."

"We need to find out all we can about her father, too."

"Can your computer do us any good?"

"You just watch me."

It was late. Time to pack it in and start fresh in the morning. I dropped C. J. at her place and promised to pick her up tomorrow since she didn't have transportation.

After I'd eaten dinner I called Albert Stewart to update him on our progress. "We've located the girl. Her name is Stacy Carson. She denies being there naturally, but we think she's lying. We need proof. Corroboration from another person would be helpful."

Stewart sounded like a happy man when we hung up.

III

C. J. called early the next morning and said her truck was ready. The car dealer's van would pick her up and she wouldn't need to wait for me.

I made a few phone calls from home which led to a trip out to Westlake High School. I received permission to talk to several of Stacy's classmates and one of her counselors who gave me some insights into the girl, and I picked up a school yearbook which had Stacy's photo in it from the school library.

When I got to the office shortly after noon, I told C. J. what I'd learned. When the school semester began a few weeks ago the counselor noticed Stacy had gained weight and wondered if the girl might be pregnant, but Stacy denied it. "The counselor told me she wouldn't swear to it, but that in her opinion Stacy was pregnant. Her school chums say she definitely was pregnant," I said. "She tried to hide it by wearing a panty girdle and big shirts. She's missed school the last two days and the rumor is that she's off to have the baby. The talk is that Benito Alvarez is her baby's father.

"The counselor also mentioned Stacy's father was a tyrant who made the girl's life miserable," I continued. "The only joy the girl had had was taking drama classes. She appeared in several community productions and was gaining a reputation as an actress."

"No wonder she was so cool," C. J. said. She had been busy, too, and found out via computer that Mr. Carson owned a successful development company and was currently involved in negotiations to develop some property in Russia. "He's been arrested for being drunk and disorderly a couple of times. In this country, not over there."

"Any history of family abuse?"

"Nothing's showed up yet, but I'll stay with it."

I retreated to my desk to clear up the paperwork left over from an employee check we'd done for a savings and loan.

Three hours later C. J. came into my office. "Tadah." She was wearing a Cheshire cat smile. "You remember little George telling you yesterday about his mother helping his sister and her baby?"

I nodded.

"How does Stacy strike you as the one having a baby?"

"Are you serious?"

"Yeah. Mrs. Alvarez and a midwife delivered Stacy's baby, but get this: the oldest Alvarez daughter plans to adopt it."

"How did you find that out?"

"A birth certificate for a little boy born the day before yesterday was registered to Stacy and Benito Alvarez," said C. J., "but the baby's being adopted by Rudy and Mary Alvarez Cantu."

"Okay, but how does this information get us to who killed Benito and Emily Jimenez?"

"I don't know yet," C. J. admitted, "but we'll find out."

The rest of the day brought us nothing new and we felt the frustration of being against a nearly impossible situation.

It was quitting time when the telephone rang and C. J. answered and listened before exploding. "Larry, you don't seriously believe him, do you?"

"What?" I asked, but she motioned me to silence.

"But it's ridiculous and you know it." C. J. listened for what seemed like a long time before saying, "Okay, but we identified the girl who Stewart saw that day—what do you want us to do?"

She listened again for a time and then told him, "Okay." She hung up and turned to me. "Albert Stewart just confessed to killing Benito Alvarez and Emily Jimenez."

"You're kidding! They don't believe him, do they? He must be trying to save Eloy."

"I know it and you know it but the District Attorney says he has to take the confession seriously. Mr. Stewart gave so many details of what happened that they all believe him."

"He knows all these details because Eloy happened upon the scene."

"Right."

"How can he explain away the fact his son was there with the gun in his hand?"

"He says his son probably figured out that he planned to kill Benito. Mr. Stewart says he left immediately after the shooting and in the meantime, Eloy showed up. Then Eloy found the bodies and the cops found Eloy."

"I can't see the old man killing Emily—for the same reason that Eloy couldn't kill her. She was only guilty of being at the wrong place at the wrong time."

An hour later we were fresh out of ideas except I did call Larry to ask if Eloy knew of his father's plans to go to see Alvarez. Larry said Eloy believed his father shot Benito.

All of this heavy thinking made us hungry and we decided a trip to the LaVista restaurant at the Hyatt to eat fajitas was in order.

The hotel is on Town Lake in downtown Austin. LaVista not only serves superb food, but has a great view. Several office buildings across the lake from the hotel were outlined in white, red, and gold lights, while the Franklin Savings is rimmed in blue. Their reflections shimmered in the water, but C. J. and I had too many questions about our suddenly incarcerated client to appreciate the sight. We did manage to enjoy the food—mostly because we'd been too busy to eat lunch.

"Albert Stewart has convinced everyone except you and me that he is guilty," I said. "Maybe he is."

"It doesn't make sense, if he were guilty why didn't he confess earlier and clear his son? Why did he hire us?" She frowned and asked, "Did you tell Albert we'd found Stacy?"

"Yes. Remember? I told you I called last night and gave him a progress report. That we were on the verge of proving Stacy was there and clearing Eloy."

"So what happened between last night and when he walked in the police station today and confessed?"

She answered her own question. "Albert must've talked to Stacy Carson. You don't suppose she told him ... Oh, shit."

"What, C. J.?"

"What if Albert went over there and begged her to help him get his son out of jail and she refused. I can see him threatening to tell her father that she'd been seeing Benito. Not exactly a young man her father would approve of, and I'm sure she wouldn't want Dad to know."

"A little emotional blackmail?"

"Possibly," C. J. said.

I counted back in my mind, "About the time Benito was killed had to be about the same time Stacy found out she was pregnant."

C. J. leaned back and thought briefly. "She goes to Benito, tells him she's pregnant with his child, and he doesn't even care. She was furious with him because he's dropped her and begun going with other girls. She goes over there hoping for a commitment of marriage and he laughs at her. Emily was there and he flaunts Emily in Stacy's face. Stacy flips out. She decides if she can't have him no one else can either and she kills them both."

"Maybe that's why she said some people deserve to die," I said. "Okay, Albert is at Stacy's house. They're arguing or he's pleading or whatever and she accidentally lets it slip that she killed Benito and Emily. And she cries and begs him not to tell."

"I'm sure she appealed to his sympathy by telling him about the baby," said C. J. "And about how she'd had to give him up and how she'd never see her baby if she turned herself in and wound up in prison."

"But Albert's concerned about his son and he's caught in the middle," I said. "He tells her he feels sorry for her but he needs his son free and he also has a sick wife in a nursing home to think about."

I thought for a moment. "So Miss Stacy comes up with a plan. She tells Albert that if Eloy takes the blame for her she'll pay him. She'll pay enough to make it worth his time if he's convicted and goes to prison. He might even get off, she says.

"Albert refuses," I continued. "He wants his son's freedom, but suddenly he realizes Stacy has offered him a way he can get his hands on some big money. He says he'll take the blame for the killing except he wants a guarantee of X amount of money."

"It would have to be enough money for Mrs. Stewart's medical expenses with enough left over so his son could have a new start at putting his life back together," C. J. said. "Maybe something like a million bucks."

"Her father can afford it if she can convince him to pony up," I said. "And Stacy could even have money of her own. Inherited from her mother's estate."

We knew it was pure speculation, but it sounded good. We decided to have a talk with Larry Hays about the whole case. He answered his pager quickly and agreed to meet us at the LaVista in ten minutes. We ordered coffee while we waited.

It was closer to fifteen minutes when I spotted Larry riding the escalator up to the second-floor restaurant. He's a tall, lanky man, pushing forty-five with sandy-colored hair, hazel eyes, and size thirteen shoes. Tonight, he looked about as tired as I'd ever seen him. "Rough day, huh?"

"I'd tell you about it, but none of it was pleasant." He sat next to me. "I haven't eaten all day or stopped more than five minutes for that matter."

After the waiter had taken his order for a cheeseburger and iced tea, he asked: "What's this new information you have?"

We explained our theory to him and to his credit he didn't interrupt or make smart remarks about our convoluted reasoning.

"You're probably close to being right about this," he agreed. "I had a gut feeling that old man was lying, but he's convinced everyone else and it's a done deal."

"You mean you won't reopen the case?" I asked.

"Not won't—can't. There's no evidence that disputes Albert's story. No fingerprints. No witnesses. And he wanted Benito punished about as much as his son did. The gun used to shoot both victims was sold to Albert. He had motive, means, and opportunity."

"He bought the gun?" C. J. asked.

Larry's food came and he wolfed it down like a starving hound. "I don't think so but he has this receipt from the flea market out on Highway 290."

"Of course, Stacy *gave* Albert that receipt," I said.

Larry drank huge swallows of tea to wash down his food. "The dealer says it's his receipt, but he doesn't remember the sale exactly. He says if Albert Stewart says he bought a gun from him, then he must have."

"Nothing can be done, then?" I asked Larry.

"Albert will stand trial. A jury will decide if he's telling the truth. He might even get off, who knows?"

"Albert Stewart is willing to sacrifice himself for money?" C. J.'s voice sounded husky.

"Sure," said Larry. "Albert's getting up there in years. Probably thinks he won't live much longer. Big money can ease all his worries. And Stacy Carson has given him an out."

"He's a nice old man caught up in lies and murder," I said. "But it still seems unfair to me."

"I agree, but no one ever said life was fair," said Larry.

"And Stacy gets away with murder. Isn't there some way to prove she was there?"

"Who knows?" said Larry. "But it would have to be strong evidence to get the D.A. to reopen the investigation, and we don't have it. The D.A. wanted this case wrapped up and in his view, it is."

"Stacy's going to have to live with all of it for the rest of her life," said C. J. "And don't forget she gave up her baby. It might not matter now, but on down the line she might have regrets." She cleared her throat. "Sometimes, there's no simple solution to murder."

I didn't have an answer to that. It still didn't feel right, but the case was closed as far as we were concerned. Whatever might happen legally was totally out of our hands.

MYSTERY ANTHOLOGIES

MYSTERY FAVORITES